SEX, LIES & WEDDING BELLS

EM Lynley

DREAMSPINNER
PRESS

Published by
DREAMSPINNER PRESS

5032 Capital Circle SW, Suite 2, PMB# 279, Tallahassee, FL 32305-7886 USA
http://www.dreamspinnerpress.com/

Sex, Lies & Wedding Bells
© 2015 EM Lynley.

Cover Art
© 2015 Ronaldo Gutierrez, Photographer.
Cover Design
© 2015 Paul Richmond.
Cover content is for illustrative purposes only and any person depicted on the cover is a model.

ISBN: 978-1-63216-808-5
Digital ISBN: 978-1-63216-809-2
Library of Congress Control Number: 2014952867
Second Edition March 2015
First Edition published by Ravenous Romance, April 2009.

Printed in the United States of America
∞
This paper meets the requirements of
ANSI/NISO Z39.48-1992 (Permanence of Paper).

To the people responsible for this story ever seeing the light of day: Emilie, Dana, Kimmy, Sue, Lasha, and Lori. Thank you for your comments, critique, and encouragement over the years.

Foreword

SEX, LIES & Wedding Bells was the first of my novels to be published. It wasn't the first novel I wrote, or even the second. But it wasn't until I wrote this that I even dared to send any of my work to a publisher and only at the instigation of several readers. Sending my first novel submission was nerve-wracking to say the least. You can imagine the thrill of being offered a publishing contract a day after sending the full manuscript to the publisher.

With any "first," there's a hell of a learning curve. Writing and publishing is no exception. There is a long list of things I wish I'd done differently with this book, and thankfully, I've had the opportunity to do them the second time around.

The gay romance genre was really in its infancy when this book came out in February 2009. You could count on your fingers and toes all the releases each month. Now you'll probably find fifty new gay-romance releases a day. Back in 2009, everyone read everything that came out. It was an incredibly exciting time to be a writer. It still is, but the landscape of readers, indie authors, and new publishers makes it feel like a completely different planet.

And I'm a different writer than I was six years ago. I'm definitely a much better writer and better storyteller. I've worked hard to improve my weaknesses and hone my strengths, and I'm very pleased with the feedback I hear from readers with each new release.

All of these changes came crashing down around me when I decided to rewrite *Sex, Lies & Wedding Bells*. I've always had an incredibly large, warm space in my heart for Jaxon Lang and Kieran Quinn. I feel like I've always known these guys. They've been in my life for more than seven years at this point.

Even so, it was an incredibly humbling experience to go back and read a book written so long ago, and a first novel to boot. At times it was downright embarrassing. I cringed at more than a few bad writing habits I've since outgrown, some shallow characterization, and a few really bad decisions I'd made in the plot.

But it was a pleasure to rework all those problems, clean the story up, and retool a few of the characters. I admit, despite all the original flaws, I have always adored this story and these two men. I love Kieran and Jaxon even more now. They've both grown over the years along with me.

So, whether you're reading this story for the first time, or you're checking out what's changed since the first edition, welcome (back) to the world of Kieran Quinn, Jaxon Lang, and Buckwheat Springs, Texas. I hope you enjoy your stay as much I have.

Chapter One

Thursday
New York City

THE FIRST thing Kieran noticed when he woke up was something warm and wet on his cock. He let out a small moan and just lay there, eyes closed, enjoying the sensations. Gradually, the night before started to come back to him. Now he remembered leaving Brut—his favorite club, just a few blocks from his place—with a model. He couldn't quite remember which one, not that it mattered. Based on what the guy was doing to his cock, Kieran had made a good choice. Slowly he opened his eyes and saw a pair of big blue eyes staring right back at him with a mischievous glint. Ah, yes. Now he remembered.

Kieran tried to recall the guy's name but drew a blank, though the face was more than familiar. Probably everyone in the city had seen it, ten times larger than life, looking down from a Times Square billboard or out from the sides of countless city buses. Now that recognizable mouth with its full pink lips was wrapped around Kieran's cock. He couldn't think of anywhere he'd rather be at the moment. Not with the way the guy—*Rod or Rob or Todd?*—swirled his tongue around the head of Kieran's cock and flicked across the sensitive bundle of nerves on the underside. He took most of Kieran into his mouth, the tip of Kieran's cock just brushing against the back of Rod's throat as he let out a groan that vibrated all the way down Kieran's cock. Warmth flooded across Kieran's belly, gradually becoming an ache in his balls. He sat up and tugged at Rod's shoulder-length blond hair. Rod looked up at him with wide cornflower blue eyes again, and Kieran pulled Rod onto his lap and kissed him deeply, his cock sliding along the cleft of Rod's ass. This time Rod moaned into the kiss and melted against Kieran's chest.

"No biting," Rod said, as Kieran scraped his teeth along one shoulder.

Damn underwear models and their rules. Kieran pulled his lips over his teeth. Rod couldn't show up for a photo shoot with teeth marks on his perfect body. Memories flooded back to Kieran: Rod mentioning he was doing a new shoot in which he'd be completely nude, with just someone's leg thrown across his crotch area. A men's fragrance ad with the tagline "It's all I wear to bed," or something along those lines. *Can't wait to see the billboard for that one.* For now, Kieran had the real thing in his lap.

Kieran put his hands on Rod's hips and lifted him slightly, settling him onto his back, legs still wrapped around Kieran's waist, heels pressing into the small of his back. Rod let out a throaty sigh and relaxed back onto the lapis-colored sheets and spread his legs wide. Kieran admired the view of Rod's even tan on smooth, firm—unmarked—flesh and reached over to the bedside table to grab a condom. Rod pulled the packet slowly from Kieran's fingers and ripped it open using his teeth, never taking his eyes off Kieran's, conveying his own need and arousal as effectively as his erection did. He rolled the condom onto Kieran's rock hardness and gracefully hooked one knee over Kieran's shoulder while he waited for Kieran to apply extra lube to his cock.

Kieran pushed one slick finger into Rod and met no resistance. He added another. Rod was more than ready, and Kieran wasted no time pressing the tip of his cock against Rod's slippery hole and plunging inside with one smooth move that overwhelmed his senses. Rod moaned as he took Kieran in, encouraging and increasing Kieran's own pleasure at the tight, hot grip of Rod's ass around his cock. It felt just as good as it had the two previous times he'd fucked Rod, before they'd both fallen into deep, sated sleep in the early hours of the morning.

On top of Rod like this, Kieran couldn't really see as much of that gorgeous body as he would have liked, so he slowed his thrusts before either of them got too close to orgasm, wanting a better view. Kieran sat at the edge of the bed, facing the large mirrored door of his closet, and pulled Rod back into his lap, back to front, Rod's legs straddling Kieran's.

"I want to see how beautiful you are," Kieran mumbled huskily against Rod's ear, "and watch you lose control." He helped Rod ease himself down onto Kieran's cock. With his hands on Rod's hips, Kieran easily moved him up and down as he watched in the mirror.

"God, yeah, just keep... fucking me... like... *that*." Rod could barely form the words and that gave Kieran even more of a thrill.

Rod's head was thrown back against Kieran's shoulder, legs splayed wide so Kieran could stroke and play with his cock and fondle his balls as Rod fucked himself down on Kieran with an uneven rhythm. It didn't take long before Rod was so fucked out he could barely move on his own, and Kieran had to do most of the work. That was fine with Kieran; he loved seeing a guy this far gone.

Kieran had Rod coming with a few skillful strokes, shooting thick creamy jets up across his chest and shuddering around Kieran's cock as he grunted and sighed with his orgasm, whispering a few mouthfuls of delightfully filthy comments. Kieran came a moment later, enjoying how Rod's aftershocks still squeezed his cock and trying to keep his own eyes open so he could enjoy watching Rod as he pumped inside him. The nearly dead weight of Rod's body in his lap intensified Kieran's own pleasure as his orgasm ripped through his body, pleasurable sensations ricocheting and reverberating along every inch of his skin and leaving him spent and exhausted and perfectly satisfied.

Kieran lay back, pulling Rod along with him. They lay quietly for a few minutes while their breathing returned to normal. Then Rod slipped out of bed and into the bathroom, and Kieran was surprised to hear the shower start. He wouldn't have minded keeping Rod company in there, but he hadn't been asked, so he disposed of the condom in a trash can next to the bed and waited, reliving the activities and enjoying his own afterglow. Rod took a surprisingly short shower and came back into the bedroom with just a few droplets of water on his beautiful nude body as he toweled his long, damp hair.

"Got any coffee?" he asked casually as he bent down to collect his scattered clothes from the floor.

"Sorry, no. I usually go out for breakfast." Kieran sat up in bed and watched Rod dress. "Want to come along?"

"I'm late as it is." Without bothering to button his shirt, Rod slipped on his jeans, socks, and shoes hurriedly before leaning down and brushing his lips against Kieran's. Rod's hand slid down Kieran's chest and gently stroked his cock one last time before Rod straightened up and left, pausing for a moment in the bedroom doorway and waving a farewell.

"Bye, Rod," Kieran said.

"*Todd*," Todd-not-Rod corrected and his smile morphed into a glare, then he turned on his heel—a move probably perfected on the catwalk—and left. Only slightly embarrassed, Kieran listened as Todd let himself out the front door and then, with a heavy sigh, padded into the bathroom to shower and get his own day started. He had to go into the magazine's office, and by the time he had breakfast, it would be close to noon. No matter, he decided as he shampooed his hair. He'd already turned in his column the evening before by e-mail. All he needed was to get final approval from his editor. Simple.

Once Kieran washed and dressed, the only outward clue to his late-night and morning activities was the broad smile on his face as he walked out the front door of his building's lobby. He rounded the corner of his street and walked half a block to the tiny diner where he had most of his breakfasts. Inside he was greeted with warm smiles and cheerful waves by the two waitresses on duty. He seated himself in a booth near the window, where he could watch people pass by on the street while he ate. He ordered a vegetable and cheese omelet, hash browns, and a fruit salad. His food arrived quickly, and while he ate, his mind went over the night and morning he'd spent with Rod… uh, Todd.

Physically, he had nothing to complain about. He'd been more than satisfied in that regard. But Kieran still felt that there had to be something more than what he and Todd had shared. Once again, here he was having breakfast—more like brunch, considering the hour—on his own, the way he did nearly every day. It was a seemingly endless parade of hot guys who had been to his place or with whom he'd gone home. Last night's guest was one of the few who'd spent the whole night, but Kieran would much rather have woken up in someone's arms than someone's mouth.

He'd even asked Rod—*Todd*, he reminded himself—to have breakfast, and that was certainly a break from the usual routine. Not that they'd had much to talk about, but Kieran had at least tried for more than a few pleasant hours in bed with the guy. *It might have gone better if I'd remembered his correct name.* Then Kieran reminded himself that Todd had turned down the breakfast invitation *before* Kieran's faux pas.

But now Kieran wasn't sure at this point how to find someone he'd even want to spend more than a night with.

Chapter Two

KIERAN FINALLY rolled into the office of *Gloss* magazine—a *New Yorker*-style literary weekly aimed at a significantly younger and hipper audience—well past noon, and got a mixed response of smiles and murderous glares from his coworkers. One person went so far as to mutter "Prima *fucking* donna" under her breath. Kieran was unfazed. He smiled his usual million-watt smile and greeted everyone cheerfully as he set his six-foot, four-inch frame at his desk in the center of an old-fashioned bullpen writers' room.

He was still in a fantastic mood after the night—and morning—he'd spent with a guy who undoubtedly everyone in this room would recognize. He had no reason to feel like he'd failed at anything just because he'd eaten breakfast on his own, right? A night like he'd had was enough to make anyone late for work, now, wasn't it?

Humming softly, he tugged at his half-tucked shirttail, fanning himself to help the air-conditioned breeze counteract the muggy mid-May Manhattan heat. *Might as well give them a show if they're still staring.* Kieran treated half the room to a nice view of his chiseled abs and the thick white waistband of his figure-hugging Emporio Armani trunks as they slid low onto the deep groove of his hipbone. Makes all those hours in the gym worth it. He smiled as he heard several feminine sighs—and at least one much more masculine—settled into his chair, and brushed damp strands of dark brown hair behind his ears.

"Kieran, nice to see you!" A loud voice behind him oozed sarcasm and irony.

"Jeff, hey!" Kieran turned toward the speaker, failing to acknowledge the sarcasm and irony in Jeff's tone.

"Kieran, what does the sign on my door say?" Jeff asked, walking around to the back of Kieran's desk and perching himself on its edge. In one hand he had a rolled-up sheaf of papers, which he thwacked against the palm of his other hand menacingly.

"Marvin Jeffries, editor." Kieran wrinkled his brow. He hadn't expected a pop quiz. Jeffries preferred to be called "Jeff" rather than any permutation of his first name; in fact, he loathed his first name, probably because of the unflattering nicknames associated with it, so it was best never uttered.

"Okay, good," Jeff replied sardonically, "you noticed that. And what does the sign on *your* office say?"

"I don't have an office?" Kieran replied, knitting his brows and wondering if it was a trick question. The conversation had attracted the attention of his coworkers, most of whom seemed to have dropped whatever they were doing to stare at Kieran. He could hear a few people still tap-tap-tapping at their keyboards, but no one spoke.

"Precisely," Jeff said cryptically.

Apparently it *was* a trick question, Kieran decided. The entire room was silent now, watching, waiting, probably *hoping* to see Kieran Quinn crash and burn.

"Are you telling me I'm getting a promotion?" Kieran asked eagerly, his grin widening, flashing his surefire dimples.

"Uh, I wonder what the Magic 8 Ball would say about that. All signs point to *fuck no*." Jeff leaned down, breathing the tuna fish he'd had for lunch into Kieran's face. Snickers and giggles echoed around the room.

"Okay, then, what *are* you telling me?" Kieran didn't consider himself a slow learner, but he still wasn't sure where this was going. He was here, and he'd turned in his column—by e-mail—well before the 5:00 p.m. deadline.

"Kieran, do you like your job?" Jeff asked, leaning back again. Someone in the far corner snorted, and Kieran darted his gaze in that direction without moving his head.

"Yeah." Kieran didn't like the way the conversation was going. He'd been thrown off because Jeff had called him "Kieran." When Jeff was angry at someone, he used his surname instead.

"Then what. The fuck. Is *this*?" Jeff demanded as he smacked the roll of papers onto Kieran's desk, punctuating his remarks. The sheets fluttered to the floor. Kieran bent down awkwardly to retrieve the document, scanning to see what it was.

"Uh, my column about the crazy things people do to find love. For Sunday's issue." Kieran wrinkled his nose as he looked at the manuscript, squinting slightly and ruffling through the pages. Jeff was old school and had started at a newspaper, hence the bullpen-style office and penchant for printing hard copies. *Waste of a goddamn tree*, Kieran thought. But it made for good drama in the office because Jeff threw papers at some poor schmuck at least once a week.

"I guess you don't like it," Kieran said as meekly as he could manage. He didn't want to antagonize his boss in front of the entire department.

"No, I don't like it," Jeff replied, mimicking Kieran's voice. "It's too fucking nice, for fuck's sake! Fuck, Kieran!" Jeff liked to say "fuck" and averaged about one use per sentence. He was clearly making up for lost "fucks" so far in this conversation.

"Nice?"

"Too. Fucking. Nice," Jeff repeated. "We don't pay you to write nice, interesting little columns with heart and hope and happy endings. We pay you to be bitchy and snarky and enter-fucking-taining, for fuck's sake. This is bo-ring! I wouldn't use it to wrap up dogshit! Come on! You talked to enough matchmakers and psychics and speed-fucking-daters and more crazy-ass lovelorn sons of bitches, and there was a fucking *fuckload* of potential for snark here. But you end up writing some fucking sympathetic piece about how hard it is to find 'love in the big city.'" Jeff used quotey fingers, which always made Kieran cringe. "Fix it the fuck up or pack your fucking desk and get a job at *Redbook* or *Ladies' Home* Fucking *Journal*. Got it?"

"Fuck yes?" Kieran ventured a grin, but Jeff didn't seem to be in a mood to joke around and didn't return the smile. He *had* managed to say "fuck" fourteen times so far, possibly a personal best for one conversation. When Kieran had first started working here, he'd found himself counting rather than paying attention to what Jeff actually said. After three years of practice, Kieran could listen and count "fucks" at the same time.

"Deadline is five p.m., which gives you four hours to get me a new draft. Or to pack. Your choice, Quinn." Jeff stormed back to his office leaving pages fluttering off desks in his wake. Heads turned, following Jeff's progress until he slammed the door behind him. Then everyone stared at Kieran.

"Thanks, all y'all, for your concern about my well-being." Kieran employed his sweetest, most drawling native Texas accent—so sugary it practically hurt his teeth just to use it. "Now mind your own fucking business!" he added in his normal, only barely-a-trace-of-an-accent-voice, and smiled a huge, pleasant, and clearly facetious smile, showing his pearly whites. He was a diligent flosser.

Fuck! Fuckity fucking fuck! Great, now Jeff was rubbing off on him. Ugh, *that* was a mental image he tried desperately to obliterate as he booted up his computer and opened the file to rework his column. Slowly, the room returned to its normal level of noise and activity as people resumed whatever they had been doing when Jeff had made his appearance at Kieran's desk.

They were all used to Jeff's weekly tirades, but Kieran hadn't been the object of Jeff's disaffection for quite a while. A lot of the other staffers thought he deserved it, the way he swanned in—never swished, despite what some people might say—at all hours of the day and consistently turned things in at the last minute. But no one disputed he was one of the most talented and most popular writers—at least with the readers—at *Gloss*. His columns invariably generated hundreds of letters and e-mails, a mixture of plaudits and complaints, but the suits and senior editors didn't care, as long as people were buying and reading it. The circulation department discovered a good number of people bought the print issue just for Kieran's column. They purposely didn't post his column on *Gloss's* web site in order to force people to buy the magazine, and apparently it worked. Circulation was at an all-time high, quite a feat given the havoc wrought by the Internet on most newspapers and magazines.

Three and a half hours later, Kieran had been to the coffee cart in the lobby three times and was so hopped up on sugar and caffeine he couldn't sit still. He furiously tapped away at his keyboard, banging one knee rhythmically against his desk and occasionally muttering to himself. Several coworkers stared at him and probably wished he hadn't shown up in the office after all. The feature writers had the option of working at home a couple of days a week, if their job allowed—the news writers clearly couldn't—but everyone was expected to be in the office on deadline day. Preferably arriving *before* noon. But now the room was nearly empty, as the writers who had already turned in their stories went home or off to live their lives.

"So, dude, how's the rewrite going?" Brad Raines asked from a few desks away. He was Kieran's closest friend at *Gloss*, and possibly in real life—or whatever you called life outside of work. He wrote for the entertainment section, reviewing films. Kieran imagined Brad's job consisted of sitting around in the dark watching movies all day then coming in on deadline day to turn in his columns. How hard could that be? But then again, Brad probably only got half the salary Kieran did, based on how many drinks Brad cadged out of him. Brad looked and sounded like a California surfer—light brown hair streaked with golden highlights, which was quite a feat considering he'd come from Vermont. Maybe he'd watched too many films and was just playing the part.

"Great, Brad. It's the best fucking thing I've written." Kieran laced his words with mock enthusiasm without looking up from his monitor.

"Really?" Brad asked. Irony was usually lost on him and not just part of the dumb surfer-dude persona.

"No, Brad, it's going to end up like Franken-fucking-stein's monster when I'm done. A little of this and a little of that, all sewn up with some bitchy snarkiness, and then some snarky bitchiness, with a teensy dollop of irony and sarcasm on top for good measure."

"So what's got your thong in a twist, dude?" Brad called everyone "dude" except Jeff, a lesson he'd learned the hard way.

"I don't know, *dude*," Kieran muttered under his breath and sprawled back in his chair. He pushed off from his desk and let the chair roll backward into the desk directly behind his where Alexa Harrington, Kieran's best friend, sat. She grabbed a handful of Kieran's hair until he yelped.

"For fuck's sake, Lex, that fucking hurt!" Kieran rubbed his head, but he smiled so she wouldn't be too offended.

"Hmm, sounds like Mr. Grumpy Pants is trying for Jeff's job or something." Alexa laughed. As *Gloss*'s restaurant reviewer, she spent most of her time in New York, but every other week she spent a few days in another city to try new restaurants, interview celebrity chefs, and follow up on food and taste trends around the country.

To Kieran she had the best job at the magazine, though Alexa insisted he had only befriended her so he could eat fantastic food for free. She constantly teased him and gave him grief for his famous appetite. When reviewing a restaurant, she typically ordered five appetizers and five entrees, plus a few desserts; *someone* had to eat all that extra food, Kieran reasoned.

Though slim, petite, elegant Alexa could actually pack away a lot more than anyone might expect, most of it went to waste unless she brought a few others along. All the food seemed to have gone to her boobs, Kieran speculated, noticing she was wearing another daringly low-cut blouse today. He might be gay, but he could certainly appreciate Alexa's allure.

"I just don't feel right making fun of some of the people I interviewed for this piece." Kieran frowned. "This matchmaker, Becky Balaban, for example. She was the sweetest little grandmotherly thing. She actually did remind me of my grandmother. I can't bring myself to mock her."

"So, just mock the people who go to her." Brad gave a half-shrug. "Or maybe you should have interviewed a few different matchmakers so you would have one you didn't like so you could really rip 'er to shreds."

"I'm surprised people even *agree* to let you interview them," Alexa said. "You're known for making people the butt of jokes or embarrassing them. How do you manage to convince anyone to talk to you?"

"It's his country-boy charm and good looks." Brad shook his head. "And the killer smile. I'm still in awe of the way you can get nearly anyone to not only want to get in your pants, but to think they actually have a chance: male, female, any age or sexual orientation. What's your secret?"

Kieran didn't bother to protest. He admittedly had abused that gift on more than one occasion—and not just to get laid. He'd been blessed with strong features, kept himself in good shape, and here in New York, his everyday Texas manners were considered the height of politeness. But he was the first to confess he'd been pretty lazy on this piece. He should have interviewed more people, but he'd really liked the matchmaker and spent far too much time chatting with her. He wanted to get at the secret to her overwhelming success at pairing up couples, many of whom had stayed together for years. She had a far better batting average than half the guys in the Baseball Hall of Fame.

Kieran had even considered asking her to help him, since he hadn't had much luck finding love in the big city. The night before aside. Then again, that wasn't love, that was *fucking*, he reminded himself, and he certainly knew the difference. With one you had someone to eat breakfast. He had to put the memory of another lonely meal behind him, or he'd never finish this damn piece.

The theme of this particular column had hit a bit too close to home for him, and he'd gone into it with entirely too much empathy for the people Jeff called the "lovelorn sons of bitches." Kieran could use some help in that department himself. He didn't want to spend the rest of his life picking up hot guys from bars. He really did want to find someone special and settle down, but he seemed to be much more successful with underwear models than with anyone who could actually be his soul mate.

He'd had a lot of fun interviewing the psychic, too. She did readings out of her tiny apartment in Brooklyn, and he'd gone over there twice after the initial visit rather than following up by phone. Of course he didn't really believe in any of that paranormal stuff, and he knew she used attention to detail to "read" his personality and what his problems might be, but she had said something that had gotten his attention. He was going to meet his soul mate sometime soon, she predicted, and it would be a complete surprise to both of them. The person would be seeking Kieran's help for a serious problem, she continued, adding something cryptic about a "baby who wasn't there," whatever *that* meant. For most single gay men, babies just didn't feature in the picture. Maybe that's what she meant.

"Earth to Quinn." Brad startled Kieran out of his musings. "You've got less than half an hour to finish that column and get your next column outlined. Are you going to manage it?" *Gloss* had writers plan out their work two issues in advance so they could manage space and advertising requirements.

"Huh? The outline is due *today*?" Brad had Kieran's full attention. "I thought that wasn't due until tomorrow?" An extra twenty-four hours could do wonders in Kieran's experience. Hell, he'd written entire columns in less time. Often, in fact.

"Oh, right, you weren't here the other afternoon when Jeff announced the new schedule," Alexa said. "Now we have to turn in the new outline along with the story for the current issue. I guess bankers'—make that underwear models'—hours can be a bitch, huh?" she teased. She knew him all too well, Kieran decided.

"Figures." Kieran frowned. "He probably said that just because I wasn't here, right?"

"Well, there was an e-mail, too, dude," Brad added in a tone that made Kieran want to smack him again.

"I never read e-mails from Jeff," Kieran admitted. Suddenly concern formed in the pit of his stomach that it wasn't the only important e-mail he'd missed. Most of Jeff's e-mails ended up in the spam folder, filtered out for having the word "fuck" in there, and Kieran tended to delete everything without looking very carefully. He'd have to be much more careful from now on.

Why does this job have to be so much work?

He loved research and interviewing people, and of course the writing, but he *hated* the planning and outlining Jeff seemed so keen on. "I don't have a clue what I'm writing two weeks from now."

"Well, do you at least have this week's column finished?" Alexa asked. "Or are you gonna pack your fucking desk?" She tried to imitate Jeff's voice and intonation but couldn't manage it.

"Yeah, just about." Kieran wheeled himself back to his desk and took one more look at what he hoped was the finished column. At that moment a trim, good-looking guy with sleek, dark, shoulder-length hair approached Kieran's desk, delivering mail from a pushcart.

"Hi, Kieran," Chris-the-mailroom-guy said cheerfully. That was how most people referred to him, sometimes even to his face. "I can't wait to read your next column; I hear it's about finding love." He gave Kieran a smile and flipped his hair back in a move probably designed to be flirtatious but ended up looking like he was swatting flies. Kieran tried not to glare at him and flashed a toned-down version of his normal smile. He didn't want Chris getting the wrong idea—although it was probably far too late to avoid that; he'd brought the guy home with him from a club one night, not realizing he'd fucked a *Gloss* employee until the next morning.

To Kieran, the whole point of one-night stands was simply that: it was only supposed to be one night. You were supposed to fuck him and forget him. They weren't supposed to show up at your desk every day making puppy-dog eyes, hoping you'd ask them out for an encore—or a real date. If he'd found any sort of deeper connection with Chris, it wouldn't have ended up as a one-night stand in the first place. Was it any wonder Kieran preferred to work from home as often as possible?

"Yeah, Chris, something like that—if I can get it done in the next ten minutes. Otherwise it will be in my portfolio as I'm looking for a new job." Kieran hoped his tone let Chris know the conversation was over without directly snubbing him. Chris didn't seem to notice the undertone and headed to the next desk, swaying his hips, possibly for Kieran's benefit. Kieran turned back to the monitor, ignoring the huge pile of mail Chris had dropped on his desk.

"Looks like love might have found you, Kieran." Brad rolled his eyes and added a smirk once Chris was out of earshot.

"No, Brad." Alexa started laughing. "That wasn't love; that was fucking." She mimicked Kieran's voice almost perfectly as she uttered one of his key phrases.

"Look, he wasn't that bad. Just not my type."

"You mean not a model?" Alexa asked.

"That's not what I meant." Chris was no model, but he was pretty good-looking. Kieran tried to recall why they hadn't clicked. It wasn't even that he worked in the mail room; most of the hot models had more of interest in their pants than their heads. But dating a coworker was never a good idea. "Hey, guys, do we have to have this conversation here, *now*?" Kieran didn't bother to hide his exasperation that his personal life was common knowledge around the room.

He glanced around to discover the three of them were the only ones left, except for the book reviewer—Bob Jones or Smith or something equally as generic and forgettable—whose desk was over in the corner. Bob was a short, balding guy with eyes that rotated independently like some kind of lizard, as Alexa had once described him. He also had a crush on Alexa and often stayed until she left. He'd hardly ever even spoken to her, and Kieran always dared her to ask him out or unbutton her top in front of his desk. Alexa didn't go much for dares, but every now and then she'd glance over at Bob and he'd scurry around his desk as though he was looking for something, or hide his head in whatever book he was supposed to be reviewing.

"I think it's so *fucking* hilarious you went home with Chris-the-mailroom-guy from a bar, and *then* found out he worked here!" Brad cried with a laugh. "And he's still got the biggest crush on you. I'll bet a week's salary he followed you to that bar in the first place, hoping you'd pick him up." Brad nearly choked with mirth at Kieran's obvious discomfort.

"You two are so *adorable* together," Alexa added in a saccharine tone, but Kieran glared at her and she looked suitably contrite.

He turned his attention back to the monitor and ignored both of them, focusing on finishing his column by the deadline.

"Okay, this is done!" Kieran announced ten minutes later and hit the enter key with a flourish as he e-mailed the final draft of his column to Jeff. Brad and Alexa applauded loudly.

"What about you guys? Almost done?" Kieran asked.

"Yeah, Jeff approved my final draft hours ago," Brad answered.

"Me, too," Alexa chimed in. "We're just here offering you moral support."

"And mocking my unfortunate sexual encounters." Kieran let out a soft snort, but he was pleased his friends had stuck around with him until he got his own piece done, even if they had distracted him more than they helped.

"We'll stay till Jeff signs off on the piece, and then we'll let you take us out for drinks to show your gratitude." Brad flashed Kieran a huge grin.

"I see money does buy companionship, at least, if not respect," Kieran replied ironically.

Chapter Three

WHILE WAITING for Jeff's final approval on his column, Kieran racked his overtaxed brain for a topic to pitch to Jeff for the future issue. As he glanced at the pile of letters on his desk, an idea began forming. Why not try a column featuring the readers who wrote him? He could pick a few choice letters, then call the readers up. He'd figure out the angle after chatting with some of them. Kieran flipped through the pile, looking for interesting return addresses or uncommon names that would make good fodder for ridicule.

One envelope caught his attention. It was made of beautiful, thick pearly beige paper that sort of glowed under the fluorescent light and had a return address of Buckwheat Springs, Texas. Kieran had never heard of it, so it must be one of the tiny towns in the middle of nowhere—with a population of five people, 500 cows, and twenty pickup trucks—that dotted Texas. It looked like a wedding invitation, but he didn't know anyone who would be getting married in Buckwheat Springs, Texas.

"Hey, I got invited to a wedding by one of my readers." With excitement, Kieran tore the envelope open and read out loud, "'Mr. and Mrs. Robert Archer request the pleasure of your company at the marriage of their daughter Danetta and Jaxon'—with a fucking *X*!— 'Lang.' Hell, I don't know these people." He peeked into the pretty envelope again. Empty. "There isn't even a letter in here explaining who they are or why *I'm* invited."

"Hang on." Alexa rolled her chair over to Kieran. "Did you say Danetta Archer?"

"Yeah," Kieran said. "Why? What the fuck kind of name is Danetta anyway? Of course she'd marry someone with an *X* in *his* name."

"I went to college with her." Alexa took the invitation from Kieran and read it, pressing her lips into a thin white line.

Kieran took another look at the envelope and saw it had been addressed to Alexa, not him. Chris obviously wasn't as good at sorting mail as he was at sucking cock. Poor guy really would have to sleep his way to a better job.

Kieran handed over the envelope. "Sorry, I didn't realize it's actually for you. It was in my pile of letters."

"Well, how interesting." Alexa shook her head as she seemed to be reading the invitation again. "The wedding is next weekend, and I'm just getting an invitation *now*? I guess I was on the second string."

"Are you going to go, dude?" Brad went over and perched on the edge of Kieran's desk.

"Me? No." Kieran shrugged.

"I was talking to Lex."

Yeah, because that was so obvious when he referred to her as "dude."

Alexa looked up from the invitation. "No, for several reasons." She paused. "Firstly, I'm scheduled to be in Napa that weekend for a winemaker's event."

"Oh, poor thing," Brad moaned dramatically. "The agony!"

Alexa ignored him. "Second, I'm more than a little miffed to be invited so late. And third, get this." She flapped the invitation in Kieran's direction. "This is the *fourth* wedding invitation I've gotten from Danetta over the past five or six years. And she's still not married yet."

"Fourth? What d'you mean?" Kieran asked.

"Well, I missed the first wedding. It was back during college before we were really friends, but I went to the next two. And at all of them she decided—at the *altar*—she didn't want to get married after all!" Alexa shrieked with laughter and grabbed on to Kieran's desk when she nearly toppled out of her chair.

"You're saying she dumped the guy in the middle of the wedding?" Kieran was dumbfounded but intrigued.

"Yeah. *Twice*." Alexa couldn't say more because she was laughing so hard. "Well, twice I saw, but I heard it happened that time when I wasn't there, while she was still in college."

"Oh, dude, that's hilarious." Brad visibly forced himself to stop laughing and wiped tears from his eyes. "Well, maybe not for the guy, but how could she plan a whole wedding and then just wait till the last minute to cut and run?"

"Well, it's too bad if it happens once, and she's done it three times so far. I haven't gotten an invitation for a couple of years. I might have missed one. Or… maybe she's serious this—"

"Hang on a minute," Kieran interrupted. "Didn't I see this in a movie?" He wondered why Brad hadn't recognized the storyline by now. Just shows he must be faking it, Kieran decided. "Does this chick think she's Julia Roberts or something? I mean, come on, no one does something like that for real."

"Danetta has," Alexa replied. "Yeah, it does sound like that movie, doesn't it? Stupid film; I loathed it."

"Lex, dude, you should go, just in case," Brad said. "Richard Gere might be there!" So he had at least heard of the film.

"Shut up, Brad!" Alexa shot him a withering look for good measure.

"What kind of shit-for-brains guy would even date her, much less propose to her with that track record?" Kieran mused, shaking his head in disbelief. Then he sat up. "I'm getting an idea here. Wait for it...." He paused, but he felt that little tingle when something good came to him. "What if I did a column on the wedding! Will she or won't she? What d'you think?"

"What's the angle?" Brad asked.

"Well, I could focus on Danetta"—he pronounced the name with scorn—"and how she's such a flake—she is a flake, right, Lex?"

"First class."

"That doesn't quite do it for me." Brad shook his head. "Real-life Runaway Bride, that's not exactly original, is it? You need a new spin to make it fly."

Kieran ignored the mixed metaphor and waited for Brad to suggest something. Waited in vain.

Wheels turned in Kieran's head as he sought a more original slant, snarky enough to get Jeff to approve a travel budget. "Okay, okay, how's this? I focus on the guy. Guys. I interview the first three, try to find out what her secret is for getting all these proposals, and then focus on the current one... what's his name?"

Alexa glanced at the invitation again, obviously holding back a giggle. "Jaxon."

"Danetta. Jaxon. How on earth do people in that town come up with these names for their kids? I never heard of either one of those. But back to business. I can hang with Jaxon a couple of days before the wedding, see how he's dealing with the uncertainty of whether or not she'll actually marry him."

"Yeah, that's good, dude." Brad nodded encouragingly. "What about some advice on how to avoid this happening to you?" Finally, he had something useful to add.

"I could even contact one of those matchmakers or relationship gurus for tips." Kieran was on a roll now with their brainstorming. "It'll be easy to make Jaxon look like a real dumbass for asking her to marry him, considering her past record. And if she bails again, I can really go to town on him."

"Kieran, I think you've done it." Alexa patted him on the shoulder. "Now hurry up! Write up the proposal, send it off to Jeff, and let's get to the damn bar." She pushed off from Kieran's desk and rolled back toward her own.

"She's having Cosmo withdrawal symptoms, I can tell," Brad said.

"Cosmos are so over, dude," she chided Brad. "It's pomegranate martinis now."

They came over to Kieran's desk and leaned over Kieran's shoulders as he worked on the outline, correcting his punctuation and mocking his overuse of adverbs while he tried to type. He did his best to ignore them, and when he was fairly satisfied with the proposal, he e-mailed it to Jeff.

"So, Kieran, tomorrow let me call Danetta and tell her you'll be going to the wedding in my place," Alexa said.

"That'd be great, thanks, Lex." Kieran rotated his head to stretch his aching neck and shoulders. "I'm going to have to spin it differently with her if I want to get a chance to interview her and Jordan before the wedding."

"Jaxon," Brad and Alexa corrected.

"Jordan was actually the name of groom number two." Alexa pressed a finger to her lips, clearly trying to recall. "I think."

"Whatever. So, how about if you tell her I'm there to do a column about how this time she's so sure, and how in love they are and...." Kieran stopped talking, eyes on the ceiling. "Hey, could she be pregnant? 'Cause if she is, she'd be more likely to go through with it this time. That would fuck everything up for the story."

"Well, I'll see if I can find out when I talk to her," Alexa said.

"Anyway, we'll make her think my angle is how *this* time it's right, and she's chosen the most amazing colors, and how special and different things will be this time with Jordan. He's *totally* Mr. Perfect," Kieran mocked in a campy tone.

"*Jaxon*," Brad and Alexa said again.

"Yeah, I know. How could I possibly forget a name like that?" Kieran couldn't help rolling his eyes.

They all turned around when they heard Jeff's office door bang open.

"Quinn, in my office, *now*!" Jeff roared out of the open door.

"How about we just meet you at the restaurant?" Brad whispered. He clearly wanted to avoid the wrath of Jeff. "Per Se okay?"

"Wow, I'm generous tonight, huh? I agreed to drinks, not dinner." Kieran frowned and got up. He walked toward Jeff's office as his friends gathered their things to go. "How about Brut instead?" Kieran shouted over his shoulder. He preferred the small champagne bar close to his SoHo apartment rather than one of the most expensive restaurants in town, no matter how good the food was at Thomas Keller's only East Coast restaurant. But the point was moot; they wouldn't get a table at Per Se.

And there was someone Kieran hoped to run into at Brut.

"Quinn!" Jeff poked his head out of his door to find himself face-to-chest with Kieran.

"I'm here, Jeff." Kieran looked down at his boss, who was closing in on six feet tall himself.

"Get your ass in here."

Kieran followed Jeff into the office and sat down in one of the chairs facing the desk. Jeff perched himself on the front of his desk and glared down at Kieran.

"Good job on fixing up your lovesick piece. I think it works now." Jeff smiled and nodded, indicating no trace of his earlier anger. Kieran rarely gave him a reason to get angry and he suspected he was actually Jeff's favorite staff writer despite Jeff's efforts not to let Kieran know it. A little bit of ass-kicking was necessary from time to time to keep him working at his peak, or Kieran had a tendency to get lazy. Kieran wondered how much of Jeff's antics were show, just so other writers wouldn't think Kieran got special treatment just because he was one of *Gloss*'s most popular columnists.

"Thanks."

"And your idea for the bride with fucking icebergs for feet? Not bad. But I'm not convinced it'll work. What's your angle if she doesn't do another runner? You can't make either her or the groom look like fucking idiots if they actually tie the fucking knot, can you?"

One, two, three…, Kieran started counting "fucks."

"Well, I considered that, too," Kieran lied, thinking on his feet. "If she goes through with it, then I'll focus on the three discarded grooms and show they weren't good enough or find something wrong with them and why this, uh, Jaxon guy is perfect for her."

"Hmm, that could work as your fallback plan. When were you thinking of going out there, to uh, Bumfuck Springs, Texas? That near where you grew up?"

Four.

"*Buckwheat* Springs. And no. I grew up in San Antonio. Full of culture and history, not some dust-bucket town in the middle of nowhere." Kieran was proud of his hometown and constantly found himself defending it while in New York. "Alexa will get me a schedule of wedding events and make sure they'll let me tag along, but I'm thinking Sunday or Monday. Wedding is next Saturday, so spending the week before in Buckwheat Springs should give me plenty of background and a choice of angles. I'd like to stick around for a couple of days after the wedding to follow up on whatever happens."

"Sounds good to me. Just keep all the receipts, and no caviar or champagne on the expense account while you're there, got it? Like they have caviar in Bumfuck Springs." Jeff threw his head back and cackled.

Five. Jeff was definitely off his game right now.

"Got it." Kieran nearly let out a sigh of relief that Jeff liked his half-baked idea. He hoped it wasn't completely obvious he'd only dreamt it up fifteen minutes earlier. He owed Brad and Alexa for brainstorming with him. Then he remembered they were eating and drinking on his tab while he was still sitting in the office, wondering whether he was out of the doghouse with the boss.

"So, go on, get your ass out of here and meet up with your friends." Jeff dismissed Kieran with a wave of his hand and seated himself at his desk. He began to sift through a pile of papers. "Where the fucking fuck did I put the fucking—" Kieran didn't hear the rest because he was sprinting for his desk to grab his jacket before rushing home to change on the off-chance he ran into his future soul mate—or the next hot underwear model—at Brut.

Chapter Four

Sunday
Texas

KIERAN'S PLANE touched down in Amarillo, in the Texas Panhandle. His knees were aching from the cramped conditions on the plane. Fucking cheapskate Jeff wouldn't spring for business class, and Kieran had found himself in coach. With a last-minute booking from LaGuardia to Dallas/Fort Worth, the plane had been nearly full and he hadn't been able to get a seat in the front row of coach, where there was at least enough room to stretch his legs. He'd ended up in an aisle seat halfway back and couldn't keep his legs in the aisle with all the comings and goings of his fellow passengers and the flight attendants. It had been four hours of agony and frustration. At least the forty-five-minute commuter flight from Dallas to Amarillo hadn't been as crowded, and he'd been more comfortable even on the model-size aircraft.

He still had to pick up a rental car and face the prospect of an hour-long drive to Buckwheat Springs. He opted for the best car available—a convertible. He'd pay the extra charge if Jeffries was going to nitpick and penny-pinch. He should have paid for an upgrade on the flight too, and would do so for the flight home.

The Chrysler Sebring was twice the price of the premium car they had available, but Kieran splurged for the extra couple of hundred dollars. He didn't have a car in New York and missed driving. He was looking forward to enjoying the sun shining on him and the wind blowing through his hair for a change.

He tossed his suitcase in the trunk of the Chrysler Sebring convertible and immediately put the top down. A wave of heat radiated off the asphalt, and he wished he'd kept it up and switched on the A/C instead. How had he forgotten this heat?

God, he was starving, and it would be too late for a meal once he got to Buckwheat Springs. Better to eat in Amarillo. He'd asked the car rental clerk for the best diner in town and ended up at the Home Plate, which true to its name had a variety of baseball memorabilia decorating the walls.

The place was crowded. He ordered a dinner platter—chicken-fried steak, the house specialty and a dish he hadn't eaten in ages—with a piece of blueberry pie and iced tea. His bill came to $12.37. He laughed as he swallowed the last bite of the delicious pie. He'd gotten a huge, filling meal for about the price of one cocktail at Brut. He'd lived in New York so long, he didn't even think twice about how much everything cost, and it was a refreshing change to be back in Texas where prices were so much more reasonable. He felt himself relaxing, and he slipped into his soft South Texas accent as he chatted briefly with the waitress before setting out on the last leg of his journey.

As Kieran drove, he reviewed what he'd learned in his research for the story. Buckwheat Springs was a former trading-post town that in the last decade had restored many of its historical buildings and tried to market itself as a "destination." The whole concept was usually a recipe for a tourist trap, but somehow Buckwheat Springs had managed to make it work without going too far into the realm of the artificially quaint. Main Street looked much the way it had a hundred years earlier; but the centerpiece of the town was the courthouse, which apparently had an almost identical twin at some equally unremarkable town in Kentucky. It seemed the architect had moved and reused the blueprints with only minor changes.

But Kieran wasn't there for history or sightseeing. He needed to focus on a strategy for approaching Danetta, Jaxon, and Danetta's trio of jilted grooms. Kieran smiled as that reminded him of the Three Tenors. Maybe they should start a musical group.

Danetta had grown up in Buckwheat Springs, then attended the University of Virginia, where she had met Alexa. Danetta majored in art history and returned to Buckwheat Springs. She got a job with the historical preservation board and was involved in maintaining historical accuracy in and attaining international recognition for the traditional Texas trading-post town's tourism marketing campaign. Danetta seemed to be responsible and competent, having held on to the job for five years.

How could someone so professionally competent be such a disaster when it came to her personal life and relationships?

Kieran realized he barely had a leg to stand on regarding that topic and scratched it off his mental list of questions to ask.

Jaxon Lang was a transplant to the town. He'd only moved there a year earlier to take a job as Buckwheat Springs High School's principal. Jaxon had grown up around Austin and attended the University of Texas as both an undergraduate and graduate. In his professional life, Jaxon had earned a reputation while working in high-level positions at two high schools as having a high success rate in improving test scores and college acceptance. Jaxon seemed to have quite a career ahead of him as an educator, but Buckwheat Springs wasn't exactly the kind of place that would look impressive on his resume. Why had he chosen to move to such a professional dead-end job like that?

It was nearly midnight, Manhattan time, by the time Kieran arrived at the Trail Dust Motel in Buckwheat Springs. He hoped the motel's name was simply intended to conjure up colorful Texas imagery and wasn't any indication of the competence of the housekeeping staff.

"I'm Quinn." He watched the gray-haired woman sitting behind the front desk, working on a quilt draped over her lap. "I'm sorry for arriving so late."

"Never you mind about the time. When you get to my age, you don't sleep all that much." She had a sweet smile and a soothing voice. She carefully put the quilt to the side, stood, and shuffled through some papers. "How do you say your first name? Ky—"

"*Keer*-un." He was used to this. He was just glad his mother hadn't used the traditional spelling of Ciaran, otherwise his name would have been mispronounced more than it was already.

"Mr. Quinn. Kier-an," she ventured, sounding it out slowly, with a smile at his insistence on informality. "I'm Marge Connors.... Why, look here! Your address says New York, but you talk like you're Texas born and bred."

"San Antonio." He nodded. "But now I work in Manhattan." Kieran could already tell he'd be explaining this all week.

"Well, you must be exhausted after such a long trip." She sounded a lot like his mother when he made his all-too-infrequent visits home. Somehow being here and talking with Marge Connors made Kieran think more fondly of home than he had in quite a while. "Breakfast is included," she continued, "but we don't have a fancy restaurant here at the motel. So if you just show your room key over at the Copper

Caboose on Main Street, they'll give you a nice meal." She leaned forward as though sharing a secret with him. "I'm particularly fond of their pecan pancakes—you be sure and try those while you're here."

"I'll be sure and do that," Kieran replied. "Thank you, ma'am." *It's true*, he mused, realizing the word "ma'am" had slipped out. *You can take the boy out of Texas, but you can't take Texas out of the boy.*

His room was large and furnished in a homey, old-fashioned way that turned out to be much nicer than the tacky Western décor—stuffed armadillos, cow horns hanging from the walls—he'd envisioned when he'd first driven up. And rather than a cowboy-print bedspread, a beautiful handmade quilt adorned the queen-size bed. It wasn't hard to figure out who had made it.

So far, his trip had been a nice change of pace from Manhattan, though he knew he still had work to do. That was why he was here. He needed to focus on Danetta and Jaxon rather than on pancakes and quilts. After washing up for bed, he slid beneath the covers and mentally ran through his schedule for the next day.

He was asleep before getting beyond the pecan pancakes for breakfast.

Chapter Five

Monday

KIERAN WOKE at ten on Monday—early for him. The comfortable motel bed left him well rested and ready to start his day. After a quick shower, Kieran dressed and wandered down the street to the Copper Caboose for some of those pecan pancakes Mrs. Connors had recommended.

On his way to breakfast, Kieran got his first good look at the town of Buckwheat Springs. As expected, Main Street had the architectural air of Victorian-era Texas. There was a moderate hustle and bustle of people who smiled or nodded or offered a "Mornin'" as Kieran passed. Shops and restaurants had old-fashioned or Western-themed names, and he fought bravely against the urge to scoff at the quaintness of everything.

There weren't many cars traveling down Main Street, and it seemed Buckwheat Springs was largely navigable by foot. Only people living near the outskirts of town would probably take their car—or truck, more likely—on a regular basis. In that regard, it was like Manhattan.

The Copper Caboose was a small hole-in-the-wall restaurant, bright and clean and decorated in a railroad theme. Kieran seated himself at a table near the window and glanced over the menu already on the table.

"Good morning!" A disturbingly perky waitress rushed over to his table with a pot of coffee. She was petite, blonde, probably in her early thirties, and wearing a nametag that said "Natalee."

More ridiculous spellings. Kieran watched her pour coffee into his mug, which was adorned with a picture of the namesake caboose. "Welcome to Buckwheat Springs! Let me know when you're ready to order."

"I already know what I want." Kieran took a sip of hot black coffee and sighed. "Pecan pancakes, double order, side of bacon, large orange juice, and fruit salad if you have it."

"Hang on, I need another pad to write all that down." Natalee chuckled and flashed a pretty smile. "Anything else?" she prompted.

"That'll do—for now."

Natalee giggled. Her laugh suited her.

"You're that reporter from New York, aren't you?" Natalee asked, her tone bordering on flirtatious.

"Columnist," Kieran corrected her. "But yes, I am he. Kieran Quinn." He held out his hand to shake hers. She took it timidly.

"Well, aren't you Mr. Big City Grammar, Kieran," she replied. "What's the difference?"

"Reporters report what they see or research, but I write what I think about things. You know, my opinions and observations. More subjective."

"And what are your observations so far?" Natalee teased, shifting her weight and cocking her hip in a way that began to make Kieran uncomfortable. He didn't mind a little playful banter, but the last thing he wanted was for her to start hitting on him. He'd have a much more difficult time getting her to gossip if she was actually interested.

"Natalee, are you gonna bring me that order or telegraph it by ESP?" the cook shouted from behind the counter.

"Sorry, coming!" She flashed an apologetic smile at Kieran before heading toward the kitchen—her own caboose shimmying—to turn in the order. She returned momentarily with the juice in a tall glass beaded with moisture and a bowl of fresh fruit salad. Kieran had his head buried in a discarded newspaper he'd found at the next table, partly to read it and partly to avoid more than casual conversation with Natalee.

"Here you go." She set the food down. "Enjoy!"

"Thanks," Kieran replied, barely glancing up from the paper.

A few minutes later, the rest of Kieran's breakfast arrived. Natalee appeared ready to stand guard and watch him eat, but the comings and goings of other customers kept her occupied. She didn't have any extra time for Kieran except to offer a refill of coffee, which he gratefully accepted.

As advertised, the pecan pancakes were delicious: large, fluffy, and full of chunks of pecan that added a delightful crunch. There was real butter and genuine maple syrup, and Kieran was in breakfast heaven. The fruit salad was fresh and juicy sweet, and the bacon was thick and meaty, not grilled to a crisp.

Positively breakfast heaven.

Kieran didn't make it a habit to be awake at breakfast time if he could help it, but if not, he required a good breakfast. The Copper Caboose served breakfast all day, and he'd happily eat all his meals here if he couldn't find any other place with decent food.

Kieran was pushing the empty plates away when the bell on the door jingled and the most beautiful man he'd ever seen walked into the restaurant. He'd seen plenty, so this was no mean compliment.

Make that most beautiful *person*, Kieran amended. He'd never seen anyone—man or woman—more attractive. Just over six feet, the object of future fantasies had short, neatly cut sun-streaked brown hair. His eyes—bright greenish-hazel, slightly heavy-lidded but in a sexy, just-fucked way—mesmerized Kieran, and just looking at his plush, full-lipped mouth threatened to give Kieran an immediate hard-on.

It wasn't simply his appearance, but the way he seemed so unaware of his power to attract. Kieran's usual playmates had no doubts about their looks, and that knowledge seeped into their personalities in all the worst ways.

This man wore a Wedgwood-blue button-down shirt fitted closely enough to make it clear he spent time at the gym, or played at least one sport, and took proper care of that amazing body.

And he was walking directly toward Kieran.

Just then, Kieran noticed the woman who had come in with the man and had pushed ahead of him as she moved toward Kieran's table.

"Are you Ky… Kee…." The woman fumbled the words, then gave up.

Kieran's eyes were still glued to the beautiful man.

"*Keer*-un." The man's voice was rich and resonant, with lovely inflections that made it distinctive and incredibly sexy as he spoke Kieran's name. "It's Gaelic, right?"

Kieran smiled, noticing a few caramel-colored freckles scattered over the tanned nose and cheeks of the man. Kieran realized for the first time in his life how much he adored freckles. At least the freckles on that face.

"Yes, it is." Kieran hoped he didn't have a stupid grin on his face. "You're probably the only person in town who can pronounce it besides me." Only natural that someone with an "X" in his name would be sensitive to another person with a slightly unusual name.

"I'm Danetta Archer." The woman practically shoved her way in front of Jaxon, blocking Kieran's view. She nodded her head in Beautiful's direction. "And this is Jaxon Lang, my fiancé." She reached out to shake Kieran's hand, and he felt obligated to take it. She gave him a short businesslike squeeze, far more powerful than her looks implied.

"Jaxon," Beautiful said, offering his own hand. Kieran took it, prolonging the contact, enjoying the warm, firm grip. Reluctantly, he let go before anyone noticed.

"Nice to meet you both." Kieran's gaze still focused on Jaxon.

Without asking, Danetta sat herself down in one of the chairs opposite Kieran. Jaxon sat down at the side of the table to Kieran's left, his knee slightly grazing Kieran's as he settled into the chair. The resulting jolt of electricity sped through Kieran's body, and he fought to keep his attention on the conversation.

"Alexa Harrington told me you'd be coming to town early because you wanted to do an article on my wedding." Danetta beamed at the word "wedding." "I'm not really familiar with *Gloss*. It sounds like it's a fashion mag, perhaps like *Vogue* or *Marie Claire*?" She paused. "You have a photographer coming, too?" Her eyes widened and flashed with excitement over the idea of her wedding being featured in one of those magazines.

Kieran shook his head. "I take my own photographs." He rarely did, preferring to paint pictures with words. "And 'gloss' actually has another definition: commentary or interpretation. It's meant to be an intellectual play on words: one connotation indicates shallowness while the other is almost opposite in meaning."

Jaxon smiled at Kieran's explanation. Danetta looked blank.

"You're familiar with the word 'glossary'? They're related."

"Oh, right," she said.

"It's very clever." Jaxon nodded.

Kieran gave a casual shrug, pleased with Jaxon's approval. "Well, I can't take the credit for it."

Jaxon turned his full attention on Kieran. "We wanted to introduce ourselves to you now, and—"

"We know you'll want to do some other interviews and I—we would be happy to schedule those for you, to help you out," Danetta interrupted.

Damn woman was already finishing Jaxon's sentences, and they weren't even married yet, Kieran thought wryly. It didn't escape his notice that Jaxon hadn't used any other pronoun besides "we," which was already disgusting in itself. Worse, Danetta had mainly used "I" and "my." Those sorts of details spoke volumes.

Jaxon might be the most beautiful name I've ever heard—even with the fucking X. Kieran forced himself to snap out of this daydream in order to participate in the conversation without drooling over Jaxon Lang.

"That's very accommodating," Kieran replied. "How did you know I was here?"

"Natalee called and told us," Danetta replied. "She knew we wanted to meet you as soon as possible. Everyone in town is on the lookout for you."

"You probably feel like you're being stalked." Jaxon's eyes twinkled in amusement. "Well, you are. I'm very sorry about that, but you're the biggest thing to happen to this town in a long time." Jaxon paused as he seemed to be giving Kieran a welcome once-over. "In more ways than one. I mean, we heard you're quite tall." A rather adorable wide-eyed look of embarrassment flashed across his face. "And everyone in town loves Danetta, so they're all very excited for our big day." Jaxon turned to her with a dopey, lovey-dovey smile that made Kieran want to puke up the fantastic breakfast he'd just eaten.

Jaxon's tone and demeanor were heading directly into Stepford territory, and it was a pretty disheartening realization that this beautiful man would be Danetta's *husband* in just a few days.

"So, Alexa said you want to focus on about how even though I was engaged before"—Danetta gave Jaxon a sideways glance—"that now I'm sure I've found true love with Jaxon. Have I got that right?"

Kieran liked how she put it—engaged, as opposed to actually *had three weddings*.

She continued, "And you want to meet the three men I didn't marry, so you can—what, compare them to Jaxon?"

"Well, I admit that's part of it." Kieran avoided Jaxon's eyes at the implied insult. "I also want to hear from you about how *you* know it's right *this* time, how you knew it wasn't right before, and, uh, decided not to go through with it."

"You don't need to beat around the bush, Kieran. You can say that I left them at the altar." Danetta gave a pretty laugh.

Kieran nodded. As much as he wanted to hate her, he admitted to liking her frankness and ability to laugh at herself.

"I thought you might want to spend some time with me while I check on the progress of a home currently being restored," she said. "It will give you a chance to meet Tom Whitfield, the builder. He was my high school sweetheart and the first man I almost married. I need to discuss a few points of business with him, and then I can leave you two for a private chat. How does that sound?"

"That sounds great," Kieran replied, glad everyone seemed to want to talk to him. He could interview people, get them to reveal their innermost thoughts and not feel resentful toward him for making them do it. People were *grateful* for the chance to tell him their most personal secrets. Then he twisted their words around to ridicule them. It made his columns entertaining, but he'd come to hate how easily he could rip people to shreds using their own words. At first it had been some sort of gift; later it became a curse. Now *Gloss* expected that from him, and after Jeff's warning, Kieran knew he didn't have much choice in the matter.

"We'd like to have you over for dinner at our house." Jaxon focused his beautiful eyes on Kieran's. "This evening."

Danetta glanced over at Jaxon. "Yes, you'll be able to get an impression of us at home. All domestic," she added, almost as an afterthought to Jaxon's invitation. Kieran spotted Jaxon's smile slip for a moment.

"So, are you free tonight?" Jaxon turned back to Kieran, one corner of his mouth now quirking just enough to reveal a devastating dimple that took the air out of Kieran's lungs.

Kieran gulped. If only Jaxon would say those words in an entirely different context. "Sounds perfect," he replied.

"Well, I better get back over to the high school before they burn the place down." Jaxon stood up. Danetta also stood and raised her face for Jaxon to give her a kiss before turning toward the door. "See you at dinner." Jaxon glanced over his shoulder at Kieran before walking out.

"I'll come get you around two o'clock at the motel, okay?" Danetta asked.

Kieran agreed. As she walked toward the door, he noticed for the first time that her skirt was almost the same color as Jaxon's shirt.

Jesus fucking Christ! Matching outfits?

Kieran had one more cup of coffee before getting up from his table. "How much do I owe?" he asked Natalee.

"Nothing." Natalee shook her head. "Breakfast is included when you stay at the Trail Dust."

"Well, I had a pretty big breakfast. I must owe something extra for that."

"Don't worry. You're like a VIP in town anyway. I doubt you'll be paying for many meals around here."

Kieran had forgotten to show his key when he came in, but apparently everyone in town knew his business. He pulled out his wallet to leave a tip. At first he grabbed a twenty-dollar bill, thinking it would be nice to leave a big tip. But concern that Natalee would get the wrong idea made him put it back and take out a five instead.

"Thanks." He waved as he moved toward the door.

"See you at breakfast tomorrow!" Natalee called after him.

Chapter Six

JAXON CLOSED the Caboose's door behind him and tried to catch his breath.

He wasn't quite sure what had just hit him, but something sure had. Something as devastating as a locomotive. Adrenaline coursed through his body, and he blinked in the morning sunshine, a little dizzy.

"Jax?" The bell on the diner door jangled his nerves as Danetta walked up beside him. "What's with that dinner invitation? I don't have time for that today." She grasped his upper arm with strong fingers, and it felt like a vise. Unconsciously he pulled out of her grasp.

"What?"

"Dinner? Tonight?"

Jaxon's brain reengaged. "Didn't we decide that?"

"We talked about it, but I'm tied up all afternoon. I'm gonna need Mama to help with dinner."

What had he been thinking? He still wasn't certain, but now he wished he hadn't extended the invitation. No, he didn't. He just wished he'd thought it through a bit more.

"Jaxon? Are you listening?"

"I'm a little preoccupied." Understatement. "Work."

"Right. I'll see what I can arrange for tonight. You'll be home in time to help too?" She glanced at her watch. "Darn it, I'm running late for an appointment." She still had her hand on his arm and pulled him in for a kiss.

Jaxon was looking through the Caboose window and missed her mouth.

"I'll call you between meetings, okay?" Danetta asked, then crossed the street at a brisk clip.

Jaxon's heart was still racing, but the tightness in his chest subsided as soon as he was alone on the sidewalk. He took an unsteady step and stopped again, trying to pull himself together. After a few quick breaths to restore oxygen to his brain, he headed for the high school, taking his time. He needed some space to absorb what had just happened.

Kieran Quinn had just landed in Jaxon's nice, calm world, like a rock on a smooth-as-glass lake. Jaxon barely understood how he'd managed to create so many ripples so damn quickly.

Jaxon had never met anyone who'd had such a devastating effect on him. Why had the sun seemed so much brighter and the whole world about to tip over when Kieran had smiled at him. And the electricity crackled when they'd shaken hands.

All Jaxon had done was say his name, "Kieran." The response was instantaneous.

And he knew Kieran had felt something too.

Jaxon wasn't sure what it was. All he knew was he wanted more. Stupidly, he'd said the first thing that popped into his addled brain. Dinner. Tonight.

With Danetta and now her parents. What had he gotten himself into?

Something about the way Danetta had tried to control the conversation, turning the topic onto herself, had rattled Jaxon's nerves. He'd never really noticed that about her before. Did she always do that? Why did it suddenly annoy Jaxon so much?

That wasn't the only question he needed to answer before dinnertime.

He was still on autopilot when he walked through the front doors to the school. He nodded as staff and students greeted him, but he didn't take in a word anyone said. Inside the safety of his office, he shut the door and locked it—something he'd never done before.

Now that Jaxon had met Kieran…. What?

Kieran had only come to Buckwheat Springs to write about the wedding.

Jaxon's wedding.

The realization opened up a deep, aching pit in his gut, and the room seemed to close in on him like he'd swallowed one of Alice in Wonderland's magical potions.

The one that turned the world completely upside down.

Chapter Seven

KIERAN SPENT the next few hours at Buck's, another little restaurant on Main Street, drinking coffee, chatting to locals, and making notes on his first meeting with Jaxon and Danetta. He'd have to spend much more time with them to get a good picture of their relationship.

He took the opportunity to ask seemingly innocuous questions of the people he spoke with and made notes. Occasionally he felt his attention wandering, thinking about Jaxon as he listened and doodled on his notepad. At one point he literally had to stop himself as he was about to draw a heart around Jaxon's name.

As beautiful as Jaxon was, Kieran had to admit he didn't see anything remarkable about him yet, beyond his looks and that intoxicating moment when they'd shaken hands and shared something ineffable. Otherwise, Jaxon appeared disappointingly average. Below average when he considered those horrifying matching outfits.

Involuntarily Kieran rolled his eyes. He needed to get Jaxon alone—not *quite* the way he'd like—to discover his real personality. He'd suggest going out for a few drinks at a local watering hole after dinner. It might be a good thing if Jaxon turned out to be a book judged by its cover but never meeting expectations.

Despite his large and late breakfast, Kieran was soon hungry again and ordered a couple of sandwiches and a plate of curly fries. The lunch crowd had come and gone while Kieran sat at the counter talking to a steady stream of Wheaties (as Kieran decided he'd call the town residents) about Danetta, her previous weddings, and their impressions of Jaxon. Kieran made copious notes, which seemed to thrill everyone.

IT WAS nearly time to meet Danetta when Kieran tried to pay his tab and was refused with a smile. He was heading back to the Trail Dust when he ran into her on the street.

"Kieran, how was your day so far?" she asked with a pleasant smile.

"Great! I met a lot of people and collected a bunch of juicy quotes. You're quite well-known around town, aren't you?"

"Famous or infamous?" She laughed. "I don't mind. I hope people were helpful. It's just a short walk to the house I was telling you about."

After a five-minute stroll, they came upon a lovely Victorian-era house set back on a shady side street filled with similar houses in various degrees of repair. Several pickup trucks were parked in front, and the sound of hammering and sawing echoed down the block. From the street, the house was as beautiful as any Victorian in San Francisco—or it would be once it had been repainted. Buckwheat Springs was turning out to be quite a surprise, full of architectural gems Kieran hadn't expected.

They walked around the side of the house to the back garden.

"Tom!" Danetta called out, and a tall, well-built man leaning over a set of blueprints turned around and gave a friendly wave.

"Kieran Quinn, this is Tom Whitfield," she introduced when he came over. Kieran reached for Tom's outstretched hand. He had a firm, friendly grip and an even friendlier smile.

Tom was well built, with a chiseled jaw, fair skin, and lively gray-green eyes. Danetta certainly had a thing for green eyes, though Tom didn't have anything on Jaxon. Kieran could see dark, nearly black hair under Tom's hard hat.

"So, Kieran, why on earth did you come all the way from New York City to write an article about Danetta and Jaxon's wedding? How can it possibly be interesting enough to people from anywhere else?"

"You have to admit it's an unusual situation," Kieran answered, "with three unfinished weddings behind her. I'm trying to focus on why this time it's actually going to happen. I hope that doesn't offend you, seeing as how it didn't work out between the two of you."

"Oh, I don't hold any of that against Danny," Tom said graciously. "I'm really happy for her and Jaxon. Our girl here deserves to be happy." Tom put his arm around Danetta and gave her a squeeze before laying a surprisingly tender kiss on the top of her head. "And I know she and Jaxon are great together."

Kieran couldn't believe that Tom could be so forgiving. Danetta looked up at Tom with a small smile, and a look flashed between them that Kieran tried to read. They still shared something. But was it sadness or regret?

"Kieran, why don't you come along while Danny and I discuss our business? This house is going to be gorgeous when the renovations are finished and I think you'll enjoy seeing it. You and I can spend some time alone after she leaves. You both need to wear hard hats in the house, though." Tom grabbed two hats from his makeshift desk and handed them out.

Properly protected, the three of them entered the house. Danetta and Tom walked side by side through the building site discussing the progress of the work while Kieran followed, alternately shouting questions about the building and their friendship over the racket the workmen made. He scribbled notes whenever they stopped to look at a window frame or alcove.

Kieran hadn't expected Tom and Danetta to still be so close and friendly. Either Danetta *wasn't* as bad as Kieran expected, or Tom Whitfield was some kind of emotional superhero.

When the tour was finished, Danetta handed her hat to Tom. "Give my best to Laura."

"Sure thing," Tom replied. "She doesn't think she can possibly survive another three weeks until the baby…." Tom left his unfinished sentence hanging as Danetta was already walking away. She waved as she made her way to the sidewalk.

"Laura's my wife," Tom explained to Kieran. "We've been married two years now, and we're expecting our first baby soon. Very soon."

"Congratulations." Kieran noticed how Tom's whole face lit up speaking about his family, and he wondered if he'd ever be that happy.

"Let's go sit out in the back for a chat. It's much quieter out there."

Kieran silently thanked him for that suggestion, though with the cacophony of power tools, Tom wouldn't have heard him if Kieran had spoken aloud.

They talked for another hour, interrupted occasionally when Tom needed to consult with members of the construction crew.

"Let me make sure I'm getting this right." Kieran flipped back a few pages in his notes. "You and Danetta were high school sweethearts and decided to get married between her third and fourth years at UVA?

What went wrong? If you'll forgive my bluntness." Kieran fully intended to be blunt. He wanted to see how Tom would hold up.

"It's nothing I haven't already heard. And I've asked myself plenty of times too." Tom took a breath and launched into the details.

"It just wasn't the right thing for us at that time, no matter how much we wanted it to be. Sometimes you just convince yourself you're making the right choice, for all the right reasons, but…." Tom glanced at something over Kieran's shoulder. "Well, she went back to school and I threw myself into work." He nodded toward the house. "I probably wouldn't have been so successful if we had gotten married, you know? It's tough to split your attention and still do two things very well. Maybe I'm boring you with all this?"

"No. On the contrary." Kieran had been scribbling notes, more about Tom's demeanor than anything he'd actually said. Kieran asked progressively more intrusive questions, but Tom answered all of them, never once saying anything critical of Danetta or Jaxon. Kieran figured he'd need to pour a few drinks down his throat before he'd scratch the surface of Tom Whitfield.

"I still don't understand Danetta's explanation for why she waited until the middle of your wedding ceremony to decide it wasn't the right thing. That doesn't sound to me like it was a mutual decision," Kieran insinuated. He'd wanted to say "excuse," but it sounded a bit too hostile.

"The reason for that is really quite personal, Kieran, and I'm afraid I'm not prepared to discuss it." Tom gave the impression he really did not want to expose Danetta's personal and private emotions without her consent. "I don't hold it against her at all. The reason she gave me was perfectly acceptable, and that's why I don't have any hard feelings about it—and why I am thrilled she's found Jaxon."

When they wrapped up their conversation, Tom offered to take Kieran over to meet Jordan Harper, or "Number Two" as they liked to tease him. It turned out that the three jilted grooms were all quite friendly with each other and were also among Jaxon's closest friends in town. This was all a bit too much for Kieran to believe. They could be putting on a show for him, but they couldn't keep the pretense up all week. He'd be able to tell pretty quickly what was real around here and what wasn't.

A ten-minute walk through the center of town later, Tom and Kieran arrived at the station where Jordan Harper was a fireman.

Tom introduced Jordan to Kieran. Again, the friendship appeared genuine.

"Kieran, say hello to Jaxon for me later on, okay?" Tom gave a casual salute and left.

"Sure thing," Kieran agreed, still looking for cracks in Tom Whitfield's armor.

Jordan's story was a bit different. He'd grown up near Austin—not all that far from San Antonio. He'd met Danetta there when she was doing a month-long architectural seminar at UT. They'd hit it off and begun a relationship strong enough to continue after Danetta returned home. After trying things long-distance for a while, Jordan relocated to Buckwheat Springs, moved in with Danetta, and proposed. Kieran pretty much knew the rest of the story.

Jordan's wedding with Danetta went as well as Tom's had. Jordan also refused to share the reason Danetta gave for jilting him, but he believed it was all for the best. He too wished Jaxon and Danetta nothing but happiness. Kieran detected no hints of jealousy—in fact, he was surprised to learn that Jordan really liked Jaxon too. Were they all brain-dead from some Danetta magic potion? Perhaps she was a witch. He'd need to be careful what he ate or drank at dinner tonight.

Jordan and Kieran had just begun a contentious discussion of basketball—Spurs vs. Mavericks—when Danetta came by the fire station to bring Kieran home for dinner.

"Say hi to Jaxon for me." Jordan gave Danetta a peck on the cheek and a look almost identical to the one Tom had given her: one of shared secrets and genuine affection, mingled with something Kieran had yet to identify. He jotted down a few notes before he and Danetta left.

Truth was, Kieran was both looking forward to and dreading dinner. He was eager to see Jaxon again, but not as enthusiastic about spending time with Danetta and her parents. But what he expected to witness tonight would make or break his column. Either there was a juicy story here, or there wasn't, and he could head home before there was any chance of his crush on Jaxon making life difficult—or interesting—for either of them.

Chapter Eight

"I CAN'T show up empty-handed. Let me stop and get some wine for dinner."

"No. No. That's fine."

"I insist. I think there's a shop this way, right?" Kieran headed toward the little wine shop he recalled on Main Street, and Danetta followed him. She was oddly quiet, and he got the sense he'd somehow insulted her with the wine, but he wasn't sure how. To make up for it, he asked questions about a few buildings they passed.

That seemed to revive Danetta's mood, and she shared more town lore with Kieran as they walked home. Kieran only half listened as he pondered what he'd learned so far. Tom and Jordan seemed to still have some feelings for Danetta, but this didn't seem to affect their ability to care chiefly about her happiness.

As they turned the corner of Surrey Street, she tripped over her words as she jabbered away, loading him down with trivia and offering nothing of substance, even repeating herself a couple of times. It was a marked change from the cool, confident exterior he'd seen so far, and it intrigued him far more than anything Tom or Jordan had said. She now had his full attention.

"Well, here we are." Danetta stopped at the sidewalk in front of the cute little Victorian home she shared with Jaxon, apparently giving Kieran an opportunity to take in the pretty façade, painted in a lovely Wedgwood color—not unlike the shirt Jaxon had worn that morning. The evening sun glinted off a gold weathervane on the roof and bathed the house in a warm glow.

"It's beautiful. Did Tom work on this one too?"

"Y-yes. You have a g-good eye." Again she stumbled and stuttered.

Danetta paused for a fraction of a second too long before she walked up the sidewalk and then lingered on the porch before opening the door. What was she putting off? Why wasn't she racing up the steps to greet her betrothed? Kieran couldn't wait to get inside and find out.

He'd already formed a strong impression of Danetta, but she suddenly became a lot more complicated—and much more interesting.

She opened the door. "Here we are." She went in first, and no sooner had he entered than he had to fight the desire to run back outside again. An unpleasant and potentially unnatural aroma assailed his nasal passages, and he curbed the overwhelming urge to choke.

The smell was an ungodly amalgamation of burnt meat, dirty laundry, and a wet bar rag. Now he understood Danetta's reluctance to enter. She must be the worst cook in Texas if that stench was coming from dinner. No wonder she'd looked shocked when Jaxon had extended the dinner invitation.

"Let me take your bag. And the bottle." Danetta reached for Kieran's messenger bag and hung it on a coat hook in the foyer. While her back was turned, he wiped tears from his smarting eyes. He'd just about figured out how to breathe without inhaling—either that or the lining of his nose had burned away any olfactory tissue.

"Danny, honey?" A middle-aged man came through to the foyer. More of the horrifying odor wafted around his body, like Pigpen's stinky cloud. "Good evening."

"This is my father, Robert Archer. Kieran Quinn."

"Bert." He reached out and they shook hands.

The name immediately conjured memories of the Sesame Street character, which was reinforced by the same wide-open eyes and perpetually bewildered expression on the living Bert's face.

"Nice to meet you, Bert." As they exchanged a few pleasantries, both Danetta and her father glanced toward what had to be the kitchen. The sounds of plates and silverware clattering came through the closed door. After a terrifying crash, the door burst open, and a woman emerged, or rather stumbled. She tottered for a moment, then pulled herself upright.

"Who's this?" The woman stared at Kieran.

"Mom, this is Kieran." Danetta threw Kieran an apologetic smile that made her seem human for the first time. "Neither Jaxon nor I could get home early this afternoon, so Mama offered to help with dinner." She blinked and gave a helpless shrug. He couldn't help but notice she was holding the bottle of wine behind her back. "Kieran, this is my mother, Lorraine."

As Lorraine moved closer, Kieran realized why. She had definitely been drinking. Close up she had the broken red capillaries common to habitual drinkers. No wonder Danetta hadn't wanted him to bring wine.

"Lorraine, honey, why don't you sit in the living room while Danny and I finish in the kitchen?" Bert steered his wife down the hall, and Danetta held out a hand so Kieran would follow.

He panicked at the prospect of being left alone in a room with this woman as Danetta and her father headed back to the kitchen. Lorraine stared at him for a moment, then fixed her gaze on a locked cabinet, drumming her fingers impatiently on the armrest of the couch.

Kieran took the opportunity to take in his surroundings, thankful he wasn't expected to make small talk. From what he could see so far, the house was lovely from an architectural standpoint, but the interior was decorated in period furnishings, a bit too flowery and feminine for Kieran's taste.

He also had time to size up Danetta's mother. Lorraine had to be at least fifty but dressed like a twenty- or thirty-year-old in a frilly skirt so short it rode dangerously up her thigh when she sat down and a blouse with a neckline far too low. She had heavily penciled eyebrows Joan Crawford would have murdered for, and old-fashioned Texas-style big hair with no skimping on the hairspray. She touched the shellacked creation and gave Kieran a very inappropriate smile. Was she trying to be seductive? She was no Mrs. Robinson. From her distillery breath, Kieran tried to estimate how much alcohol she had consumed before he arrived.

Danetta's hesitation on the steps made perfect sense now.

"Did you want a drink, Jasper?" Lorraine asked, eyes still fixed on that cabinet. "Get me one while you're up?"

Who's Jasper? Did she think he was Jaxon or Jordan, one of Danetta's exes?

Lorraine repeated the question, changing her intonation, perhaps to imply he might have an IQ in the single digits.

"I'm fine," Kieran replied, never meaning it less.

He felt a rush of joy when he heard the front door open and spied Jaxon entering at the other end of the hall, and not for the reasons he would have guessed only fifteen minutes earlier.

Jaxon came down the hall, grinning as he entered the room and spotted Kieran.

"Kieran, good to see you." Then Jaxon noticed Lorraine on the other sofa. "Evenin', Lorraine," Jaxon added with a polite nod that every male born in Texas learns practically before he can walk.

"Oh, Jasper!" She sputtered a little on the "sp" and Kieran was glad he wasn't close enough to get sprayed. "Want a drink?"

"I'm good," Jaxon replied and turned toward Kieran again. "Can I get you something?"

Did Kieran imagine the little inflection in Jaxon's voice? Probably. But Jaxon did seem pleased to see Kieran here. He was just enjoying the caramel-colored stubble on Jaxon's well-shaped jaw when Danetta's heels click-clacked in the hallway.

"I'm just about to serve dinner." She slid an arm around Jaxon and used the other hand to bring his mouth into position so she could plant a wet kiss with unnecessary sound effects. Jaxon pulled his gaze away from Kieran only when Danetta's mouth made contact. When she let him go, she turned toward her mother. "Mama, come help me serve dinner?"

When they left, Jaxon settled next to Kieran on the sofa and leaned back, unwinding after what might have been a difficult day. Or it could just be him taking a moment of reprieve after finding his future mother-in-law in his house. He undid the second button on his Wedgwood-blue Oxford, and Kieran didn't resist the urge to look, enjoying the sight of a few golden hairs peeking out.

"Kieran, I'm sorry about dinner." Jaxon licked his lower lip in a manner that made Kieran ready to forgive him anything. "I intended to get home early and cook, but there was a last-minute disaster I had to deal with." He glanced toward the dining room, where Bert was setting down a pitcher of tea, perhaps steeling himself for another disaster.

"Not a problem. If life went according to plan, it would be boring." Kieran gave a tiny shrug.

"In that case, there's never a dull moment around here. Consider that a promise, not just a warning."

"Okay." Kieran let out a soft chuckle. "I'm game."

Jaxon nodded and shifted position so he was facing Kieran, causing his knee to brush up against Kieran's, and he didn't move it away. Kieran tried not to read anything into the movement.

Jaxon looked into Kieran's eyes and pressed his lips together for a second, as if thinking something through. There was a warm radiance surrounding him, an inner glow that made his eyes appear even more intensely green. He opened his mouth, clearly having decided what to say. Kieran couldn't wait to hear it.

"Dinner's on the table!" Danetta sang out from the dining room.

When Kieran looked back at Jaxon, that glow was gone.

DANETTA SERVED Kieran a glass of wine rather than bringing the bottle to the table. From the way Lorraine sniffed the air in his direction, he wished he hadn't stopped to buy it. No one else drank.

Between Lorraine's near-constant bickering—though mostly one-sided—and Danetta's possessive hold on Jaxon, Kieran couldn't wait for the meal to end. She touched Jaxon's arm or leg constantly. Occasionally she leaned over to kiss him. Kieran saw Jaxon give her hand an affectionate squeeze as if understanding Danetta's need for some kind of reassurance. Kieran could have used a squeeze too.

Danetta balanced the conversation between dealing with her mother and telling Kieran about the upcoming wedding in excruciating detail. She prefaced everything with "we wanted this" or "we decided on that," though Kieran doubted Jaxon had had much of an opinion on the topic. But Jaxon nodded and agreed as though he'd rather plan a wedding than have tickets on the fifty-yard line at a Cowboys game.

If it hadn't been for Lorraine's disruptive outbursts, Kieran might have lost respect for Jaxon fast, but the way he supported Danetta actually raised him in Kieran's esteem. It balanced out the offensive smoochiness, which Jaxon didn't seem to mind. Kieran found that behavior somewhat inappropriate, considering he was a guest the couple had just met.

Lorraine berated Danetta's father, Bert, every chance she got, including criticizing the food and the way he held his knife. For his part, Bert seemed like the kind of guy who would have to look up to a doormat. The man was innocuous, nearly invisible, saying nothing besides "Please pass the potatoes." Bert and Lorraine were easily the most dysfunctional couple Kieran had seen outside of television. They were a walking advertisement for divorce.

And the food was barely edible. There was a hard disk of meat covered in a dark brown sauce with the consistency of school paste. After one taste, Kieran surmised that paste probably tasted better. It was especially galling after being subjected to hearing about the entire mouth-wateringly delicious menu they'd serve at the wedding.

Halfway through dinner Bert got up and left the room. He came back a few minutes later with half a glass of wine, which he set in front of Lorraine. Her eyes lit up and she quieted down and sipped. It worked like magic, and Lorraine joined in the conversation.

"But Jathper, honey." Lorraine turned to Kieran in a moment of almost lucidity. "You've hardly touched your pork chop."

Pork chop? More like a reject from the quality control line at a hockey puck factory.

"Sorry, I'm actually trying to become a vegetarian, so I try to limit the amount of meat…."

"Well, in that case, have some more potatoes!" Lorraine responded and piled on more of the runniest mashed potatoes Kieran had ever seen. Maybe it was just potato soup gone dreadfully wrong. There was so much salt on everything Kieran could feel his blood pressure rising. He smiled and chatted along politely, expecting a nomination for a Tony award for his performance in the near future.

Kieran hoped Danetta hadn't learned her culinary skills from her mother, or Jaxon would starve or be poisoned before their first anniversary. As it was, Jaxon barely touched his dinner, and Kieran didn't feel so bad leaving most of his on the plate as well. He was even hungrier by the end of the meal and hoped his protesting stomach wouldn't growl and give the game away.

He desperately wanted another glass or three of wine, but that wouldn't be appropriate. As soon as was decent, Kieran tried to extricate himself from the dinner party—a very loose term as far as the evening was concerned. He wanted to figure out a way to ask Jaxon to go out for a drink, to see what Jaxon was really like. Kieran wasn't sure anything was real inside that house; he certainly hoped it wasn't.

"I hope you won't think it's rude," Kieran began as they moved into the living room after dinner. Bert was clearing the table and apparently doing the dishes. Too bad he hadn't cooked, Kieran concluded unkindly. "I was hoping I could steal Jaxon away for an hour or two and—"

"Good idea, Kieran," Jaxon agreed, interrupting not only Kieran, but Danetta, who had her mouth open to speak. "Danny and her friends have monopolized you. We haven't had a chance for our one-on-one interview yet."

"Sure. Did you want to go now?"

"Yeah, we can check out the Lone Star Cafe over on Third Street," Jaxon replied.

Kieran wasn't in the mood for coffee, but he would follow Jaxon anywhere. They were on their way five minutes later.

"Do you want to grab a beer and maybe some dinner, too?" Jaxon offered with a smile as they headed, again on foot, for the center of town.

"Fuck, yeah!" Kieran replied and was rewarded with a deep laugh from Jaxon. *Maybe he's not such a robot, after all.*

"We'll go to Sam's," Jaxon said. "They serve food and booze."

"Not Lone Star Cafe?"

"I said that because Danny doesn't drink, and she doesn't like me to either, especially at Sam's. Mainly because Sam doesn't much like *her*." Jaxon gave a shrug.

Kieran gave Jaxon a guy respect point for having misled Danetta, then immediately felt like a heel. But he understood why Jaxon would need to escape the asylum now and then.

"What's he got against Danetta?" Kieran couldn't wait to meet Sam, the only one in town he'd heard about so far not completely enamored with Danetta. Not that Kieran didn't like her; he just didn't understand who she was yet and without a neutral opinion, he wouldn't. He intended to spend plenty of time with Sam.

"Sam's not a 'he,' but we're already here." Jaxon led Kieran into a place with a sign hanging outside that read simply "Saloon." The word described the place to a T. Worn, honey-colored wooden floors and walls, a shiny dark wood bar, and the air of a place that hadn't changed in a hundred years. It was rustic like something from an old Western, but without the desperate need to illustrate its origins with horseshoes, lassoes, or chaps hanging from the wall. Kieran expected someone to settle onto the bench at the old upright piano and belt out "Git Along Little Doggies" or "Don't Fence Me In."

It was a million miles away from the elegantly hip Brut.

Kieran loved it.

Jaxon nodded to the woman behind the bar. "Sam, meet Kieran Quinn. Kieran, Sam Alexander."

Sam was in her midthirties, with shoulder-length brown hair, lively almond-shaped hazel eyes, and a sly but infectious smile. She had a few extra pounds around the middle of her small frame, but

Kieran got the impression she had muscle and power beneath a deceptively soft exterior.

"Good to meet ya, Kieran." Sam dried her hands on a towel, then held one out and shook Kieran's with an unexpectedly strong grip—he'd been right about the power. She had a slightly husky voice—the kind that came from too many cigarettes, too much whiskey, or both. It suited her perfectly.

"Same here, Sam," Kieran said.

"Can I get a cheeseburger, some curly fries, and a couple of beers?" Jaxon asked.

"Same for me."

"A couple of beers for you, too?" Sam asked with a chuckle.

"Let's start with one each," Jaxon said.

"I think I'll have a couple of cheeseburgers, though." Kieran could probably eat three at this point.

"You're not going vegetarian?" Jaxon cocked an eyebrow as he teased Kieran.

"I've got some nice local ale, pale ale, and wheat. What'll it be, fellas?"

"Wheat for me," Kieran answered. Jaxon chose ale. They waited while Sam opened bottles, then Jaxon led Kieran over to a tall wooden table toward the back of the room and they settled themselves on stools. They sat for a few moments in silence while they worked on their beers.

"I never heard of this beer, but it's pretty good." Kieran glanced at the label after draining half the bottle.

"Local brewery over in Amarillo. Not bad at all. So what do you think of Buckwheat Springs so far?" Jaxon asked.

"It's full of surprises, actually." Kieran wondered whether now that they were alone, Jaxon might become much more interesting. Kieran enjoyed gazing at the freckles and enchanting green eyes again. Even in the dim bar light, they seemed to sparkle, and not in a teen-vampire way. More like a reflection of something burning under the surface. "It's a much nicer and livelier town than I expected. People have been really friendly, and the restoration is fantastic."

"Definitely true. I know I didn't expect much before my first visit, and I found plenty to like about this place." Jaxon paused. "It's not Dallas or Austin, but it's really great for a small Texas town."

"If you like having everyone knowing your business all the time." After the anonymity of New York, Kieran cringed at the mere thought.

"That is a drawback, but mostly I like everyone around here."

"How do you get on with the three former fiancés?" Kieran asked. *Might as well jump right in,* though he would have preferred to just chat with Jaxon and not be reminded the reason he was here was work and not a date.

"We all get along well, oddly enough. I didn't expect them to like me; I figured they'd be jealous or hold a grudge now that I'm with Danny. But that's not the kind of guys they are. They're probably my closest friends here, believe it or not."

"How are you all able to get along so well?" Kieran asked.

"Because we all care about Danny, and we want her to be happy." Jaxon's gaze seemed fixed at something behind Kieran. "They've all realized for one reason or another things didn't work out with her, but they want her to be with whoever will make her happy. No one's jealous that she thinks I'm that person."

Kieran was content to let Jaxon keep talking. It was the secret to a great interview. Never stop the flow of words. You never know what someone will say when they start rambling. He'd gotten absolute gold by simply listening and nodding. Thankfully, Kieran had the sort of memory that could almost recall a conversation verbatim. He didn't want to pull out his pad and make notes.

One thing stood out from Jaxon's comments about Danetta. He never once said that being with her made him happy. Was he so focused on making her happy that he hadn't noticed? Or was he the sort of man who consciously put her happiness first? Jaxon seemed to care for Danetta, but he didn't have that madly-in-love look about him. Kieran wanted to know why.

Just then Sam brought their food and set the platters and two more beers on the battered surface of the table. She took away the empty bottles from the first round.

As if by mutual consent, Jaxon and Kieran ate silently, savoring each bite of food. The burgers were delicious: juicy, thick, and char-broiled, with real cheddar and toasted buns. Kieran tried not to think about Jaxon's lips as he watched him push fries into his mouth. And when Jaxon put his lips to the beer bottle, Kieran *wasn't* wishing they were wrapped around his cock instead.

Jaxon finally broke the silence. "I'm really sorry about dinner. Lorraine… well, she thinks she's helping. She'd been dying to meet you, but if it were up to me, that would have happened much later. I hope you won't mention her in the article…." He gave a sad sigh and fixed Kieran with a mesmerizing gaze.

Kieran forced himself to focus. He was surprised Jaxon had mentioned Lorraine's behavior, though so far he'd avoided the elephant in the room—her drinking or psychological issues or both. Kieran further reconsidered the low opinion he'd formed of Jaxon originally.

"Unfortunately, Jaxon, I've had worse."

"Lorraine can't cook to save her life—quite the opposite in fact. So far no one's actually died, though there's a rumor someone did end up in the hospital from one of her dinner parties back when… well, a while ago. Way before I lived here, so I can't say for sure." Jaxon chuckled again. "But Danny never complains; I guess she grew up with Lorraine's cooking and is so used to it she knows there's no point in saying anything."

Jaxon's ability to criticize his future in-laws demonstrated that maybe he had some balls after all.

"Luckily Lorraine doesn't cook for us very often. If I'd known in advance she was cooking instead of Danny picking something up, I would have delegated that last meeting and gladly have made dinner for you myself. But you know Texan hostesses: wouldn't dream of serving a guest something that wasn't homemade."

Kieran had cleaned his plate, while Jaxon had only eaten about half his burger and fries, but he seemed to be finished. Kieran was eyeing the fries, and before he knew it, he'd reached out and grabbed a couple. He'd felt so comfortable with Jaxon, it almost seemed natural.

"Oh, sorry." Kieran paused before he put the fries in his mouth. "That was rude."

"It's fine, help yourself." Jaxon smiled but didn't push his plate toward Kieran. Kieran felt impertinent taking the plate, so he reached over to grab a few more. It seemed an oddly intimate gesture for near strangers, but Jaxon didn't seem to mind. In fact, Kieran wondered if that was what Jaxon intended. *Stop projecting!*

"So, tell me the truth." Kieran hated disrupting this newfound intimacy, but he had to ask. "Are you worried at all about Saturday?"

"No, I'm not." Jaxon shook his head without a trace of concern. "I know Danny loves me as much as I love her. Why should I worry?"

"But it's not enough, is it? I mean the other three guys believed exactly the same thing, didn't they?"

"That's true." Jaxon appeared to pause, then frowned as he considered his words before continuing. He pushed his bottom lip out a bit, making it look even more lickable. "I know she's really ready to settle down now. With me."

"What makes you so sure? What's different about you?" Kieran probed.

"It's really rather personal, and I don't want to discuss the details, but she and I share something that she didn't share with anyone else, and it's enough to give us an unbreakable bond. The kind of thing that either breaks up a relationship or makes it strong and permanent."

BDSM? Alien abduction? Liking John Denver? Kieran ticked off a list of curiosities. He also realized how odd it was that Jaxon used nearly the exact same words Tom and Jordan had when they explained why they didn't resent the way Danetta had treated them. Kieran was convinced it wasn't just coincidence. But was it a conspiracy? He calmed his imagination, but he smelled a good story here, and if he could dig in the right place, he'd unearth it. He was determined to figure it out by the wedding on Saturday afternoon.

Sam came by to remove their plates, bringing another round of beers. This was a woman who knew how to take care of her customers.

"I just have to say, I'm relieved that I'll probably never have to go through anything like what you're going through right now, or what happened to the other three." Kieran worked on his third beer. "It'll never happen to me."

"Not big on marriage?" Jaxon asked.

"Getting married is still a bit complicated right now—even if I found someone I wanted to marry." Jaxon wrinkled his brow in confusion, and Kieran added, "I'm gay."

"Really?" Jaxon's tone betrayed a mixture of amusement and irony.

Kieran hadn't known what to expect, and Jaxon's response both pleased and concerned him. He'd been careful not to be completely obvious. This was Texas, after all, where the GOP was openly in favor of antigay therapy. He'd taken a chance mentioning it to someone he barely knew here in Texas, but for some reason Jaxon made Kieran feel like taking chances. Those mesmerizing green eyes had robbed him of normal brain function, but for the time being, Kieran wasn't complaining.

"Yeah, really. And right now, same-sex marriage isn't embraced in every state, yet."

"Or Canada," Jaxon added.

"Right, it's just marriage in Canada, no matter who you're marrying." Kieran was impressed that Jaxon knew that. "That's just a matter of time, but most people I know haven't really gotten used to it being a real option for our future. A lot of guys are still of the mindset that relationships are better when temporary."

"But there isn't anyone you'd want to marry?" Jaxon asked.

"Not at the moment," Kieran answered. There never had been, but he didn't need to tell Jaxon that depressing detail. Hence Kieran's particular interest in the matchmaker and the rest of the people he'd met researching that last column.

"That's a matter of time too." Jaxon smiled and raised his bottle to clink against Kieran's.

Kieran hadn't yet gotten his mind around the idea of marriage either, but he knew he wanted to find love. For him that would be a start. Marriage wasn't anywhere on his radar, not like it must have been for Jaxon.

"You're already living with Danetta. What difference do you think getting married will make in your life?"

Jaxon stared at his beer bottle for a long moment while he worked at peeling off the label. "There's so much fuss about the wedding, you know, but who really thinks about what happens after that? You're kind of wrapping up your life in a shiny mauve—or puce—or whatever the fuck color she picked out—ribbon." Then he looked up, directly into Kieran's eyes. "It makes it all permanent."

Jaxon drained the rest of his beer and motioned to Sam for another round. He didn't say anything until half of that beer was gone. Kieran wondered what was going through his brain right now. Maybe once Jaxon trusted him more, he could find out.

Almost as if by mutual agreement, the conversation shifted to less personal topics, and they talked for another hour about all sorts of things: from how Kieran liked New York to baseball, with a few more of Kieran's personal questions—most of them for the column, but a few private curiosity—thrown in here and there in a way that wouldn't make Jaxon suspicious of Kieran's angle for the piece. But Kieran didn't learn anything that would help him unravel the mystery of Danetta's hold over the men of Buckwheat Springs.

Then Jaxon leaned forward into Kieran's personal space, their knees touching. "So, what's it like?" Jaxon asked, obviously more relaxed from the alcohol.

"What's what like?"

"Kissing a guy?"

"Huh?"

"What's it like to kiss a guy? Jesus, you hard of hearing or something?" Jaxon scooted his chair around so he was almost next to Kieran and spoke softly, evidently conscious that this wasn't a conversation either of them would want overheard. No one was seated near enough to them to be a concern, and Kieran certainly didn't mind when Jaxon closed the space between them.

"No, it's just a strange question, that's all."

"Why?"

"Fuck, you ask more questions than I do, and I get paid for it." Kieran grinned.

"You're obviously not very good at your job, are you?" Jaxon laughed. "So answer!"

"I never considered the topic in the same way you do, that's why it's hard to answer. I think about kissing someone I'm attracted to and kissing someone who gets you really hot. I realized that I wanted to kiss boys and not girls. That I thought about guys in a way most guys think about girls."

"When did you realize that?"

This conversation was not going at all the way Kieran had expected. He wasn't sure why Jaxon was asking.

"A long time ago."

"Hmm. So what kind of guy attracts you? What about that guy?" Jaxon pointed to a nice looking, well-built blond sitting across the room at a table with two other men.

"Don't point at people!" Kieran grabbed Jaxon's arm. "Fuck, didn't your mother teach you any manners?" But he was laughing, both at Jaxon's pointing and at his suddenly insatiable curiosity about Kieran's sex life.

"Aha, that guy must be your type, or you wouldn't make such a fuss," Jaxon teased.

"He's not actually," Kieran replied. He didn't realize he still had his hand on Jaxon's arm. Suddenly, Kieran was very aware of the heat radiating through the thin cotton of Jaxon's sleeve. Jaxon didn't seem to notice that Kieran was still touching him. Reluctantly, Kieran pulled his hand back, somewhat embarrassed at the fantasies about Jaxon now racing through his head and traveling rapidly in the direction of his cock. He shifted in his seat as his jeans began to feel uncomfortably tight.

"Oh, you can't fool me, Kieran," Jaxon went on in a taunting tone that only exacerbated the growing problem in Kieran's pants. "Looks like you're kinda shy and blushing over there. Maybe I'm right after all, huh?"

"Fuck off!" Kieran responded, wondering what the fuck his body was telling him.

"Anyone else here you're attracted to?" Jaxon asked with a sly smile. Was it Kieran's imagination or did Jaxon just get a lot closer to him? Their legs weren't just brushing together; now Jaxon's leg was pressed up against Kieran's, sending more pleasurable shockwaves to his cock. And Kieran was enjoying that entirely too much. *Is Jaxon doing this on purpose?*

"Uh, yeah, a few guys," Kieran replied, trying to decide what to do. Jaxon seemed so curious about Kieran in particular, or had he just misinterpreted Jaxon's interest?

"Well, who?" Jaxon insisted.

Kieran turned to him, meeting Jaxon's eyes directly, and then wished he hadn't. Those eyes that ranged from green to hazel were at this moment a glittering emerald color that somehow took away Kieran's ability to think and speak, and possibly even breathe. They were beautiful and electrifying. And that was just the man's eyes. Kieran didn't even want to think about his lips, not while he was this close to Jaxon.

"What's it to you?" Kieran asked, hoping that Jaxon hadn't just asked out of mere curiosity.

"Well, making conversation, for one. You know, go out drinking with your buds and maybe talk about the hot girls. Only you don't want girls, so I'm trying to accommodate that." Jaxon sipped more beer. "Second, I admit, I'm just curious. No one in this town is gay, at least not openly, so I don't know much about it, except from movies and TV. I'm just trying to deepen my knowledge. I'm an educator, remember?" Jaxon's dimples emphasized how much he was enjoying the conversation.

"And you're planning on including this in the curriculum of the local high school?" Kieran teased.

"Okay, you've got me. It has nothing to do with my quest for erudition." Jaxon gave a guilty shrug.

"You do know the best way to find something out is to experience it yourself?" As soon as Kieran said it, he wished he hadn't. He'd meant it, and he wanted Jaxon to take him up on it in the worst way. Or, it could completely backfire.

Jaxon stared into Kieran's eyes for a moment, then glanced down at his watch. "Fuck, it's much later than I realized. I better get home." Jaxon's tone betrayed nothing of what he might be thinking. He was all business again. "It's a school night," he added, and Kieran couldn't help reveling that Jaxon hadn't mentioned Danetta as the reason he had to get going.

"Right. Speaking of school," Kieran began, "would it be okay if I came by your office tomorrow and spent some time with you while you're working? Get an idea of who you are professionally?" He certainly couldn't ignore what had seemed like a moment of mutual attraction to Jaxon, but the moment had passed. Mentioning it was out of the question.

At least because of the column, Kieran could spend a lot of time with Jaxon and not arouse any suspicion, and maybe he'd find out if it was just his imagination and whether he'd misinterpreted Jaxon's behavior as *attraction*. He'd enjoyed talking with Jaxon almost as much as he liked looking at him and imagining him in bed. When they'd been with Danetta, she had controlled the conversation, and Jaxon didn't get much opportunity to show his true personality.

"Sure. How about meeting me at Tumbleweeds for lunch, and then you can come back with me for the afternoon? Most of the trouble happens after lunch anyway, and it might make for a more exciting visit for you if I can suspend someone or break up a fight. I have to impress you somehow." Jaxon's grin went straight to Kieran's crotch—again. "Besides, I get the idea that you're not much of an early riser."

"Not at all." Kieran gave an unapologetic smile. "What time tomorrow?"

"Eleven work for you?"

"I can manage to get up in time for that." Kieran nodded. "See you at eleven."

They walked to the bar, and Kieran asked for the check as he pulled his wallet out.

"On the house." Sam pushed his hand away when he offered her some cash anyway.

He stuffed a twenty into the tip jar before they left.

"I can't get anyone to take my money around here," Kieran said when they were out on the street.

"Stop carping." Jaxon gave Kieran a friendly punch on the arm. "Good night."

"Good night." Kieran turned in the opposite direction from Jaxon, not letting himself look back at Jaxon heading away.

Back in his room at the Trail Dust, Kieran spent an hour entering notes about dinner and the bar on his laptop. He was distracted by his attraction to Jaxon, but it wasn't so bad to be actively interested in someone worthy of interest, no matter how unattainable. Jaxon was educated, well read, and interesting to talk to. He *wasn't* particularly interesting when he was with Danetta, however. Kieran was eager to see what Jaxon was like with his students and how he interacted with the staff. It would illustrate what kind of man Jaxon really was.

Kieran decided not to blame Jaxon for the kissy-face, lovey-dovey bullshit. Jaxon hadn't mentioned Danetta during their conversation in the bar, except when Kieran specifically asked about her. Truly pussy-whipped men constantly mention their significant others, Kieran theorized, even when it's totally inappropriate. It seemed Danetta ramped up the PDA at dinner for Kieran's sake, as a means of convincing him she and Jaxon were really in love. Kieran found it suspect and was sure Danetta was hiding something.

Kieran washed up and slid under the covers of the comfortable, fresh-smelling bed. He couldn't get images of Jaxon out of his mind: his beautiful face with its charming freckles and pouty, perfect mouth. The idea of Danetta enjoying Jaxon's body was downright depressing, but so far, he had no proof that she didn't deserve it.

Kieran had only his suspicions and a gnawing in the pit of his stomach. He tried not to picture Jaxon with Danetta and went back to dreaming about Jaxon's pink, pillowy lips, wondering what they would feel like on his cock. Kieran was instantly hard.

Imagining more things he'd like Jaxon to do to him, it didn't take many strokes for Kieran to come. But afterward, as he drifted off to sleep, he felt lonelier than ever.

Chapter Nine

JAXON WATCHED Kieran walk back toward the Trail Dust. It was after midnight, and he should get home, but his feet felt like cement blocks as he tried to turn in that direction. He sucked in some cool night air.

What the hell had he been saying—and doing? Why had he steered the conversation in such a dangerous direction? Asking about Kieran's sex life had been so far out of line. But Kieran didn't seem to mind. He'd welcomed Jaxon's curiosity and hadn't evaded the truth.

At this point Jaxon wondered if that was a good thing.

Or a very, very bad one.

Definitely the latter if he'd guessed the thoughts racing through Jaxon's mind as they sat there, close enough to touch. Close enough to kiss.

God, he'd wanted to know what Kieran's lips would feel like. Even as Jaxon walked home, the memory of that desire aroused him and heat flowed through his body.

The only way to stop himself from imagining things, from wondering too much, had been to keep bringing up Danetta. She was like a circuit breaker. The only thing guaranteed to keep that delicious current from igniting and turning Jaxon's world into a deadly inferno.

As he rounded the corner of his street, Jaxon turned the other direction. He wasn't ready to go home yet. He wandered the silent streets of town and considered all the forces that had brought him to this place at this point in time.

Could someone invent time travel before Saturday?

When the buzz of beer and the sensory overload from sitting so close to Kieran subsided, Jaxon turned for home. He unlocked the door quietly.

The unpleasant odors from the pork chops from hell still permeated the air as he tiptoed up the stairs. On second thought, even the devil might consider Lorraine's pork chops a punishment too cruel and unusual.

He lay down so as not to disturb Danetta on the other side of the bed and stared at the ceiling. Even up here he could smell the stench from dinner. It made his stomach churn.

It wasn't the booze; it was the knowledge that this was his future, all tied up in that fancy ribbon, and there was nothing he could do about it.

Was there?

Chapter Ten

Tuesday

A KNOCK sounded on Kieran's motel room door. He opened it to find Jaxon standing on his doorstep. Wordlessly, Jaxon came in and closed the door quickly behind himself. Taken completely by surprise, Kieran let Jaxon shove him roughly against the door and kiss him hungrily, fingers playing through Kieran's hair.

That mouth. Those lips. Kieran wanted to suck on Jaxon's gorgeous lower lip, but couldn't because Jaxon had taken control. Kieran was hard as a rock as Jaxon moaned into his mouth, tongue greedy and demanding. Kieran realized Jaxon was actually trying to say something but wouldn't stop kissing Kieran long enough to speak.

"Want. Your. Cock." Jaxon breathed the words out between kisses, his voice little more than a rumble in the back of his throat. Just the sound had Kieran desperate for them to get their clothes off as quickly as possible.

"God, yes," Kieran moaned in response, starting to unbutton his shirt.

Jaxon dropped his hands to Kieran's belt, then leaned away to unbuckle it. With his hips glued to Kieran's, his erection dug into Kieran in a most agreeable way. Kieran helped Jaxon with the button and zipper on his jeans, and soon Kieran's jeans and shorts were down around his ankles. Jaxon slid down Kieran's body, letting his hands play and linger along Kieran's chest and abs before he took hold of Kieran's cock.

Kieran moaned as Jaxon's fingers touched him, and he looked down as Jaxon's obscenely beautiful lips parted to take Kieran's cock into his mouth. Jaxon licked and sucked, tonguing the crown, poking his tongue into the slit, and making deliciously wet, dirty sounds.

Kieran knew he wouldn't last long and gave himself over to Jaxon's surprisingly skilled mouth. *God, this guy learns fast.* Jaxon used one hand to cup Kieran's balls as a finger explored farther back.

Jaxon's other hand wrapped around the base of Kieran's aching hard-on. Kieran put his own hand over Jaxon's, and they stroked together. Kieran held Jaxon's gaze, mischievous green eyes dark with arousal as they glittered under thick eyelashes.

"So close," Kieran began before he was interrupted by the shrill ring of his cell phone. It was on the night table by the bed, far out of reach. Kieran closed his eyes, concentrating on Jaxon's mouth and hands, but the phone wouldn't stop. Kieran finally opened his eyes to find that Jaxon was gone. *A dream!* Kieran lay in bed, alone, with only his own hand on his painfully hard cock and the phone still demanding his attention.

"Fuck!" Kieran tried to press the "ignore" button on the phone, and finally it went silent.

Who the fuck could be calling?

He wanted to murder whoever it was because they had interrupted that deliciously realistic dream. Kieran kept stroking himself, not quite as close to orgasm as he'd been before the phone had intervened. But the ringing started again. Kieran grabbed it and checked the display. *Alexa.*

"Lex, lemme call you back, okay?" Kieran growled into the phone.

"Are you alone?" she asked.

"Yes." As soon as he said it, he realized he should have lied, then she'd stop bothering him. "I gotta call you back."

"No! Don't hang up. Just listen, it'll only take a minute," she insisted.

"Hang on just a sec." Kieran let the phone fall to his chest. He turned his attention back to his cock. With a couple of strokes, he was nearly there and tried not to moan as he attempted to finish.

"Kieran!" Alexa's voice was tiny but still audible. "Are you jacking off? You are! I can't believe you!"

Kieran laughed as he came, noisily.

"Kieran! Did you just come? Eww!" Alexa was still on the line, so she couldn't be that offended.

"I told you it was a bad time to call, didn't I?" Kieran picked up the phone again, still somewhat breathless and his voice a bit gravelly. He grabbed a handful of tissues from the box near the bed and started cleaning up. "So what is so all-fired important?" he asked almost cheerfully.

"Jesus fucking Christ, I can't believe you made me listen to that!" Alexa said indignantly.

"You could have just hung up." Kieran smirked even though she couldn't see it. "You deserve whatever you heard."

"Okay, fair enough. Hey, does this mean I've had phone sex with you?" She chuckled, her own voice low and flirtatious.

"Yes."

"Wow, that makes me the only woman you've had sex with in a long time. I feel really special."

"Only woman *ever*. And you should. Now why did you call?"

"I wanted to know how your first day in Bumfuck Springs went?"

Had he only been here one day? Why did it feel like so much longer? "You interrupted me for that?"

"Well, I didn't know I was interrupting, did I? So how'd it go?"

"Pretty good. I met Danetta and Jaxon."

"Hmm, *Jaxon*, huh? I can tell by the way you said his name that he's already made quite an impression on you. He's hot, then?"

"*That's* an understatement." Kieran paused, still catching his breath. "I think he's sickeningly in love with Danetta. And he's not worried about Saturday—he's convinced she's gonna go through with the whole thing. Danetta acted pretty certain of it, too. Maybe she is pregnant," he joked. "Did you ever ask her about that?"

"I hinted around at it. She clammed up, said it wasn't any of my business, but if I really wanted to know, then no, she wasn't pregnant. She got pretty annoyed at me even though I tried to play it as a joke. So what'd you find out?"

Kieran briefly described his day, his talks with Tom and Jordan, and the disastrous dinner.

"Oh, Danetta's parents are really something, aren't they?" Alexa remarked. "I remember them from the two weddings I went to. Her mom is fucking scary, and her father is like the perfect servant, always there but never really seen or heard."

"Yeah, that's a great description," Kieran agreed. "They'd make anyone think ten, twenty times before getting married. Why didn't you warn me about them?"

"Now that would have ruined all the fun of you meeting them yourself, wouldn't it?" she said breezily.

"Bitch!" Kieran replied. They were close enough she wouldn't be offended. Kieran glanced at the clock. "Oh, damn, I need to get going. I'm meeting Jaxon for lunch, and then I'm spending the afternoon at the school with him."

"Is that a date?" Alexa teased.

"Only in my mind." Kieran gave a self-deprecating laugh. "Talk to you later, okay? I might have a few things I'd like you to look up for me, if you can get to it before you leave for Napa?"

"Sure, just give me a buzz. If I'm too busy, I'll get Brad. Enjoy your date!" Alexa said sarcastically, then added a loud smoochy kiss.

"Hey, Lex?"

"Yeah?"

"What're you wearing?" Kieran asked in a deep, sexy voice.

"Fuck off!" Alexa hung up.

Kieran hopped in the shower and was dressed and ready to go with plenty of time to spare. He wasn't the most punctual person at the best of times, and he chalked this up to his inappropriate desire to see Jaxon again. It was only a five-minute walk to the restaurant, so he spent some time going over his notes from the previous day and making a list of topics he wanted to cover while he was at school with Jaxon.

When Kieran walked into Tumbleweeds at eleven on the dot, Jaxon was already there waiting for him. *Very punctual*, Kieran noticed, which said a lot about Jaxon. Maybe he was looking forward to spending more time with Kieran. *Wishful thinking.*

"Morning," Jaxon said as Kieran sat down.

"Hey." Kieran didn't get any further because a waitress was hovering with a menu. She had shoulder-length brown hair and a nametag that proclaimed "Howdy, I'm Erica!" Probably not from around here, otherwise her name would be spelled *E-r-i-k-u-h* or something equally as ridiculous. Oblivious to his opinions, she smiled and handed Kieran the menu.

As Erica walked away, Kieran noticed that she was wearing a *very* short cowgirl skirt and Western boots. He glanced at the menu and noticed the items all had ridiculous Wild West-inspired names. He tried not to roll his eyes at the overwhelming cuteness of it all. On the other hand, there was a busboy who would look very good in a male version of the waitress outfit—and even better out of it.

Forget busboys. He was here with Jaxon!

"Despite the kitschy décor and the theme, the food is good here." Jaxon had picked up on what Kieran was thinking, though hopefully not on the part about the busboy. Only then did Kieran notice the table was made from a wagon wheel. *Christ!*

"Can I get a turkey club?" Kieran asked when Erica came by again. "I can't figure out what you call it here, sorry." Kieran gave her his brightest smile, useful for extricating himself from any trouble he might have gotten into.

"Oh, that's the Rustler, and it comes with fries or coleslaw." She had a smile that made Kieran wonder what she was thinking. Well, maybe it wasn't a complete mystery because she let her eyes linger on Kieran's face and chest before treating Jaxon to the same once-over.

"Can I possibly get both?" Kieran flashed his dimples.

"Absolutely!" she replied, obviously swayed by Kieran's charm and the power of his dimples. "Something to drink?"

"Iced tea, please." Kieran looked over at Jaxon, waiting for him to order.

"I've already ordered," he replied.

Erica quickly returned with two iced teas and swept off to another table, hips swinging and skirt flaring up in a way that didn't interest Kieran all that much but caught the attention of just about every other guy she walked past—except for Jaxon. Kieran glanced around at the western décor. So this was where the cow horns and stuffed armadillos ended up. Cowboy hats and boots had been artfully arranged on the walls and part of an old covered wagon took up one corner, all things that sometimes made him wish he wasn't from Texas. This was a New Yorker's idea of Texas.

He took a minute to size up the other customers. The place was nearly packed, so the food must be as good as Jaxon had said. Most people smiled when Kieran caught their eye, but a few gave him a look that made him very uncomfortable. He'd seen that look way too many times before, and it always worried him.

"Jaxon." Kieran kept his voice low, causing Jaxon to lean in to hear him. "Did you tell anyone what I told you last night? About me?"

"About being gay?" Jaxon whispered back, only mouthing the last word. He'd clearly picked up on the looks Kieran was getting, too.

"Yeah. I'm getting a bad vibe here."

"No. Well, I told Danny; I didn't think that would matter." Jaxon's voice was still little more than a whisper. "But no one else, and I don't think she would say anything. Why would she?" That was clearly meant as a rhetorical question. "Maybe someone overheard us in the saloon?"

"Maybe, but I didn't think anyone was close enough." Kieran had been paying more attention to Jaxon than to his surroundings.

"Are you worried if people find out?"

"A little," Kieran said. "This is Texas, after all." He wasn't sure how he'd be treated in the small town but worried it might deter some people from talking to him. And there was always the threat of physical harm from people who didn't think his life was worth much. "Should I be? What's the attitude like here?" he asked Jaxon.

"Well, I don't know of anyone in town who's gay, so I don't have a good feel for how people will take it. I've never heard any homophobic comments, except the typical locker-room shit."

"What did Danetta say when you told her?"

"Nothing. She's lived away from here, so she's open-minded. She was mainly interested in knowing what we talked about last night, so I just summed up our conversation. I left out the discussion of her parents, though." Jaxon gave a conspiratorial grin.

Erica came by with the food. As Jaxon and Kieran ate in comfortable silence, Kieran went over what he'd asked Jaxon the night before. He'd tried a few ways to wheedle out that mysterious and maddeningly secret bond to Danetta that Jaxon mentioned, but he didn't think Jaxon picked up on it enough to let Danetta know what Kieran was trying to get at.

They stuck to small talk for the rest of the meal, which Kieran finished off with warm homemade peach pie with the flakiest crust he'd ever eaten, topped with two scoops of vanilla ice cream—after he'd again eaten the rest of Jaxon's fries. When Kieran asked for the bill, the waitress told him it was "on the house." So far, nothing had significantly changed from the day before, Kieran concluded as he and Jaxon left the restaurant and headed for the high school.

KIERAN SPENT the afternoon in Jaxon's office, watching him go about his work, which consisted of speaking with teachers and students and one conference with the parents of a suspended student who faced possible expulsion. Kieran sat unobtrusively out of the way, after Jaxon made sure no one minded. Kieran was impressed with the way the staff respected Jaxon, even though he was much younger than many of the teachers.

Even the students seemed eager to earn his approval, including two sophomores caught fighting. Jaxon listened attentively and responded with obvious sincerity, offering Kieran a glance at why Jaxon had been so successful in his career.

After the two budding boxers left, Kieran continued with his interview. "So, when is the end of the school year?"

"Two more weeks of school, then another two of administrative wrap-up before I get my summer break."

"You're postponing the honeymoon to next month, then?"

"Next week, actually," Jaxon replied. "It's exam week. The staff won't need me for that. Mrs. Reddick, the vice principal, can handle it. I'll be back for graduation and then the admin work I mentioned."

"Where are you going?"

"Hawaii—Kauai, to be exact. It's supposed to be beautiful."

Something in Jaxon's tone struck Kieran, as if Jaxon wasn't entirely convinced he would enjoy the trip.

"It's gorgeous. I've been once before," Kieran said.

"You'll have to tell me the best things to do and see while we're there."

"Let me think on it and see what I remember. It was a few years ago." He wondered why Jaxon needed to find activities to do on his honeymoon. "Any big plans for summer break?"

Why did he keep asking these ridiculously inane questions? Even Jaxon seemed like he'd rather be talking about any other subject. But any other subject would be dangerous. Kieran kept the focus on Danetta, if only to remind himself that Jaxon was off limits.

"Danny is attending some seminar in Savannah, so we'll go there for a couple of weeks, then maybe visit some other historical southern towns. We haven't planned anything else. The wedding's been our priority so far." The answer came out as if he'd rehearsed it. Wasn't Jaxon looking forward to any of this?

"You seem to have taken a pretty active role in helping Danetta with that, from what she was saying."

"Are you kidding?" Jaxon let out a peal of genuine laughter. "She doesn't want or need my help. She's been through this three times before, so she knows what she wants and how to do it. I'd just be in the way." He turned and looked Kieran in the eye. "I honestly don't care one way or the other about any of it," he added, and Kieran added a few more respect points. "But she wants to make me feel like I'm involved." Jaxon's tone verged on sardonic.

The office phone rang—Danetta calling to say she'd arranged for Kieran to meet Marc, groom number three, and that she'd be by to pick Kieran up in ten minutes.

As much as Kieran wanted to meet Marc, he was disappointed he wouldn't get to spend the rest of the afternoon with Jaxon. And just when he was getting beneath Jaxon's outwardly cheerful façade. That must have been obvious from the look on his face, Kieran realized with alarm, when Jaxon continued to stare at him. What else had been so obvious to Jaxon?

A short knock sounded at the door, and Jaxon's assistant popped her head in tentatively. "Jaxon, Jerry McAllister's father is on the phone again. If you don't talk to him, he's coming down here."

"I'm just leaving anyway." Kieran stood and collected things.

"Terri, tell him I'll call back this afternoon."

"But—"

"If he wants to come by, let him." Jaxon turned to Kieran. "I'll walk you to the front door."

"I can see you're tied up here." Kieran moved toward the door.

Jaxon came around the desk with the same disappointed frown that Kieran must be wearing. "It can wait."

They walked through the oddly silent halls at a leisurely pace. The students and staff who passed by nodded or offered polite greetings to both of them. Kieran noticed paper flowers, hearts, or other decorations on some of the lockers. None of the graffiti he'd gotten used to seeing at the New York schools. Was Jaxon a strict disciplinarian, or did the kids just behave better here?

Kieran intended to find out. "It's so much quieter than I remember from my high school. And much cleaner and neater than New York schools. Decorations rather than graffiti."

Jaxon smiled as he turned a corner Kieran didn't recall passing on the way to Jaxon's office. "Our students have more respect for their school than the average. We give prizes for the best locker decorations or the cleanest classrooms. Gift cards for books or music. It's reduced some of the problems that most high schools face."

"Were those your ideas?"

Jaxon gave a shrug. "I wouldn't say that."

They came to the end of the hall and out through the double doors that led to the sports fields behind the school. A gym class was playing soccer, the kids shouting and cheering when one scored a goal.

"Where's Danetta meeting me?"

"Oh, out front, I guess." Jaxon sounded distracted, as if he'd completely forgotten Kieran's next appointment. He moved away from the building and into the sun, which gave his hair glittering golden lights.

To Kieran he could have been a modern-day Greek god. With longer hair and out of the button-down shirt, it wouldn't be difficult to imagine. But not a particularly good idea.

"How's the football team?" Kieran asked, glancing toward the stadium situated beyond the soccer field. High school football was a religion in some parts of Texas.

Jaxon smiled again, looking even more golden. "They're pretty good. No championships. But our team has the highest GPA in the state."

They both laughed. GPA didn't mean a damn thing to most football recruiters, especially in Texas.

"We're working on a recruiting program to bring in some better players who aren't necessarily good enough to get a top football scholarship."

"That might bring the GPA down."

"True. But it will help our winning average a hell of a lot more."

"That bad?"

Jaxon shook his head and gave Kieran an adorable grin. "I'd get booted out of here if I didn't do something on that account. This is still Texas."

They'd been strolling slowly past the soccer game, and Kieran's stomach tightened as they meandered toward the front of the building. He could spend the rest of the day here, with Jaxon, getting to know him. He wanted to. Jaxon suddenly stopped before they turned the corner.

"Kieran, would you like to meet up at Sam's again?" Jaxon asked

Kieran's spirits rose more than he should have allowed. He was being ridiculous. Jaxon had been talking about Danetta much of the afternoon. He couldn't possibly have any interest in Kieran beyond being cooperative for the column, could he? Again, Jaxon's smile seemed more than merely friendly, but maybe that was Kieran's overactive—and admittedly more than slightly horny—imagination.

He forced himself to pause before blurting out an immediate yes. "Sure. Tonight?"

"Good. How about eight o'clock?"

"Yeah, sounds g-good." Kieran stopped himself from saying "great," but he couldn't help searching Jaxon's gaze for a hint of emotion. Was that a brighter smile, or was he just squinting in the sunshine?

"I wondered where you had gotten to." Danetta's voice startled Kieran and seemed to have wiped the smile off Jaxon's face. The sparkle in his eyes didn't look as bright. Maybe it wasn't just the sun after all.

"Sorry, I got distracted." Jaxon didn't sound that sorry. Or that distracted.

Kieran kept his glee to himself. He expected to find out more later that evening.

Chapter Eleven

MARC ROSSITER was the assistant DA for the county. His office was in the famous courthouse Kieran had read about online. Though he'd passed by it probably a dozen times so far, this was his first time entering.

As before, Danetta gave a running commentary on the historical accuracy of the furnishings and fixtures in the building all the way down to the paint. She seemed to really enjoy her job. Kieran nodded while tuning out nearly everything she said on the topic.

This would be the last appointment he'd allow Danetta to plan for him. He didn't want to risk her manipulating not only the information he might discover at these chats, but also the impression the men had of him.

Danetta's heels echoed off walls and a high ceiling as they took a curving marble stairway up to the second floor. Away from the rotunda, the air was thick and warm. When they got to a door with gold painted letters announcing the Office of the District Attorney of Buck County, Danetta strode in as if she owned the place.

Inside it was much cooler, thanks to the ubiquitous air conditioning.

"Hey, there, Danetta," the receptionist said. "Got everything organized for Saturday?" The woman was in her thirties and had impressive light brown Big Hair, but nothing like Danetta's mom's. Lorraine had probably been County Hair Queen back in the day.

"Pretty much, Sue Ann. I can't wait to tell you! First, though, this is Kieran Quinn from *Gloss* magazine in New York City."

"I've heard all about you, Mr. Quinn." Sue Ann turned her head slightly away in that coy way Texas girls seemed to learn in kindergarten. "You enjoying Buckwheat Springs?" She turned back to him in order to give him a good look-see.

"Yes, I am." Kieran wouldn't venture to guess why he was enjoying his visit, but he didn't have to lie. "Everyone's just *so* nice."

"I think Marc's expecting us, Sue Ann."

"Oh, right." She pulled her gaze off Kieran. "Y'all go right on in."

"I'll be back in a minute to tell you about the flowers!" Danetta's voice rose in excitement and her face crinkled up into the picture of happiness.

Sue Ann responded with a feminine squeal.

Kieran gave a polite nod before he followed Danetta past Sue Ann's desk. They barely paused at the inner door as Danetta gave a quick knock and entered.

"We're a teensy bit behind schedule...." Her voice trailed off.

A very tall, very thin man with straight, short dark hair and lively blue-gray eyes came around from behind his desk to greet them. He held out a hand to Kieran.

"Nice to meet you, Kieran." He even pronounced it correctly. "I have to admit, I'm a fan of yours. Got a subscription to *Gloss*." He nodded and gave an open grin as he wrung Kieran's hand with more strength than could be expected from someone so thin.

"Thanks. I don't get to meet many of my readers."

Marc let out a snorty kind of laugh. "I don't imagine you would."

Danetta had been standing to the side while they greeted each other, but now she spoke. "Why's that, Marc?"

Marc looked at her with a gentle smile. He got a softness at the corners of his eyes, a genuine affection such as Kieran had seen from Tom and Jordan. "Probably because they don't live in New York."

She nodded and smiled. "I'll leave you two for a chat. Sue Ann wants to hear about the flowers." She gave Marc and Kieran another sweet smile and left, shutting the door behind her.

"Danetta's really something, isn't she?" Marc asked. He wore an expensive, well-tailored suit, more than a notch above the professional attire Kieran had seen so far in the courthouse, probably a holdover from Marc's former life before Buckwheat Springs. And he made Kieran feel underdressed even in his designer cargo pants and thin button-down. He'd be right at home in the Hamptons.

"Oh, yeah. She's something," Kieran agreed, though he hadn't figured out exactly what yet. He hadn't been able to distinguish between the conflicting personality traits he'd seen so far. Admittedly, he'd been spending more time with the grooms than with the bride.

Marc sat back in his chair, one of those big executive-type things that dwarf most men. Given Marc's height, he fit the chair well. He inhaled and pressed his palms together.

"I won't beat around the bush here." His tone had changed from the breezy, good-natured one he'd used in front of Danetta. Kieran wouldn't want to be on the other side of the aisle from him in a trial. "I have read your work. That was no lie. But I'm no fan of yours. I don't much like your game, and I won't have you coming here and doing a number on Danetta the way you usually do with your articles."

Kieran opened his mouth to respond, but Marc wasn't finished.

"I'm prepared to go after you for libel if necessary. I'll call your publisher so fast your head will spin and make the little girl in the *Exorcist* look like she ought to be selling Girl Scout cookies. Got it?"

Kieran counted through the first five things he was tempted to say while trying not to look like he'd been kicked in the nuts. "Sure, Marc." He put on the smile that worked with 99 percent of the people he'd tried it on, suspecting Marc was in the 1 percent. "I haven't written anything yet, and I don't even have a good enough idea of anyone's personality or interests—except yours. I'm not sure what you're accusing me of at the moment."

Marc nodded. "I just want to spell things out first, before I say a word to you. This isn't an idle threat. It's a warning."

"Duly warned." Kieran was torn between smoothing Marc's ruffled feathers and riling him up enough to find out what he was trying to hide. He'd go with the former for the moment, but not rule out the latter. What had become crystal clear was that there was something mighty juicy to uncover. And Kieran was going to figure out what it was before the wedding.

"Good." Marc's smile returned, like an animal hiding its deathly sharp teeth. "It's possible I've overreacted a bit here, but I'd rather piss you off than have you upset Danny." Marc's tone had softened, and he leaned forward again, like an eager student waiting for the professor to test his knowledge of a favorite subject.

"Danetta has inspired an incredible degree of loyalty among the three of you. I get it with Tom, since they were high-school sweethearts. Jordan I haven't quite figured out yet, but you moved here from Dallas, giving up a promising high-powered position in the prosecutor's office. Maybe you were that much in love at one point." Kieran paused, watching Marc's face for any telltale movements that would key him in to which way to push. "We've all been there," Kieran lied. He'd never met anyone worth changing his entire life for. "But after she dumped you, why didn't you just go back? What are you still doing here?"

Marc's pupils contracted to tiny dots, and Kieran expected to feel claws sink into his throat. Instead, Marc let out a peal of laughter. "Okay, fair enough. I deserved that." He grinned and Kieran felt the tension between them dropping away again; this time for good.

"It's true. I met her in Dallas, and she stole my heart, and I gave up a lot to move here with her. But I found I liked small-town life. I grew up near Dallas and couldn't wait to move into the city. The whole bright lights, big city thing many of us have when we're too young to realize what we want, or appreciate what we do have."

Kieran looked up from his notepad. He wasn't writing, just doodling. People seemed to feel more important if they saw him taking notes. "You didn't like Dallas?"

"On the contrary, I loved it. Loved the pace, the pressure, the competition." Marc sat back in his chair again and turned up one corner of his mouth. "Where did you grow up?"

"Near San Antonio."

"Ah, a big city that's a small town. Are you glad you moved to New York?"

"Yes."

"Every single day?"

It was Kieran's turn to laugh. "Not every day. But most."

"That's what it's like here. I like the slower pace, the chance to get to know people, not just pretend to recognize them."

"Do you have a woman in your life now?"

"Do you?"

"Fair enough. Though your track record definitely includes at least one woman, so the question wasn't entirely out of line."

"Didn't you dig up *all* the dirt on my love life?" Marc's tone was unreadable. Was he flirting or just ribbing Kieran?

"Not yet, but I will. I need to defend myself against that libel suit you threatened me with." Kieran smiled so he wouldn't seem as much of a hardass as Marc had been.

"I'm not seeing anyone right now. But it's got nothing to do with Danny."

Marc's sudden change of mood intrigued Kieran. Could he be gay, or at least bi? It would be interesting to ask some more specific questions, but they'd gone far astray from what Kieran really had come to discuss. Danetta. "Right, let's get back to her. I'd like to understand this loyalty the three of you have for her. Help me out here."

"I still really care about her, and I want her to be happy."

"Why did she leave you at the altar?"

"That's one question I'm not prepared to answer."

"Would a few drinks change your mind?" Kieran offered his most charming smile and a dimple. If it didn't get him laid, it often got him a date. And it usually got him the answers he wanted.

"Not a chance. I'm not fool enough to drink around a journalist."

"Now you just sound like a politician."

"Ouch." Marc put his hand over his heart. "Truth is that question isn't mine to answer. Did you ask Danny?"

"Not yet. But I will. Do you think she'll answer me?"

"I don't know. All I'll say is that she wasn't ready to get married to me, just as she wasn't ready with Tom or Jordan. Until she's ready to talk about what happened before, I'm not sure she'll be ready to marry Jaxon either."

Now that was interesting. Kieran waited to see if Marc would say anything else.

"I hope she's talked to him, but I'll risk repeating myself: I wouldn't like to see it splashed on the pages of *Gloss*."

Kieran's reporter radar was flashing like crazy at what this big reason could be.

"So how do you feel about the wedding? Do you think she'll go through with it?"

"I think Jaxon's the best of us, so I hope like hell she does. I couldn't be happier for the two of them." Marc's gaze fell to Kieran's hands, gripping the pencil, but not moving. "You can quote me on that."

Kieran questioned whether Marc could honestly be as thrilled as Tom and Jordan had been about Danetta marrying Jaxon and began to wonder if Danetta had passed out scripts.

Speaking to the ex-grooms wasn't getting him anywhere. He had to bring in the big guns.

Chapter Twelve

BEFORE LEAVING Marc's office, Kieran paused in the doorway.

"Just one more thing."

"Is this your Columbo routine?"

"No. Something I just thought of." Kieran smiled again, but he didn't think Marc had bought the lie. "Who are Danetta's girlfriends? The bridesmaids, or anyone else in town I should talk to?"

Marc pursed his lips and pressed his palms together like he was praying for the answer. Then he listed half a dozen names, and Kieran made a point of writing them down and double-checking spelling.

"Thanks, then. I'm sure I'll be seeing you again soon," Kieran said as he left the office. Marc Rossiter hadn't offered to walk him to the hall. Just as well. Kieran stopped by Sue Ann's desk.

"Did you have a nice chat with Marc?"

"Yes. What about Danetta's flowers?" He winked.

"Oh, they're gonna be beautiful. I can't wait till Saturday."

"What are the colors?" He'd learned in a short span of time what kind of questions to ask, though he couldn't care less.

"Gold and pale pink."

"Are you a bridesmaid?"

"Oh, no." She shook her head. "I'm not good enough friends to be asked."

"That's too bad. You'd look beautiful in a pale pink dress."

Sue Ann gave a surprisingly girlish giggle, coloring a little at the compliment. "You're sweet to say so."

"Who are the bridesmaids?"

Sue Ann rattled off eight names, and Kieran wrote them down. "Thank you. Now you'll be sure to save a dance for me at the reception?"

Now her cheeks flamed. "Okay, I sure will."

God, he felt like a heel at the moment. But he had at least one sure-fire contact and another source of information about Marc Rossiter. And a dance partner for Saturday night. He'd need someone to keep his mind off seeing Jaxon holding Danetta and gazing lovingly into her eyes. Sue Ann was a much safer choice than any of the men who'd caught his eye in town.

BACK AT the Trail Dust, Kieran found Mrs. Connors quilting again behind the desk. He asked for a local phone book. When she realized he wanted to call Danetta's friends, she told Kieran where they all worked and suggested that he'd have better luck visiting them there.

Armed with his list, Kieran headed for the closest one, Penny Martin, who worked in a tiny vintage clothing shop on Main Street. Penny was a petite girl with beautiful almond-shaped brown eyes and sleek dark brown hair that fell in a glossy wave over her shoulders.

She was as beautiful as any model he'd met in New York, but she had a sweet innocence about her, as if she was unaware of her beauty. It was refreshing after his experience of vain and vacuous beauties— male and female.

Penny had been friends with Danetta since childhood and was more than happy to discuss Danetta, the weddings, and the grooms, and seemed quite candid answering the few questions he'd asked.

"Penny, there's customers to ring up!" A high-pitched female voice carried across the entire store. Penny's shoulders rose, and she squeezed her eyes shut for a split second.

"I have to get back to work."

"I wouldn't want to get you in any trouble." Kieran grabbed a pretty teal silk scarf with gold fringe and took it to the counter. Lex would love this.

Penny shook her head. "You don't h—"

"It's a present for a friend. Now, how about if I take you and the rest of the bridesmaids for dinner tonight? I know it's kind of short notice, but—"

"Oh, that would be fun!" She gave an adorable shrug and beamed. "Let me call the girls and arrange it. I'm sure they'd all be happy to change whatever plans they had for a chance to talk to you! Now where did you want to go?"

"You decide. I don't know many places. What's your favorite place?"

"Well, La Piñata has like twenty different flavors of margaritas."
Penny's eyes widened. "Would that be okay, to have margaritas too?"
Apparently she hoped it was.

"Of course. Sounds fantastic!" Kieran mirrored her excitement,
happy to provide as many margaritas as the job required. At this point,
he could use one himself.

NINETY MINUTES later Kieran found himself at La Piñata with most
of Danetta's bridesmaids, a rainbow of margaritas arrayed in front of
them. It turned out that Erica, the Tumbleweeds waitress, was among
the group. The girls happily sipped and chattered. Kieran flirted
shamelessly with them and kept ordering margaritas, food, anything
they wanted. They were all thrilled about the wedding and being
bridesmaids.

"Just out of curiosity, are you wearing the same dresses as any of
the previous weddings?"

"No," Erica said. "But Danny's real good about pickin' dresses
we'd want to wear somewhere else."

"Oh, they're beautiful this time!" Cassie, a lively blonde with a
head full of glossy curls said. "Look." She pulled her phone out of her
purse and showed Kieran her dress, a pearly pale pink.

"Here's mine." Kristin held up her phone and the others
followed suit.

"Gorgeous." Kieran noticed each dress was a slightly different
style that flattered each girl's figure. It was rather thoughtful of
Danetta. In Kieran's limited experience of weddings, bridesmaids all
wore the same style, which sadly didn't suit most of the girls and
seemed to make each girl's figure flaws glaringly obvious as guests
compared them.

"Here's the one from last time." Jessica pushed her phone under
Kieran's nose.

For the next two hours, Kieran brazenly asked as many questions
as he could get away with, hoping to pin down a less-rehearsed picture
of Danetta and her secret.

"We don't have a clue," a bubbly redhead called Lizzie said.
"We'd love to know how Danetta can get all of these hot guys to fall in
love with her and want to marry her. She just has some natural charm

or something. I mean, she goes on these trips for work, and like within a few months, a new boyfriend decides to move to town."

"Yeah, and then a month or two later, she's got another ring on her finger," Penny added. "Well, you know, not all the rings at once. Like, a different new one," she clarified, slightly slurring her words. She'd already worked her way through about half the rainbow. Kieran hoped he'd get something sufficiently juicy to justify the bar tab to Jeff.

"She got some sort of formula for catching a guy in six months or less, it seems." Dinah, a serious-looking blonde girl with tortoiseshell glasses sipped something alarmingly blue. "She really needs to share the secret with us," she added, glancing around at the others, who nodded in agreement.

"But Jaxon, wow, he's really the best of all," Lizzie added dreamily, and the others agreed loudly and went on to list all of Jaxon's charms, most of which Kieran had already discovered or suspected. But the idea of Danetta having a six-month formula stuck in his head, and he jotted down a few notes of points to follow up on in his research.

A glance at his watch reminded Kieran he needed to get going for his "date" with Jaxon, and he thanked everyone for coming to dinner.

Outside on the sidewalk, Penny tugged on his sleeve. "Kieran? Don't tell Danny we drank all those margaritas, okay?" She wore her wide-eyed worried look again.

"Wh—don't you worry. I won't say a thing." He held a finger up to his lips and she mirrored the gesture. "Are y'all okay to get home?"

The girls nodded and assured him they were all walking and lived nearby. He waved as they tottered on their heels, holding each other up and giggling. Penny's request had caught him off guard, and then he remembered that Danny didn't drink—at least she hadn't at dinner the other night. Memories of Lorraine's behavior came back to Kieran with startling clarity. It also explained why Danny didn't like Jaxon going to Sam's.

And he'd better get his ass over there, just a couple of blocks away.

He'd gotten as much information as he was going to get tonight, and now the girls liked and trusted him. Next time he might get one to lower her guard so he could extract something really useful.

Kieran wished he'd left La Piñata earlier so he'd have time to stop at the Trail Dust and change, but he didn't want to be late getting to Sam's. He arrived with two minutes to spare, but Jaxon was already at the bar, working on a beer.

"Sorry I'm late. I got stuck at dinner." Kieran nodded to Sam, and then settled with Jaxon at a table near the back of the place, farther from the bar and the door than they'd sat the previous night. He chose a spot where they could both face the bar, and Kieran could get an idea who might be listening to their conversation, as well as watch the other patrons. He felt safer that way.

Sam came by and took his order, then returned a few minutes later with a bottle of Jester King weisse. Kieran smiled at the label showing what looked like an anthropomorphized female bear wearing cat-eye glasses and a blue bikini. He took a long swig, enjoying the bite of the wheat.

"I've definitely been away from Texas for too long. These craft brews are something else." Kieran took another draw as he looked at Jaxon.

"I like that one too."

Jaxon's hair was a bit damp, and Kieran's brain conjured images of naked, wet Jaxon soaping himself up. The temperature was definitely rising. Kieran drank another quarter of his beer, trying to cool down.

But Jaxon did smell nice and clean, with the light, fresh scent of a cologne Kieran couldn't name. Had Jaxon taken a shower just for him? Or had he just fucked Danetta and washed up after? Technically, that was still a shower for Kieran, wasn't it?

"You already ate?" Jaxon asked. Apparently this was one event about which word hadn't yet traveled around town.

"I took the bridesmaids out for dinner and twenty flavors of margaritas."

"And you still want beer?"

"I didn't actually drink any margaritas. Penny might have tried all twenty herself."

"La Piñata, I'll bet." Jaxon chuckled. "Ah, that explains it," he added cryptically.

"Explains what?"

"Your perfume. Unless you were wearing it for me or something." Jaxon raised his eyebrows and grinned.

With all the hugging, Kieran definitely smelled of bridesmaid—or at least their perfume. It was certainly embarrassing to smell so girly around Jaxon, and hopefully no one else had noticed.

Sam appeared out of nowhere with a tray and put a plate in front of Jaxon: a grilled chicken sandwich and curly fries.

"I went to the gym after school and didn't get a chance to eat yet." Jaxon bit enthusiastically into the sandwich. "I gotta lay off the cheeseburgers." He patted his stomach.

From what Kieran could see—and he had definitely looked—Jaxon was in good shape, with a firm, flat stomach. Tonight he was wearing a button-down shirt close fitting enough to give a clear impression of his well-built upper body. Not that Kieran was really looking now. Much.

"What about the fries?" Kieran tried to divert attention from the fact he was staring at Jaxon's body. He couldn't help being relieved to know Jaxon hadn't been with Danetta before he'd come out to meet him.

"Oh, those are for you." Jaxon rotated his plate so the fries were within easy reach for Kieran.

Jesus, Kieran thought. This was too much. What was Jaxon playing at here? He was being awfully friendly, but nothing so obvious that Kieran could interpret it as more. Still, Kieran was sure there was *something* in Jaxon's smile and his continued interest in making plans with Kieran, especially after that detour past the sports fields that afternoon, as if Jaxon wasn't ready to let Danetta take him away.

Kieran glanced at Jaxon while he was busy eating, wondering how much was imagination and how much was real. He'd have to wait for Jaxon to let him know exactly what it was.

The conversation quickly moved to sports, sizing up the Mavericks' chances at another championship, Kieran dissing the Cowboys, and Jaxon questioning what the Yankees were thinking with A-Rod.

After a couple of beers, Kieran ordered shots of the best tequila Sam had behind the bar and a couple more of a middle-quality tequila. They knocked back the cheaper shots quickly, then sipped at the smooth *añejo* while they talked.

"Hey now, I'm not a Yankees fan," Kieran said. "Still love my Rangers, no matter what."

"Even when they're at the bottom of the division?"

"Hell yeah. My dad used to take me to games whenever he had weekends off."

"What's your dad do?"

"Works for a tech company. They always seemed to have some big project that was due yesterday, so he worked a lot of Saturdays. What about yours?"

"Accountant." Jaxon sipped more beer. "Pretty boring life except when his firm was involved with some of the Enron mess. He was away for a few months, coming back a couple of weekends a month. My mom's a high-school English teacher."

"Is that how you got interested in education?"

"Yeah. She was always complaining about the administration. Rules that didn't have anything to do with kids learning. I know some schools are dealing with really bad behavior issues, but rules that treat kids like the enemy don't do much to encourage them or reward them for success." Jaxon suddenly stopped talking. "Sorry, I'm getting on my high horse again."

Kieran liked hearing him so passionate about a subject, and he liked the way Jaxon's eyes softened when he spoke about his parents. It appeared Jaxon's family situation was much better than Danetta's.

Jaxon reached for a fry just as Kieran did, and their hands bumped. Kieran felt that electricity and heat again. Did the whole place just light up, or was that just him?

"You have it, Jaxon."

"No. I really don't need fries."

"You look great. I don't think a few fries will do much damage." Oh shit, how had that popped out? Tequila, of course.

Until now the conversation had been easy, comfortable. Just two guys getting to know each other, not once touching on the subjects of Danetta, the wedding, or anything to do with why Kieran was even in Buckwheat Springs.

"It must be hard settling down here in a small town after Dallas and Austin." Kieran still couldn't fathom why Jaxon would have even considered moving here in the first place, especially when he'd only been seeing Danetta for a few months at the time.

"Yeah, it's taken some getting used to," Jaxon agreed. "There aren't that many problems at the high school, and we're well on the way to dealing with those, so it practically runs itself. Not much challenge for me professionally at this point." Jaxon frowned slightly, and Kieran sensed there was much more to that statement. He'd sit back and listen.

Jaxon went on, "Maybe I'll run for city council or something, just to make things more interesting."

"Why don't you just move somewhere else?"

"Danetta's job is here, and she really loves it. I don't think she could find something similar anywhere else. I wouldn't want to make her leave just for my career," Jaxon said. "Plus, her parents." He didn't elaborate.

There had to be plenty of historical towns she could consider, many of them near larger metropolitan areas, where Jaxon would easily be able to find an appropriate school administrator position, maybe even teaching at a college or university. It was unconscionable that Danetta let him lock himself away in this tiny town, no matter how cute the place was or how happy *she* was here.

There had to be something else behind Jaxon's apparent lack of motivation regarding his own career. "That's the whole reason? That *Danetta's* happy here?" Kieran probed.

"That's enough for me. I'd do anything to make her happy, and if she wants to stay in town, I'm prepared to give up a few things to make that happen. I owe her...." His voice trailed off, and he stared at something over Kieran's shoulder with a blank expression that wasn't just the result of a few drinks.

But Kieran held his tongue. What did Jaxon feel he owed Danetta? Did it have to do with that secret something that kept the men around here wrapped around her little finger?

During the pregnant pause, Jaxon glanced around the room and shuffled his feet on the rungs of the stool. Was he leaving?

"How about another round of tequila?" Kieran grasped for something to keep Jaxon here longer, as well as hopefully loosen his tongue.

"Until tonight, I can't remember the last time I drank tequila. You know Danny...." He didn't need to finish the sentence.

Kieran noticed the alcohol was beginning to affect him. Danetta probably didn't let Jaxon go out drinking with his pals very often. Given her home life, it made sense, but it was overly restrictive for a responsible adult like Jaxon.

"Well, we should try other brands, and you figure out which one you like best."

"I'm not sure I could handle any more." Jaxon was still smiling and hadn't made another move to leave.

"Next time," Kieran said.

"Okay. Next time." Jaxon sounded as if there absolutely *would* be a next time.

Kieran tried not to get too excited about that prospect or read too much into anything. He had to keep reminding himself Jaxon was getting married in a few days and that he'd be going back to New York.

"So, Kierrrran, can I ask you something personal?" Jaxon hadn't quite slurred his words, but Kieran liked the way his name sounded on Jaxon's lips.

"Yeah?"

"So, you never... ya know... with a girl?" Jaxon asked, the alcohol probably having lowered his inhibitions. His voice was quiet, and Kieran had to lean in to hear him, their faces only an inch or two apart.

"I didn't say that."

"You must not have liked it much, didya?"

"I didn't say that, either."

"Well?"

Oh God. Kieran was way too close to those mesmerizing green eyes, the scattering of freckles, and Jaxon's clean, fresh scent to start talking about sex now. He wasn't sure he could handle it. He tried not to watch Jaxon's mouth as he spoke, but Kieran didn't have that much self-control. He didn't really have any lately, it seemed.

But Jaxon's stare forced an answer out.

"I never found girls particularly arousing. I figured things out pretty early on."

"You think that's easier?"

"Definitely. No hurt feelings or bruised egos trying to make something work that never will."

Jaxon opened his mouth, then closed it and inhaled slowly before replying. "And you weren't at all curious, just to make sure you weren't into girls?"

Kieran paused a moment. This discussion was going to strange places. Was Jaxon asking what Kieran suspected he was, just reversing their situations? Jaxon looked so serious; he wasn't just making conversation now.

"I never tested it out with a girl because with another guy it felt so right, not like something was missing. That's me, but it's different for everyone. I've always just said that if you're into someone—or not— you know. Then having sex with that person is taking it to the next level. I happen to only like men, but plenty of people enjoy sex with both men and women."

"Well… I think there's more to it than that."

"Are you asking me about sex or about love? Because there's a difference."

"Yeah, there is a difference. A big difference," Jaxon said. "I guess sometimes you can confuse them, huh?"

"Are you still talking about me, now?" Kieran asked with a smile.

"Yeah." Jaxon was quiet for a few moments as he took another sip of tequila. "Did you ever love a woman?"

"Romantically? No."

"And you didn't get turned on by them. Is that why you tried guys?"

"I wouldn't say it's exactly like I 'tried guys.' I never consciously—at least at first—chose men over women. I just knew that I didn't get that spark with women." Kieran didn't want to think about sparks. There were far too many when he was around Jaxon.

"Spark." Jaxon smiled and nodded, as if he'd just learned something significant. "But that's about sex again, right? I'm asking about love this time. Have you loved a man?"

Kieran closed his eyes and pressed his lips together. Why was Jaxon getting so damn personal now? Kieran would rather talk about sex than admit he knew fuck-all about love. "No." He took another breath and shook his head.

"Do you have a boyfriend?"

"Okay, now who's interviewing whom?"

"You can't call this an interview, not when you buy me tequila. That's got to be against some sort of journalistic code of ethics."

"There is no journalistic code of ethics when it comes to alcohol," Kieran said, laughing. "But I suddenly feel that the tables have been turned here. No one's ever asked me this many questions before."

"Ha, now you're on the other end of the question, it seems really nosy and personal, doesn't it?"

"Yeah, it does."

"Well, I'm not writin' an article. Just askin' outta *personal* curiosity. Okay?" Jaxon asked and Kieran nodded. "Just friends talkin'."

That snapped Kieran back into reality.

Friends? Kieran asked himself. They weren't *friends*. They couldn't be friends, no matter how much he enjoyed Jaxon's company. He was here to do a job, and part of that included Jaxon looking like a fool for falling for Danetta. If she ran, that would be simple. But Danetta seemed too concerned about appearances to agree to the column and introduce Kieran to her exes only to bail in the middle of yet another wedding, knowing it would be in a national magazine.

At this moment, Kieran was nearly positive that Danetta was planning to stick around and actually marry Jaxon. But he still didn't understand why she ran the first three times. He had plenty more digging to do, and it had nothing at all to do with talking to Jaxon.

Kieran knew he had to step back from Jaxon. Literally and figuratively. The idea of Jaxon spending the rest of his life with Danetta here in this one-horse town was becoming harder and harder for Kieran to accept. Writing the column would be so much more difficult than he'd anticipated.

Despite all of Jaxon's questions about figuring things out, Kieran wasn't prepared to risk his job for one or two nights with a bi-curious guy who would be married by Saturday, a guy looking for some last fling before settling down to reality. In the past Kieran might have taken Jaxon up on an offer of ephemeral mutual enjoyment.

Now, it wouldn't do either of them any good. Continuing his behavior of serial bed hopping was never going to bring him the permanency or love he'd come to crave.

There would be no way Kieran could write the column he needed if he got too emotionally invested in these people—especially Jaxon. He'd learned that much from the last column, and he hadn't even wanted to sleep with any of the people he'd interviewed for that one.

Kieran glanced around the room, needing to look at anything—or anyone—but Jaxon, sitting so close, smelling so good, and taking such a close personal interest in Kieran's sex life.

When he pulled his attention off Jaxon for more than a split second, Kieran noticed a couple of guys watching him. This wasn't the disapproving, potentially dangerous kind of look that he'd seen earlier. This was something far preferable. He smiled back at a guy wearing black jeans and sky blue, long-sleeved T that fit him very, very well.

"Hey," Kieran whispered to Jaxon, "you said no one in this town is gay."

"They're not, as far as I know."

"Well, a couple of them are giving me… looks."

"Like they want to beat you up?"

"No, just the opposite. Like they're interested; cruising me." Kieran spotted another, nice looking, about Kieran's age, slim, sandy-blond hair and alluring cornflower blue eyes. They'd met in the coffee shop the day before, but Kieran couldn't remember his name. The look was unmistakable.

Maybe Buckwheat Springs was more interesting than he'd expected. A little time with one of these hunky locals would allow him to take the focus of his sexual energy off Jaxon. Or at least keep him from fantasizing quite so much.

"Are you sure?" Jaxon was about to turn around, and Kieran grabbed his shoulder to stop him.

Bad idea. He felt Jaxon's firm warmth, and lightning struck again. Kieran had to consciously peel his fingers off Jaxon and not give in to the urge to stroke his arm and wrap his hand around that bicep.

"Maybe I'm reading too much into it." Kieran glanced at Sky Blue, and the look turned into more, an *invitation*. One way to find out.

"Gimme a minute." Kieran got up from the table and headed toward the bathroom.

Chapter Thirteen

JAXON SAT at the table waiting for Kieran to get back from the bathroom. He turned their conversation over, his brain not too muddled to recognize he was stepping into dangerous territory.

It was one thing to enjoy spending time with Kieran, another to invite him to lunch or to Sam's, but asking about sex and sexuality? That discussion, those questions, steered his interactions with Kieran into perilous waters.

Over the years, Jaxon had had some cravings and fantasies, but never anything approaching an official *urge*. At least not until he'd met Kieran Quinn. Suddenly, the world Jaxon inhabited had become uncomfortable and unfulfilling. He'd been more and more restless with Danetta, but he'd attributed that lack of passion to the sudden changes in their relationship and the impending wedding.

Now, Jaxon examined his life in a whole new light. What had Kieran said? "If you're into someone—or not—you know." Just because Jaxon wasn't as "into" Danetta as before didn't mean he was into men.

He still had to convince himself he wasn't into Kieran, because while his brain might still be questioning, Jaxon's traitorous body had decided the issue. All he could think about was being with Kieran, getting close to him, kissing him. Had he felt such overwhelming physical need for Danetta?

The answer eluded him.

What hadn't eluded him was his history of relationships: he'd never stuck with anyone very long, and he probably wouldn't have followed Danny to Buckwheat Springs if—well, no sense in rehashing that. What's done was done. And Saturday was a few short days away.

Sam brought two more beers to the table, rousing Jaxon from his unsettling reflections.

"Ready for another round? On the house. Haven't seen you here two days in a row since... forever." Sam's cheerful grin and husky voice seemed oddly comforting at the moment.

"I think I've hit my limit."

"Well, you only live once." Sam winked as she set two more bottles down on the table. "Don't forget that."

He was still trying to figure out what she meant when Kieran returned. He looked a little flushed as he settled back on the stool and gulped down some beer.

"Ooh, nice and cold. Just what I needed."

"Hey, worried you fell in or something." Jaxon let out a laugh. "You should probably eat more fiber."

"I eat plenty of fiber." Kieran let out a chuckle. "I was... uh... detained."

Jaxon didn't say anything for a moment, then understanding dawned. "You just *fucked* some guy in the bathroom?" Why did his chest tighten as he waited for a reply?

"No."

And why did that make breathing easier, at least for a moment? "Some guy fucked *you*?"

"No... uh, blow job."

Jaxon had been interrogating Kieran about his sex life, but he hadn't expected to get this much information.

"You're joking. Who?"

"I can't tell you—that would out him."

Jaxon glanced around the bar, trying to figure out who it had been.

"Not cool, Jax. Don't. How do you think he'd feel if *everyone* knew?"

"What do you mean 'everyone'?"

"This is a sort of stealth gay bar. I didn't pick up on it last night. There's a mixed crowd, but the gay men find each other easily enough."

"What?" Now Jaxon took another casual glance around the room. He spotted a few people he knew, mostly sitting together at tables. At the bar were three guys, with an empty barstool between each one and the next guy. The singles started to take on a new significance. "Shit. All this time? Should I be offended no one ever hit on me?"

"If you came in alone, I'm sure Sam let them know you were off-limits."

Jaxon felt a little insulted. He glanced around, but no one caught his eye except Sam, who nodded and smiled. "Jesus."

"He probably wouldn't be caught dead here."

The line was delivered so drolly that Jaxon let out a pent-up explosion of laughter.

What if he *had* known? Would anything be different? He sucked down more beer, his good mood waning. Since Kieran had returned, the room didn't shine so brightly, the electricity between them had ebbed away to nothing.

"You can just do that with a complete *stranger?*" Jaxon couldn't stop from asking. At least he'd been able to keep his voice steady.

"Yeah," Kieran replied, not meeting Jaxon's gaze. "I reckon you might not want to hear that."

"How can you separate sex out like that, so it's totally removed from having any feelings about a person?"

"Sometimes that's all you want." Kieran turned his gaze fully onto Jaxon. "Sometimes you can't have who you really want, so you find someone you *can* have, and it makes that easier to accept." Kieran put his empty bottle down, never taking his eyes off Jaxon.

"What's your excuse tonight?"

Kieran's silence was all the answer Jaxon needed. His heart pounded, and he could barely breathe. He put his hand on Kieran's elbow and took a deep breath.

"What if you could have that person?"

Kieran focused his attention on his beer bottle. He didn't say anything until he'd scraped off most of the label.

"Even if I could, I shouldn't."

"Why not?" Jaxon asked in a whisper, trying to keep the hurt out of his voice. Kieran had just fooled around with some random guy, but he wasn't interested in Jaxon? Had he been imagining everything for the past few days? Hadn't any of it been mutual?

Why had he drunk that tequila? He couldn't think straight—that made him laugh, and Kieran raised an eyebrow.

"Aren't you interested, Kieran?"

"God yes." Kieran's voice wavered and his lips trembled.

Jaxon wanted to kiss them even more. "Then, why not?"

"So goddamn many reasons, Jax."

Jaxon's cell phone announced a text message. Fuck! Why now? He glanced down at the caller ID.

Danetta

"I bet that's one right now." Kieran looked as miserable as Jaxon felt.

Jaxon glanced at the text message, wrinkling up his mouth. "It's about Lorraine. Danny needs my help." He slipped off the stool and pulled his wallet out.

"I'll cover it. You need to leave."

Jaxon stood immobilized for a moment. He considered hurling the damn phone against the wall. Instead, he jammed it into his pocket and walked out.

If it had been any other reason... *any* other....

He couldn't be sure what he would have done.

Chapter Fourteen

As KIERAN watched Jaxon walk out of Sam's, he recalled the famous opening line from *A Tale of Two Cities*: "It was the best of times. It was the worst of times."

Summed today up to a fucking T.

Yay, Jaxon returned at least some of Kieran's feelings.

Fuck, Jaxon returned at least some of Kieran's feelings.

He scuffed his feet over to the jukebox that until now had been spewing mostly country tunes. It was blessedly silent. Kieran stuffed a dollar bill in there and selected a few songs, then went to sit at the bar.

"What'll it be, stranger?" Sam asked, but she wasn't smiling.

"A shot of your four cheapest tequilas." That should be enough so he wouldn't be able to think much before he passed out at the Trail Dust.

"Honey, I can't do that to ya. Nothin' is *that* bad."

She poured four shots of the top-shelf stuff. He'd be fucked up, but maybe he would feel marginally less like a shit sandwich in the morning.

He sucked the first one back like water. As he held the second, he sang along to one of the songs he'd picked out. "Hotel California," because right at this moment, it was both heaven and hell.

Sam came back over and put a hand over the shot glass before Kieran could down it.

"You see it, too, dontcha?" Sam asked, her frown deepening.

"See what?"

"That Jaxon doesn't belong with Danetta."

"Under-fucking-statement," Kieran responded and gently knocked her hand off his shot.

"She's got her poison into him somehow. She's gonna break him and win. I don't want to see that happen either."

"What kind of poison is it?"

"Hell if I know. But I can see your mind's working on the problem. After tonight, you sober up till you figure it out." She handed him the third shot glass and walked away to serve another customer.

Kieran knocked back the next shot, needing the harsh burn scorching his throat as he swallowed, and picked up the last one immediately. As he raised the glass to his lips, a tiny germ of an idea planted itself in his brain.

Someone had said something significant to him today, but his brain hadn't fully processed the information yet. He decided not to drink the rest of the tequila after all, slapped the shot glass back onto the surface of the bar, where it sloshed and spilled.

Sam was right. Kieran was the only one who could rescue Jaxon. And he couldn't if he let himself stay drunk till after the wedding, which had seemed like a good plan until Sam made him see what a sorry ass he was being.

First thing tomorrow, he'd get his shit together.

At the moment, he wasn't sure he could find the door without a GPS.

Chapter Fifteen

LORRAINE HAD cut herself on a broken bottle. After a trip to the ER and a couple dozen stitches in her hand and wrist, she was released. Danny insisted on staying with her and dropped Jaxon off at home to get some sleep before he had to work in the morning. That was only part of the reason; Danetta had sighed and shaken her head when Jaxon arrived home with alcohol on his breath. She knew he hadn't been at the Copper Caboose.

Lying alone in bed at 3:00 a.m., Jaxon felt like he'd let her down. She frowned on drinking. And he'd led her to believe he was somewhere else. Worse, he hadn't been much help with Lorraine because the tequila had kicked into overdrive by the time he'd raced home.

Now, he went over the evening with Kieran. How much more upset would she be if she knew Jaxon had let Kieran know he wanted to—what? Jaxon didn't even know what he wanted from Kieran.

What he did know was that he'd fallen down the rabbit hole that was Buckwheat Springs, and he couldn't get up. It looked nice from the outside, but appearances were deceiving. He hummed a line from that old song "Hotel California," about being able to check in but not being able to leave.

He was in Hotel Archer, with Lorraine some crazy desk clerk who'd locked up the keys.

What would it feel like to kiss Kieran? To lie next to him, wrapped in his arms? Touching him sent electrical signals bouncing from Jaxon's brain to his dick and gathering in his balls. Just the sight and scent of him, and now even the memory of his smile and laugh, produced what should have been a pleasurable physical response.

Now, just a few days from his wedding, Jaxon hurt like hell wondering about what might have been.

Kieran had been right; it would only make matters worse if Jaxon acted on any of his desires now. He'd promised to marry Danetta, and he would. He'd never cheated on anyone before, and until a day ago, he wouldn't dream of doing that. But now he began to understand how someone might justify it.

Which was worse? Cheating on Danny and discovering they really didn't belong together for the rest of their lives, or marrying her and turning into Lorraine and Bert?

Both alternatives frightened Jaxon.

Maybe he'd discover that those sparks with Kieran were just beer induced and situational, not a sea change.

Yeah, right.

Chapter Sixteen

Wednesday

WHEN KIERAN woke up he was face down on the pillow, and he discovered a feather in his mouth. He tried to blow it out, but even afterward his mouth tasted like there'd been a whole duck in there, and not the kind with plum sauce. Beer and tequila had combined to produce an award-winning headache, so he swallowed a few Tylenol, grimacing at the bitterness.

Brushing his teeth helped extinguish the flavors of tequila, feathers, and medicine. If only he could wash his head out. That strange conversation with Jaxon came back to him. Maybe he'd only imagined Jaxon's interest in getting to know each other in the biblical sense.

After eating an order of the Copper Caboose's pecan pancakes, bacon, and fruit salad and guzzling about a pot of hot black coffee, his head had stopped threatening to explode.

It was time to clear his mind not only of the remnants of alcohol from the night before, but of his foolish attraction to Jaxon. Some fresh air wouldn't hurt. Such a beautiful day was perfect for taking his rented convertible out for a nice, relaxing drive. The sun shining on his face and the fresh air would do him a world of good. He missed driving, and the long straight roads in this part of Texas were just what he needed.

BACK AT the hotel later, Kieran began work on his column. He wanted to get as much as possible written before he saw Jaxon again. *If* he saw Jaxon again. Kieran had intended to make Jaxon and the other grooms look ridiculous for falling for Danetta, and it was getting nearly impossible to remain detached. He'd go with his first impressions, and then later on, if he found out Danetta's secret, he could work it in.

Midafternoon, when he got hungry, Kieran called Sam and asked if she'd deliver some food. Kieran wanted to avoid any chance of running into Jaxon on the street or at Sam's.

He wasn't prepared to see Jaxon just yet.

Too much temptation, at least on Kieran's part. Maybe in the light of day and sober, Jaxon would regret telling Kieran he was interested. He might genuinely be facing questions he'd never worked through before, but as much as Kieran wanted Jaxon, acting on the attraction would be treacherous for both of them.

Kieran called Sam back not five minutes after he'd hung up the phone.

"Throw a bottle of some decent tequila on my order, please." He was going to need it to get to sleep again tonight.

"Sorry, hon, we're all out of tequila." Then she hung up and didn't answer when he called back three times in quick succession. But he appreciated her concern, and her cooking.

After demolishing a BBQ brisket sandwich and a tub of cool, creamy coleslaw like his mother used to make, Kieran focused his full attention on the column for several hours. Jeff was expecting a teaser for this week's edition, just a hint of what was to come. That was easy enough, so he sent it off and worked on a draft of next week's column.

His aching neck and shoulders reminded him to take a break every couple of hours, or he would spend the rest of the day happily tapping away once he got back into the rhythm of writing. He stood and stretched for a few minutes and read back what he'd done.

It was too nice. He'd been enjoying himself and the people he met far too much. Jeff would sack his ass in a New York minute if he turned this in. He imagined Jeff's voice booming, "You don't get fucking paid to write for the fucking travel section, for fucking fuck's sake."

Nope. He had to go back to the drawing board.

That required tequila. He grabbed his key and went around the corner to a little shop selling smokes and booze and bought a small bottle, for professional use only.

Kieran drank a couple of glasses of tequila and tried again.

Jeff would approve of the second version: his initial impressions of Jaxon, Danetta, and her family, as well as the three ex-grooms. He'd achieved the right mix of sarcasm and condescension his readers loved. Jeff was going to eat this up.

Danetta came across as a teetotaling amalgam of witch and Svengali, and Kieran painted the grooms as having fallen under her spell. Based on Kieran's dinner with Jaxon and Danetta, she certainly seemed to be pulling Jaxon's strings. He tossed in a few gems about Lorraine and Bert for comic relief.

The big problem was Tom, Jordan, and Marc liked Jaxon, with no evidence of *schadenfreude*—glee that Jaxon might crash and burn the way they had. He intimated that the three of them had some information they were keeping from Jaxon. Outwardly, they were nice to him, but in reality, they weren't sharing the intel. Because of Danetta's continued influence over the three men.

Considering his growing friendship—if that was the correct word—mocking Jaxon sufficiently proved difficult. Luckily, Kieran had already worked up his first impressions, the matchy-matchy outfits and overuse of the pronoun "we," to characterize him as Danetta's willing puppet.

He felt a twinge of guilt over what he'd written, particularly considering how kind everyone was to him; but he'd come to do a job, and he was going to do it well. Before he could change his mind, he e-mailed the draft to Jeff. It was exactly what Jeff had been looking for: cutting, sarcastic, condescending, and very, very critical of just about everyone and everything he'd seen in Buckwheat Springs.

It was a good thing he'd scared Jaxon off the night before, Kieran decided, pouring another glass of tequila. Emotional attachments here could only lead to disaster. Without needing to spare anyone's feelings, Kieran was free to ridicule everyone, then return to familiar professional and emotional territory in New York.

He still needed to stay friendly enough with Jaxon to attend the rehearsal dinner, the bachelor party, and then the wedding. Kieran could keep his attraction to Jaxon hidden for a few more days.

On Sunday—after recovering from a Texas-size hangover from getting as drunk as possible if the wedding went as planned—or Monday, he'd write the follow-up and aftermath of whatever happened on Saturday. He had to avoid becoming one of the casualties after Danetta and Jaxon flew off to Kauai for their tropical honeymoon.

A knock sounded on Kieran's motel room door, surprising him out of his musings. He was even more surprised when he opened it to find Jaxon on the doorstep.

Wordlessly, Jaxon came in, closing the door behind him.

Kieran blinked, thinking he'd found himself back in the dream from the previous morning. Surreptitiously, he pinched himself. He blinked a few more times.

Jaxon was still there.

Chapter Seventeen

JAXON'S HEART was pounding so loudly he couldn't even hear himself speak. Part of him had hoped Kieran wouldn't be here, but there was no going back. He looked up at Kieran, who was wide-eyed with surprise. He glanced toward the couch, then back to Jaxon, but he didn't say a word.

But seeing him again, close enough to feel the heat from his body and smell the spice of tequila on his breath, Jaxon was certain. Needed to be here. "I had to see you, talk to you."

"Have a seat." Kieran paused at the table and slapped his laptop closed as Jaxon sat down.

What was he hiding on the laptop? Porn? Kieran didn't look flushed or like he'd adjusted his clothes in a hurry. But Kieran hovered by the desk as if he didn't want to get too close. Maybe it was easier this way. With Kieran any closer it would be difficult to think. Even *more* difficult.

Was this how a skydiver felt before he jumped out of the plane? Once you were out, you couldn't get back in.

Enough stalling. Jaxon took the plunge and stepped out into the unknown. "I spent a lot of time this week thinking. Not just last night. Talking with you reminded me of so many things I had forgotten since I came here."

Kieran finally sat down on the couch with Jaxon. "I'm not sure what you're saying, Jaxon."

Jaxon noticed the tequila next to the laptop on the table where Kieran had been working.

"Gonna offer me a drink?"

"Okay. Let me find a clean glass." He got up and moved into the bathroom. Jaxon heard the water running, then Kieran returned with a glass. He poured some tequila and handed it to Jaxon.

Water droplets still clung to the glass. Jaxon stared into the amber depths, inhaling the wood and spice aroma. He took a sip. The liquid tingled as it wrapped itself around his tongue. Then Jaxon downed the rest in one anxious gulp.

Kieran hadn't poured any for himself. He stood watching as Jaxon put the glass down on the table. Oh God, his fingers were shaking. Could Kieran see that?

"If you need a drink to say what you want to say, what does that tell me?" Kieran sat back down on the couch with Jaxon and put the bottle down on the table in front of the couch. He was smiling when he turned his gaze back on Jaxon.

The smile helped settle Jaxon's nerves. "It should tell you that I'm going to say something important, or I wouldn't be so anxious."

"Fair enough."

"Can I ask you something about last night?" Jaxon paused. "About the guy you, uh, fooled around with?"

"Ask away, but if you're that curious about my sex life, there's a better way to find out." It was part challenge, part invitation. Kieran's mouth turned in a mischievous smile.

"I know I keep asking a lot of questions, but I am curious." Why had he used *that* word? "About...." Jaxon looked at his hands, then back at Kieran. "About *you*."

"Why?"

Goddamn Kieran, couldn't he make this a little easier? No wonder he was single. He could be an ass. A tall, gorgeous example of sex-on-legs ass. And for some reason Jaxon wanted him even more because he didn't take the easy route.

Screw all those people who say "no pain, no gain."

"We have a lot in common. We've both moved far from home, not necessarily in physical distance, but in lifestyle. You went to a much bigger city, while I came to a little town. It's a big transition, figuring out where you fit into a place where things are unfamiliar, and life happens at a totally different pace. Slowing down is just as hard to get used to as speeding up."

"I hadn't thought of it that way." Kieran looked thoughtful. "So much for my writer's incisive powers of observation."

Jaxon could smile at that compliment. "In New York, there are so many paths to choose from—all crisscrossing and twisting around each other—it can be hard to find the right one." He paused. "And here, for me, there's just one path. I'm on it; and there's nothing but that one path. Sometimes it feels like that path was waiting for me here, before I ever arrived. I'm just blindly following it, taking the same steps many people before me took."

"Are paths supposed to mean people in this convoluted metaphor?" Kieran went back into ass mode.

"I hadn't meant it that way, but it could."

"You mean marrying Danetta?" Kieran asked, thankfully finally helping Jaxon along.

"Yes." It felt like a weight lifting to finally be able to say this to someone. The words came more easily. "Three other guys went down that path before me, but they never got to the end. But they were still on the very same path."

"I thought you loved that path... I mean, Danetta." Kieran shook his head. "You can drop the path thing. Please just tell me what you're thinking."

"I want to marry her, but somehow it's not about love now. I don't even know how I feel about her anymore. I've never loved anyone before. What if I'm wrong? I've missed out on a lot of things because I got on this path too soon. I *think* it's the right path, but I need to see what else there is before I get to the end. I want to step off the path." Jaxon's heart was doing that jackhammer thing again. He looked into Kieran's eyes. "With you."

Kieran looked all serious, lips pressed together. Not the reaction Jaxon hoped for. Had he expected Kieran to rip his clothes off or something?

"Jaxon, I'm flattered as hell, and I'm this close to carrying you over to that bed, but I don't think it's a good idea."

"*Yes*, it's a good idea." At least Kieran wanted to rip his clothes off. That was a start.

"Under any other circumstances, I'd be all over you." He took hold of Jaxon's hand and rubbed his thumb across the back of it. It felt so good. "Hell, I'll sing Tom Jones songs or do somersaults, if you ask. But I want you to think about what this is really about." Kieran looked down at Jaxon's hand in his, then back into Jaxon's eyes. "Is this about you, or me, or Danetta?"

"There's no right answer to that question, is there?"

Kieran shook his head.

"And any answer is going to be wrong."

"Yeah."

"It's about all three." He swallowed and steeled himself. "I've never been with another guy, but I've thought about it. I even went to a gay bar in Austin, but I didn't know what I was doing or how to act, and I didn't see anyone there who caught my interest enough to get over my fear and confusion."

He looked at Kieran, who stayed silent, giving Jaxon space.

"I thought that meant I wasn't gay. Like I'd passed some sort of test. I met Danny a week or so later, and I had fun spending time with her. We didn't just jump into bed. It was comfortable and easy. Now I look back and wonder why I didn't want to get her into bed sooner. She's beautiful. Well, things progressed, and here I am." He'd left a whole lot out, but he wasn't going to tell Kieran everything right now.

"What's changed, Jaxon? Why are you ready to step off the path now? Is it because the wedding is in a few days? Last chance for the big gay test?" Kieran gave a soft laugh, but his tone wasn't mocking or sarcastic. For some reason it was easy to talk to him. He wasn't judgy or disparaging of Jaxon's thoughts and doubts.

"You, Kieran. I met you." Jaxon paused, waiting for the constriction in his chest to return, but it didn't. "I met you and something inside me snapped into place. It's not even something sexual—at least not completely. It's just that you make me feel good in a way no one else ever has. I think about you all the time. I never felt like this with Danny. Compared to the emotions you've unleashed, she's like a friend. A close friend."

"So, you came over and figured we'd fuck and then you'll go home to dinner?"

Jaxon pulled his hand away like it was on fire. "No. Why—"

"Or maybe we'd fool around and you'd realize you really don't want to fuck guys?"

"What the hell is wrong with you? Why're you being such an asshole right now? Don't you know how hard this is to say?"

"Yes, Jaxon. I do. It's going to be the hardest thing you do in your entire life. Because you have to be sure. A thousand percent sure. Before you do anything. Before I'll do anything."

"A thousand percent?" Jaxon laughed. He couldn't take this anxiety.

"Okay, five hundred percent. Jaxon, you have no idea how difficult it is for me to say this, because I want you to be here. In my room, in my arms, in my bed. Everything you feel, I feel too. But unless you know for sure who you are, it's just sex, and it's cheating."

"You said yourself it's possible, even preferable in some cases, to separate sex from love."

"Would this be just sex to you?"

"No."

"You've just answered your own question." Kieran's shoulders sagged.

"I want to be with you."

"Just take that one step off the path and then go back?"

"Yes. No. Maybe. I don't fucking know yet. But I take full responsibility for the cheating part. I need to know."

"This is just research?" There was a stridency in Kieran's voice. A new emotion Jaxon hadn't heard yet.

"I don't know."

"How do you think I'll feel after you walk out of here and go back to Danetta?"

"Don't you sleep with random people?"

"Jaxon, nothing about you is random. You and I are so past random here, you can't even see it in the rearview mirror. You feel it and I feel it, and you're lying if you think you can just get back on the path to Danetta. But, you'll break me too."

The words were like a slap in the face. Kieran felt this same pull, this unstoppable attraction that went far beyond a physical ache. It went deep into the bones. Something Jaxon had never felt and never thought he would. Could he do this to Kieran? He saw now how selfish that would be.

But neither could he go home and spend the rest of his life with Danetta, who would never be this to him, who even in a million years would never get into his heart and soul the way Kieran had in only a few days.

"Please, Kieran, show me what I'm missing. Show me what I really need." Jaxon's whole body trembled.

"You're sure?"

"Five hundred and one percent."

Kieran smiled and pulled Jaxon into his arms, enveloping him in an aura of heat and booze, hard muscles, and overwhelming masculinity. But he stopped short of bringing his lips up to meet Jaxon's.

"How far off the path do you want to go? Column A, which is the beginner stuff, or column B, where we do things together you'd never ever forget and that would make Danetta cry herself to sleep for a month if she knew."

Column B sounded frightening but oh, so tempting. "I want to taste everything on the menu."

Kieran looked down at him, eyes dark, breath already raspy. The sight turned Jaxon's insides to mush, but it made his cock swell.

"Let's start with a kiss." Kieran pressed his mouth to Jaxon's so softly, a caress of lips. How could such a gentle touch ignite every fiber of Jaxon's body? Then Kieran pulled back and traced a finger first along Jaxon's upper lip and then the lower, a delicate butterfly touch that made Jaxon's pulse race, and suddenly he couldn't remember how to breathe.

The feel of Kieran's lips was electric, and Jaxon let himself be kissed, let Kieran give or take whatever he wanted. Jaxon brought his right hand up to caress Kieran's cheek, fingers tracing the strong jawline before moving to rub through the bristly hair of Kieran's sideburns. He didn't let himself worry about whether it was right or wrong, just how good it was.

Kieran parted his mouth, inviting Jaxon in, and Jaxon traced Kieran's lips with his tongue, licking at them with more and more heat, before finally darting inside. There was nothing gentle about it now, and Jaxon's mouth plundered Kieran's, devouring it with an intensity and passion he'd never imagined. How could he ever get enough of this, of Kieran, of this incredible high?

He felt off balance, as if the world were spinning, moving at warp speed, with light and sound and amazing sensations that only began where Kieran's mouth touched his and sang through Jaxon's entire body. It was the very definition of mind-blowing.

Matching Jaxon's intensity, Kieran returned the ardor, his arms circling Jaxon and pulling him in closer. Jaxon forgot how to think, how to breathe, how to do anything but kiss and be kissed until Kieran pulled away and suddenly the world was still again, no longer bright and shining and spinning. They were back on the couch in Kieran's motel room, in each other's arms. Jaxon found himself in Kieran's lap, though he couldn't remember how he got there.

"No one's ever kissed me like that before," Jaxon gasped when he was finally able to form words. His chest was heaving from lack of oxygen, and his brain wasn't fully functioning yet. "I've never felt anything like that, either. Never wanted a kiss as much as that."

"Ditto."

"God, you writers have such a way with words."

Kieran laughed, and Jaxon joined in, breaking the tension. "I can barely remember my name, much less say anything eloquent."

Jaxon glanced away, not sure if he should believe the compliment. How could he do something original for an experienced guy like Kieran?

Kieran turned Jaxon's face up with two gentle fingers that left a trail of heat as he caressed Jaxon's cheek.

"Is that it?" Jaxon's voice was low and raspy.

"We haven't even started," Kieran whispered between shallow breaths.

Then Kieran again pressed his mouth to Jaxon's, letting him explore the lips and mouth he'd been dreaming about for days, at first gently, then more desperately, licking and sucking at them, wanting to memorize everything about the way they tasted and felt so he could remember them forever. He drank in the sweetness and heat of Kieran's mouth, their tongues dancing and darting, giving and taking, until he had to stop and breathe again.

Kieran looked down at Jaxon, eyes glittering darkly with arousal and more emotion than Jaxon expected. He was so hard it hurt, and his erection was as obvious as the bulge in Kieran's jeans.

"Are you ready to take another step?"

Jaxon was silent. Kieran watched him, his eyes playing over Jaxon's face and body. Jaxon's lips felt bruised from their combined passion, face raw from Kieran's end-of-day stubble. Kieran caressed Jaxon's chin, trailing his fingers down Jaxon's throat, making Jaxon's entire body shudder at the touch and pleasure he promised.

Jaxon leaned his head back, exposing his neck and throat, and Kieran moved in to kiss and lick at him, making Jaxon groan. With trembling fingers Kieran undid the first button on Jaxon's shirt. He peeled back the fabric and stroked Jaxon's chest lightly. Jaxon sighed, arching into the touch, craving the electrifying touch. One more button. Kieran's fingertips played softly at Jaxon's nipple, and he felt it harden and tingle, then throb and ache, pulsing along with his swollen cock. Jaxon closed his eyes and moaned as Kieran gently pulled and pinched at the nipple. Then he let go.

Jaxon let out a little moan. "More," he thought he said.

The pleasure intensified, as if Jaxon's nipple was connected by a wire to the base of his balls. Then wet heat closed around the nipple and sent even more devastating shockwaves through Jaxon's body.

Kieran's hand traveled down toward Jaxon's lap, brushing gently over his erection. Jaxon nearly leaped off the couch in response, and his eyes shot open. He watched as Kieran pulled Jaxon's belt open and popped the first button on his jeans.

Jaxon couldn't get air. He felt hot, on fire, and if Kieran so much as breathed on his cock, he'd shoot his load. It was too much, too fast, and far, far too good.

"Stop." Jaxon could barely whisper.

Kieran took his hand off Jaxon's zipper. "Stop as in slow down, or stop as in *stop*?"

Jaxon pulled himself up to a proper sitting position again, still in Kieran's lap. He didn't want Kieran to stop. But he needed to stop.

"You okay, Jaxon?"

"This—you—oh God, it's so *good*. It's too good."

"Do you want to go back to kissing? Take this more slowly?"

Jaxon's breath was coming in gasps. "It's… it's…. Now I know what it must feel like to take drugs and be unable to stop. You're like a drug. I have to stop before we even start."

Kieran slid Jaxon off his lap. "I take it that's not a compliment."

"I don't know what I was thinking. You were right. I can't do this. I can't…. If we go any further—and I want like hell to get to Column B—I'll be lost in you. It would be so easy…." Jaxon stopped. He wasn't sure what he was saying. His body ached with a heaviness, an emptiness, because he knew this was all he could have.

"I'm sorry if I pushed you."

"You didn't push. I'm the one who came here wanting you. I'm sorry I can't give you more, but…." Jaxon paused. "You're right. It's not just about sex for me, either."

"Maybe it's for the best." The look on Kieran's face, the sorrowful tone of his voice, belied the words. "Like I said, I would have a hard time letting you go back to Danetta."

The mention of Danetta's name was like an ice wave crashing over Jaxon. He sat up stiffly and buttoned his shirt, moving away from Kieran on the couch and not meeting his gaze.

All he knew for sure was he couldn't let Danetta down. She needed him in a different way than Jaxon needed Kieran. "I can't cheat. I made a promise to her, and I am going to follow through." Jaxon felt the words and the obligation pulling him down like a weight around his neck. "I have to go." He got up and adjusted his jeans, his erection still obvious and painful. He untucked his shirt in an effort to hide the bulge, smoothing the shirttails with trembling fingers.

When he got to the door, he stopped. "I'd still like you to come to the rehearsal dinner tomorrow."

"Are you fucking kidding me?" Kieran asked.

"No. At least I'll be able to see you again. I still want that. But I can't trust myself alone with you. I'm sorry."

"I can't go. I don't want to see you with her, and I can't be around your families. I know I'll do something or say something, or *feel* something, and everyone will figure out my feelings for you."

"Don't you need to do more interviews for your column?"

"Bastard. Don't do that to me. I'll find another way to get the information I need."

Good-bye wasn't the right word for parting, so Jaxon opened the door and left without a sound, only one last glance at Kieran sitting on the couch, looking as lost as Jaxon felt. The door shut between them, a necessary barrier.

It had been selfish to invite Kieran to the rehearsal dinner; Jaxon shouldn't have done it. Kieran was right. People would see it in Jaxon's face, too much emotion for Kieran and not enough for Danny.

What the fuck was he going to do?

Chapter Eighteen

Friday

KIERAN WENT to the window and, like a fool, watched Jaxon walking away. When he was out of sight, Kieran pressed his head against the door, trying to calm the explosion of emotions racing around his brain and body.

Jaxon had to leave tonight. It couldn't have ended any differently or any better if he'd stayed, and it would probably have been a whole lot worse for everyone involved. There couldn't be a more inappropriate person to be falling in love with. Jaxon was supposed to be getting married in three days, while Kieran was only here to do a job, not to fall in love with the subject of his column.

Life in Buckwheat Springs went on before Kieran got here, and it would go on long after he'd written his column and left. He was supposed to pass through as an observer. Kieran had no right to come here and change anything. He was like a time traveler, warned not to do anything that might alter the future forever.

He'd already made everything harder for Jaxon all around. Would anyone guess the bond that had formed between them? Jaxon's life would be ruined if anyone suspected he was gay. Buckwheat Springs didn't have the rainbow flag flying at all, unless you counted the margaritas at La Piñata.

Poor Jaxon.

He didn't belong with Danetta, that was for damn sure. But now it had nothing to do with Danetta. Jaxon wouldn't be happy with her, and that would eventually make her miserable. Better to cancel a wedding than deal with an unhappy marriage and divorce. Or no divorce. Danetta's parents hadn't taken the escape route when plainly they should have.

But Jaxon would never tell her, because he was clearly so concerned about not hurting her. How ironic, considering Danetta had hurt so many men before Jaxon—men who still cared for and protected her.

The best thing he could do for Jaxon was to find out Danetta's secret before the wedding. If Jaxon knew what it was, he'd reconsider his decision to marry her. When Kieran had first arrived, he was focused on whether Danetta would go through with the wedding. Now he was convinced she would—and it was the worst possible outcome he could imagine for everyone involved.

If only Kieran could get out of going to the wedding. Impossible. But he would be an emotional basket case watching Jaxon make the biggest mistake of his life. Jaxon's sense of duty and obligation would take him down the wrong path, and it would be a very long road.

Kieran poured a large shot of tequila into his glass and downed it, the throat-searing pain distracting him from Jaxon's visit, from the way he'd felt in Kieran's arms, and how he'd responded to Kieran's touch. More tequila seemed to be the only thing that could keep Kieran's thoughts from wandering to what Jaxon was doing and thinking right now.

Better to sit here in a tequila-flavored cloud of loneliness.

Chapter Nineteen

Thursday

KIERAN WOKE up around noon. His pounding headache didn't compare to the horrifying sensation of knowing his attraction to Jaxon was mutual. It hurt a million times worse than the uncertainty of the previous day. Now he knew exactly what he was missing out on.

Jaxon stated he was going to marry Danetta no matter what, despite recognizing he wasn't ready to get married. What mystical hold kept Jaxon with Danetta?

Kieran grabbed a notepad and itemized his data. Danetta's "formula" mentioned by the bridesmaids became his starting point. Danetta and Sam didn't care for each other, making Sam a potential ally in the search.

When talking with her exes, there had been a look between each one and Danetta. Something shared, something unspoken. Danetta hadn't been able to hide this, though she'd played everything else just about perfectly. It added to his developing theory.

Next, he made a list of specific data he'd have Alexa research.

Under the guise of follow-ups for the column, Kieran spoke again with Dinah, the bridesmaid who had spotted a pattern in Danetta's relationships, Sam, who didn't hold back her animosity, and once he had a clear line of attack, Tom.

That particular chat required all of Kieran's subtlety and charm to avoid alienating Tom or causing the other exes to steer clear of Kieran. Tom ended up providing Kieran with an important clue. Then he called Alexa for advice on how to proceed.

Unfortunately, Kieran also needed to speak with Danetta's parents. He dropped by their house to discuss Danetta's career. They answered freely and effusively, never suspecting what he'd really been getting at. Thankfully, he was able to leave before he was forced to eat or drink anything Lorraine prepared.

While Jaxon and Danetta attended the rehearsal dinner, Kieran spent the evening going over everything with Alexa. They could already see the outlines of the big picture, and Kieran knew precisely which pieces were missing.

He only had one more day to get the proof that could save Jaxon.

Chapter Twenty

Friday morning

KIERAN WAS on the road to Dallas well before the ass-crack of dawn. No time for coffee or pancakes. But he was on a mission, and it was worth every lost minute of sleep. It was even worth the $300 speeding ticket he got on the way to meet with several of Marc Rossiter's friends and relatives. These interviews couldn't be handled by phone.

By lunchtime Kieran had discovered what Marc had been hiding, but could he get Jordan or Tom to confirm his theory? A few more phone calls, some well-placed lies, and plenty of charming chitchat got several people to reveal information they mistakenly assumed he already knew.

By midafternoon, Kieran knew Danetta's secret, how she'd been able to get four men to propose to her, regardless of the fact that she'd previously left grooms at the altar again and again. Everything fell into place: why the three men moved to Buckwheat Springs, uprooting their lives for a woman who, while beautiful, was still rather average in every other way. Maybe he wasn't the best judge of that, but it all fit.

He knew why three men, even after Danetta jilted them in the worst possible and most humiliating way, didn't hold it against her and still refused to reveal to anyone her explanation of why she'd done it. Danetta had a nearly foolproof plan to snag a husband.

Or so it seemed. But she hadn't gone through with any of the weddings. The men were all good-looking, kind, successful, and definitely husband material—and every single one of them had clearly been devoted to her. They still were.

Kieran hadn't actively disliked her, even though she wasn't the right partner for Jaxon. At times Kieran had even felt a little sorry for Danetta's complicated, almost tragic family situation.

But now the truth turned Kieran's stomach, and Jaxon needed to hear it before he married Danetta. Would Jaxon believe him, or would he consider this a ploy to get him away from Danetta? There was only one way to avoid destroying whatever new affection they'd formed for each other.

Danetta had to tell Jaxon herself.

All Kieran had to do now was to figure out *how* to make that happen.

On the drive back to Buckwheat Springs, it came to him. As much as he hated what he was about to do, it was the only way. He was doing this for Jaxon, not for himself and not for his column.

With the excitement of his discoveries, he'd practically forgotten his column. He phoned Jeff from the road.

"This is Jeff. I actually have a life, so I don't have time to talk to you. Leave it at the beep." Kieran cursed as the voice mail message played.

"Look, Jeff, I found out something that changes the entire spin of this piece, so I want to make some changes on what I've already sent you. I'm pulling it back for the time being. *Don't* do anything with it yet. Don't even read it, okay? Get back to me as soon as you can. Thanks."

He focused his concentration on the road and put his foot down on the gas pedal, trying to get back to Buckwheat Springs as quickly as possible, even if it meant another ticket.

Chapter Twenty-One

Friday evening

KIERAN DROVE straight to the Victorian house Danetta and Jaxon shared. Tonight was Jaxon's bachelor party, and afterward he was staying at the Trail Dust. Danetta decided it would be more seemly if they didn't leave together in the morning for their wedding. At least he wouldn't run into Jaxon here.

Kieran parked crookedly in front of the house. He fought the urge to jump out of the car immediately. He calmed himself down and pulled the hotel notepad out of his case. He wrote down the bones of what he'd found out, and folded it up. If Danetta wouldn't tell Jaxon herself, Kieran would give him the note at the bachelor party and leave.

But first he wanted to give Danetta a chance to do the right thing.

He stuffed the note in his pocket and ran up to the door, jamming his finger repeatedly on the doorbell and banging on the door for emphasis a few times. Danetta finally opened the door. She was wearing pink and green gingham pajamas. No wonder Jaxon didn't want to have sex with her.

"Hi, Kieran," she said with a look of confusion. "What's your emergency? I expected you to be at the dinner for Jaxon."

"I have to take care of something first." He paused, meeting her gaze. "With you."

"Why, Kieran, you're attractive and all, but aren't you gay?" she asked, smiling.

Narcissistic bitch, Kieran thought, though that wasn't the worst name he'd called her in his mind that day.

"I need to *talk* to you." He shoved his hands in his pockets to keep from curling them into fists and punching her.

"Well, come on in." Danetta moved out of the doorway to let him pass. "A couple of bridesmaids are coming over for a girls' night in, so I hope this won't take long, or do you want to take some pictures of the bachelorette slumber party?"

Kieran didn't reply as he followed her into the house. The stench from Lorraine's dinner had dissipated, replaced by a fresh floral scent. Other than that, the place looked exactly the same. But in the few days in between, nearly everything had changed for Jaxon.

"We missed you at the rehearsal dinner. It was very elegant. Jaxon was hoping you'd get to meet his parents."

Was this all she could talk about? The goddamned wedding? Then he remembered his main purpose for coming here was to write about said wedding and not to fall for the groom. It was perfectly natural for her to assume *he* wanted to talk about the fucking wedding.

"I was pursuing a different angle. But I have more questions for you."

She let out a pretty laugh. "Haven't I already told you I'm not having second thoughts about tomorrow? I'm more in love with Jaxon every day. And I *am* going to marry him. I know that's going to ruin your article, isn't it?" It might have been a trick of the light, or Kieran's biased attitude, but the light reflecting off her toothy smile reminded him of some kind of nocturnal hunter, sensing its prey.

She led him to the back sitting room. Last time he'd been here, he'd been left alone with Lorraine. He wondered where she was tonight. Probably at the bachelor party, already under the table.

"You don't have any idea why I'm here? Are you fucking kidding me with your hopelessly in love routine?"

"I don't care much for your language, Kieran."

Kieran wasn't fooled by this prim-and-proper act. He knew who and what she really was, and now he had proof.

"Are you trying to get me to stand Jaxon up at the altar? You're wasting your breath."

"You're right. I don't want you to go through with it tomorrow."

"I'm not going to leave *him*. I'm definitely marrying Jaxon tomorrow, so you can stop trying to manipulate the situation just to get a good story. Go and get along and party with him tonight, because once the wedding is over and you leave, there won't be any more late-night drunk fests with the boys." She smiled. "You've been such a bad influence on him."

"I'm here to keep you from marrying him."

"Of course your article will be so much more interesting if I do another runner, but I thought Jaxon's your friend. Why do you want to hurt him like that?"

"No, Danetta, this has absolutely nothing to do with my column. I'm only trying to save him from a life of lies and deception with you."

She paused a fraction of a second too long. "What on earth are you talking about?"

"I know all about the baby."

"Baby?" Danetta repeated, as if she didn't know what he was referring to. "There's no baby."

"Exactly. It's the baby that wasn't there." It finally twigged what the psychic's words meant. "I'm talking about the fake pregnancy story you used to get Marc—then Jaxon—to propose to you."

Danetta opened her mouth to say something, then closed it again. For once she was speechless. Would it be this easy to get her to admit what she'd done? At least she hadn't denied it.

"I know all about what you did with Marc, and I discovered you did the same thing with Jordan, and now Jaxon. Tom wouldn't admit anything, but Marc and Jordan are enough of a pattern. I remembered how strangely you acted when Tom mentioned his wife was impatient for their baby to be born."

"Marc *told* you?"

"Everything." Marc was so antagonistic, even after Kieran presented the facts, but his reaction only confirmed what Kieran had already learned.

"He told you why he moved here, and why I didn't marry him?"

"Yes," Kieran lied. *Well, close enough.*

"He prom—" She stopped herself, visibly clamping her mouth shut. "I don't believe you."

"Well, you've just confirmed it by your reaction." Kieran had pictured himself shouting "Aha!" and pointing dramatically as if they were in some Agatha Christie production, but this was all too serious to joke about. "I've pieced together what you did, and I'm disgusted by it. You need to tell Jaxon the truth. If you really do love him, you owe him as much."

"What do you think you know?"

"I talked to a lot of people and put some random facts together. It seems you've been refining your plan over the years. You meet someone while you're out of town on an extended business trip. You see him a lot during the time you're there. With Marc it was Dallas, with Jordan and Jaxon it was Austin. You say you're in love with them and don't want to end things when you come back here. They accept a long-distance relationship for a time, seeing you as often as possible, but never here. You always visit them. Everything's fine until you sense the distance is starting to be a problem, and then you gauge their interest in moving here. You encourage them. Somewhere along the line, in order to keep things going, you tell the guy you're pregnant. You want to keep the baby, because you love him so much."

Danetta didn't say anything. She looked small and frail against the couch. Her skin took on a sallow cast that clashed with the wild colors of her pajamas. This didn't feel as good as Kieran thought it would. It was like beating up the Easter Bunny.

"You say you want his baby so much, you'll raise it on your own. Of course none of them can let you do that. They're all kind, generous, and principled. So they move here, rebuilding their professional lives, for you, and then not long after, there's a 'problem' and you 'lose' the baby. You're so distraught that somehow you get them to propose, because you've gotten them so thrilled at the idea of having a baby, and they really love you and want to protect you. That's how you got men to keep proposing; because it's something lots of men would fall for."

"Are you finished?"

"There's more, but I guess I don't need to tell you."

She shook her head.

Kieran was out of breath and completely worked up, but Danetta didn't shout or cry or deny anything. She blinked a few times, on the verge of tears, but that was the most he got out of her. He expected more.

"Did you tell Jaxon?"

"Not yet. I think you should tell him yourself. If you don't, I will." He pulled the note out of his pocket and showed it to her. "Jaxon doesn't deserve the lies and the deception. He's a kind, gentle person who only wants to take care of you and make you happy—even at the expense of his own happiness. How could you lie and trick the others into wanting to marry you, and then jilt them at the altar? Did you even love any of them?"

"You're right. None of them deserved it. They are all kind and loving and would have done anything I asked." Her voice was so tiny Kieran had to move closer just to hear her.

"I did love them. I really loved all of them. I want to get married, have a family, and have a happy ending. Who doesn't?" She looked directly into Kieran's eyes. "But I was also afraid of being married. I mean, look at my parents." She gestured vaguely in the air with one hand, as if conjuring up their presence. "You saw how they are together? My mother is constantly nagging my father, getting him to bend over backward, and he keeps doing it—no matter how badly she treats him. I don't want that. I don't want to *be* that! I don't want us to grow old and hate each other, or for *my* husband to turn into a doormat. I convinced myself I was deeply enough in love with each of them, and it couldn't happen to us." Her voice faltered.

Kieran waited for her to finish.

"And then, at the altar, I was standing there, in a beautiful dress and next to a man I loved with all my heart, and I glanced over at my mother, with her frilly dresses and big hair and too much makeup, who loves the bottle more than anyone or anything else. I saw my dad, so miserable, but he won't leave her. He says he promised 'till death' and they're both still living. Living, but not *alive*." She blinked and swallowed loudly before continuing. "I saw my future. I panicked. I saw *my* future there, and I couldn't run away fast enough. I couldn't do that to those wonderful men."

Now the tears began to fall.

Kieran felt like a dick for throwing that all in her face.

"My mother... well I won't go into all of it, but she told me no good man would want me, or want to move here—but I can't move away and leave my dad on his own with her, even though...."

Kieran grabbed a box of tissues and handed them to her. He almost felt like hugging her. He couldn't imagine living with her family. Jaxon was a saint for not running as soon as he met them.

"You know, maybe it doesn't mean much, but with Tom, I really was pregnant and I really lost our baby."

"What about Jaxon?"

"When I met Jaxon, he seemed perfect, and I used the same lies. I didn't want to risk having him leave me, so I lied to be sure he would stay and marry me. He's been so good helping with Mama, and he's given me a lot of strength. With him I think I could move away and have a real life. I'm going to tell him on the honeymoon we should leave Buckwheat Springs."

Kieran wanted to dredge up some famous quotation about irony, but he was crap at remembering things like that. Of course the least suitable groom turned out to be the one Danetta would finally marry.

Not if Kieran had anything to do with it.

"Danetta, I'm sorry about your mama. It's been rough on you and your dad, but lies and trickery aren't the way to start a marriage. You'll still be trapping him, just like your dad is trapped. Tell Jaxon the truth and let him decide whether he still wants to marry you. If you don't tell him, I will."

"No, Kieran! Please don't say anything to him! I want to marry him. I know he'll make me happy."

"What about making *him* happy?" Kieran raised his voice. "Doesn't Jaxon's happiness mean anything to you?" She still saw everything from her own selfish perspective. He felt a wave of pity for whoever ended up married to her and prayed it wouldn't be Jaxon.

"He'll be happy with me. He's happy now, isn't he?" She sniffled and grabbed more tissues. "He's so good at taking care of me, and making me happy, makes him happy."

Kieran bit his lip to remain silent, remembering how Jaxon had come to his hotel room two nights earlier. About the secrets Jaxon had been keeping from Danetta.

"Jaxon's different from the others, and he's made me different. He's got a certain confidence about him, but not in a way that makes him arrogant or overbearing. Perhaps it comes from working with teenagers. He earns their respect and trust, and he encourages them to do their best. I love seeing him with his students." Danetta's smile blossomed as she spoke. Kieran could tell she was sincere.

"Jaxon's too much of a catch for his own good." Kieran shook his head. That made it even worse someone as undeserving as Danetta would be getting him. Jaxon should be with someone who loved him the way he *deserved* to be loved, without playing tricks on him.

"If I didn't know better, I'd say you're falling in love with him, too, Kieran."

"I am," Kieran admitted. What harm could saying it do now?

"He likes you a lot."

If she only knew.

"Did you sleep with Jaxon?"

What *did* she know? "No." It was the truth.

"Is he gay?"

"I don't know." He shook his head. That was true too.

"I thought that's why he likes going over to Sam's."

They sat together for a few moments in silence, in some unspoken truce.

"I'll tell him the truth. I promise."

"Against my better judgment, I'm going to trust you." He held up the note and crumpled it, then stuffed it into his back pocket.

"So, what are you going to do now? Are you going to put all of this in your article?"

"No, I'm not that cruel. But I might change my mind if you don't tell Jaxon the truth about everything—before the wedding. I'll bet the others would rather have the whole mess of lies revealed than let Jaxon be tricked into marriage. Or you can just do a runner tomorrow and save yourself any potential embarrassment. No one would bat an eyelash around here if you stood Jaxon up. Then you can keep your secrets. I'll let you decide."

"I understand."

Kieran stood. "Now, I'm going to a bachelor party. I hope I *don't* see you tomorrow at the church." Without waiting for a response, he walked out the front door.

He spotted a couple of the bridesmaids coming down the sidewalk dragging rolling suitcases and giggling. What kind of bachelorette party would they have now?

Chapter Twenty-Two

KIERAN HADN'T seen Jaxon since he'd run out of the motel room on Wednesday, so he had no idea how Jaxon would react to seeing him at the bachelor party. If Jaxon gave any indication he didn't want Kieran around, he'd just leave quietly without making a fuss.

By the time Kieran got to La Piñata, Jaxon was already more than a bit tipsy. Marc, Tom, and Jordan had ordered plenty of drinks for him, and they sat half-drunk in front of him in the big booth.

"Good to see you." Tom reached out for a vigorous handshake. Jordan and Marc gave him guarded looks, so before sitting down, he stepped away from the table with Marc.

"I talked to Danetta, but I won't tell anyone else. Not even Jaxon. She's promised to tell him the truth before the wedding."

"Don't print any of it." Marc's tone had softened compared to their previous encounters. "It'll kill Danny."

"I don't want to hurt anyone. I want what's best for both of them. And it's not marrying Jaxon."

"I won't argue with you."

Kieran picked up on something in Marc's voice he should have noticed sooner. Marc was still very much in love with Danetta, despite the lies. It explained some of his hostility and anger.

Jaxon hadn't eaten much of his meal yet, so after Kieran scooted in the booth next to him, he grabbed a fork and took a bite of enchilada from Jaxon's plate.

"Kier, you finally made it! I was worried about you." Jaxon was smiling and laughing and had passed tipsy twenty miles ago. But he acted genuinely glad to see Kieran. Then he smacked Kieran's hand. "Get your own dinner!"

"You don't seem to be eating this one, so I'm making sure it doesn't go to waste." He took one more forkful of food, stuffed it into his mouth, and relinquished the fork. He didn't care who saw the intimacy of their interactions.

"I'm eating, I'm eating!" Jaxon took a few bites of food. "See?"

"Don't feel the need to show me, okay?" Kieran teased. "You're acting more like one of your students."

A waitress came by. Kieran ordered his meal and turned back to the table.

"So, Kieran, where ya been? No one's seen you since yesterday afternoon," Tom said. "We were taking bets at lunch that you'd gotten lucky with a secret lover, and that's why you missed the rehearsal dinner. We've been trying to figure out who else is MIA around here." Everyone laughed, except for Jaxon, who glanced over at Kieran shyly. Was there a hint of jealous curiosity in his gaze?

"I was working, believe it or not. Writing isn't all about sitting on your ass. I had to go to Dallas to interview a few people." He didn't say who or what it was about, and Marc didn't volunteer any information.

"Dallas?" Jaxon exclaimed with a mouthful of food. Kieran was glad to see he was eating, or he would pass out before too long. "Who were you talking to? All of my friends and relatives are here for the wedding. You've hardly even talked to my family for your column."

"I can't reveal my sources." Kieran laughed and took a sip from one of the drinks arrayed in front of Jaxon, earning another playful slap.

"Hey!" Jaxon said with mock anger, pouting slightly, and Kieran forced himself to ignore the way Jaxon's lips looked even more irresistible. It was difficult because all Kieran could think about was how much he'd really like to suck on Jaxon's lips again. Right now.

"You have more than enough, and I need to catch up to you."

"Well, at least ask first, my stuff isn't just here for the taking, ya know. But if you ask nicely…." Jaxon's tone was almost flirtatious, and Kieran suspected he wasn't just talking about his dinner and drinks. *Wishful thinking.* They'd tried the other night, and Jaxon had been the one to put a stop to it. *Has he changed his mind?*

Jaxon treated Kieran to a beautiful dimpled smile and took a gulp of green margarita, licking stray grains of salt off his lower lip as he swallowed. Kieran felt himself hardening as Jaxon swept his tongue across his lip. He refused to believe Jaxon was completely oblivious to the effect he had on Kieran; but there was nothing he could say or do with Marc, Tom, and Jordan across the table from them.

Surprisingly, Kieran enjoyed the rest of the dinner. It was good fun as Jordan, Marc, and Tom joked with Jaxon about how or when Danetta would decide to run the following day. Apparently several people were running pools on how far she'd get down the aisle this time. Half the folks in town had played.

Jaxon laughed, unconcerned his bride would get cold feet. Was he wishing as much as Kieran that she would? With the amount he'd drunk so far, Jaxon probably didn't know his own mother's name.

When they finished eating, the five of them got ready to go. Tom paid the bill, and they stumbled down the street to Sam's saloon.

Inside, cheers and shouts greeted Jaxon. His other friends, acquaintances, a few younger relatives, and some teachers from the high school had come to give him the party he deserved.

It was nice to see so many people here for him. After spending most of the past week with Jaxon, Kieran had concluded he didn't have many close friends. Jaxon spent most of his time at work or with Danetta but was probably closest to the other three grooms. Kieran was pleased to see so many people had turned out to wish Jaxon the best. Or not, as it turned out. Nearly everyone who came up to greet Jaxon offered a drink and a rude remark about Danetta. Jaxon shrugged off the remarks good-naturedly.

"Jax, I need to tell you something important." Kieran separated Jaxon from the crowd of well-wishers by gently pulling him toward the pool tables at the back of the bar. If Jaxon got any drunker, the conversation wouldn't do any good.

"Okay, what is it?" Jaxon's balance wavered and he leaned back against the wall for support.

"I need to tell you something about Danetta. Something really important."

"Look, I'm getting enough shit from everyone else around here. They think it's all in fun, but it's getting to me now. I don't need you badmouthing her, too. I thought we were pals, that you understood what I have to do."

"We are, which is why—"

"You know I told you I was going to marry her, no matter what we...." Jaxon paused, suddenly unable to meet Kieran's gaze. "Can't you just be happy for me now? Be optimistic that everything's going to be fine? I don't want to talk about Danetta with *anyone*, especially you. I just want us to have some fun."

"I honestly want you to be happy, Jax, which is why you need to tell her the truth and let her decide for herself—"

"If you want to be happy for me, you'll come back to the table and have another drink and stop thinking so much, okay? It's only going to hurt both of us now. I shouldn't have said or done anything the other night. I need for you to let it go, like it never happened."

"Okay." But Kieran would never forget it happened or that Jaxon had been the one to want it in the first place. He couldn't just sit quietly as Jaxon ruined his life and Danetta's. But it wasn't Kieran's truth to tell. The best he could do was to appeal to Jaxon's sense of honesty.

The party continued until it was clear Jaxon needed to get to bed if there was any chance of him being awake and sober at his wedding the following afternoon. Kieran offered to get him back to the Trail Dust, since he was going there anyway. They headed off in the direction of the hotel as the party went on without the groom.

Chapter Twenty-Three

INSIDE JAXON'S room at the Trail Dust, Kieran helped him get ready for bed and forced him to drink a couple of glasses of water. He pulled down the bedcovers, and Jaxon practically fell onto the bed. Kieran knew Jaxon was drunk, but it was hard to tell *how* drunk.

"Jaxon, you need to listen to me. For just one minute." Kieran had to try again.

Jaxon put his hand over Kieran's mouth, staring up into his eyes. Jaxon's green eyes were dark and pleading. His fingers were warm, and Kieran fought the urge to kiss them. He was sure Jaxon wouldn't mind, but Kieran was determined not to take advantage of Jaxon's drunkenness.

Kieran didn't make a move, even though he knew he might regret the decision forever. If only he could expose the truth, get Jaxon and Danetta to talk to each other and realize on their own that they were both marrying for the wrong reasons.

Would Jaxon stand by his promise to Danetta once he found out what she'd done?

"No, Kieran. No more important stuff. Not now." Jaxon shook his head vigorously, fingers still pressed to Kieran's lips.

"Jax, don't go to sleep yet." Kieran shook Jaxon's shoulder. "Do me one favor, please?" Kieran pleaded. "I'm going to leave you a note, okay? Please, please, read this before the wedding. Will you promise me? You need to do something very important before you make a final decision."

"Yeah," Jaxon mumbled, more asleep than awake. "Promise, I'll read it," he slurred, but he opened his eyes and gave Kieran another look that tore at his heart. A look that said he wished things could have turned out differently, but that he wouldn't break his promise to Danetta. Then Jaxon closed his eyes.

Kieran watched him sleep for a few minutes, then grabbed the hotel notepad and pulled a pen out of his breast pocket.

Jaxon,
Danetta has something very important to tell you
before the wedding. Call her when you wake up.

He folded the note and leaned it against the clock so Jaxon would see it first thing in the morning.

Then, against his better judgment, he leaned down and pressed his mouth to Jaxon's soft, beautiful lips, lingering much longer than a simple brush, but not enough to disturb Jaxon. It was much less than what Kieran would like from Jaxon, but it was more than he should have, considering the situation.

Just as he was pulling away, Jaxon's arms came up around Kieran's waist and held him tight then Jaxon slid one hand down Kieran's ass. If only this had happened yesterday.

"Stay here tonight, Kieran? Show me something I'll never forget."

Kieran pulled Jaxon close, gathering him against his chest and pressed his lips to Jaxon's throat. He inhaled, taking in his last breath of Jaxon, nose pressed close to the warm flesh he would never taste or touch again.

Then he laid Jaxon back down and headed for the door. He spotted the tuxedo hanging off the wardrobe. Jaxon would look fantastic in it. Seeing it brought home to Kieran that the wedding tomorrow was a reality, and it was still going to happen—unless.... Kieran just hoped Jaxon would keep his promise to read the note.

When Kieran got to his room, he slipped a hand into his back pocket for the hotel key but it wasn't there. He tried the other back pocket, all the front pockets, and his jacket. He hated waking Mrs. Connors, but she shuffled from the back room to the front desk wearing a quilted robe and handed him a replacement without any complaint.

"Guess that's one hell of a party tonight?"

"Hell of a party." He tipped an imaginary hat and hurried to his room before his willpower faded and he went back to Jaxon's.

He'd come to Texas to write a story and ridicule a group of people who a week earlier he hadn't even known. *Do I have the right to mess with their lives beyond that? Do I have the right to interfere with Jaxon and Danetta?*

Did it matter that both of them were living lies? *Is* ignorance truly bliss?

The answer to that one was above his pay grade.

Chapter Twenty-Four

JAXON WOKE up to Rod Stewart shouting into his ear. He most certainly did not think Rod was sexy, so he smacked the clock radio right off the nightstand. Rod kept singing anyway, and Jaxon realized he was in the motel room alone except for an awful hangover. The tux hanging off the wardrobe reminded him he couldn't lie in bed all morning even if he wanted to.

Stomach churning, head pounding, he dragged himself into the bathroom for a shower. Most of the night before was a blur, at least the latter part of the party. His memories trailed off during dinner, and the only thing he could remember with any clarity was that he threw himself at Kieran again.

But Kieran hadn't taken him up on it. Jaxon wasn't sure whether he was relieved or disappointed. Could they be friends after today? Did Kieran want that? Jaxon wasn't sure what he wanted.

Still wasn't sure. He'd had the expected prewedding jitters. Then Kieran Quinn had arrived and the jitters were more like earthquakes. He'd turned Jaxon's world upside down and left it there, with Jaxon hanging off the edge by his fingertips. Did he want to hang on or let himself fall into an entirely new world that beckoned far more strongly than he'd ever allowed himself to imagine?

The one thing Jaxon was sure of was that if Kieran hadn't come to Buckwheat Springs, today would be the happiest day of his life. Wouldn't it?

Probably. It was supposed to be.

Jaxon wished he didn't have to work so hard to convince himself.

He dried off and pulled on blue-and-white striped boxers. He'd just grabbed the first thing in the drawer when he packed the previous day. Should he have picked different underwear for such a momentous day? If Danetta had packed, she'd have chosen something significant. Every little thing at the wedding had some sort of significance that was lost on him. Was he not interested enough, or was that just normal for a groom? He should have asked Marc or Tom.

A knock sounded on the door as he was pulling his jacket on.

"Quit jacking off and open up," Marc's voice boomed as Jaxon opened the door to let him in.

Before closing it, Jaxon looked out the door and down the hall in both directions. Would Kieran stop by?

"I'm almost ready."

"You haven't even got this tied properly." Marc reached up and retied the bow tie. Then he stepped back to look at the finished product.

"Do I pass muster, Sergeant?" Jaxon gave a lame salute.

"What do you think?" Marc swung Jaxon around by his shoulders so he could look in the full-length mirror on the bathroom door.

Jaxon looked at himself. The tux was nice. It was sleek and elegant, and the tie looked so much better after Marc had fixed it. "Not bad. I don't think I'll scare her away."

Marc chuckled and hummed the "Wedding March."

Jaxon looked at his reflection, and instead of picturing Danetta on his arm, he wondered what it would be like to walk down the aisle with Kieran. Not in Texas, of course, but in almost every other state now.

Kieran had been the gentleman, not pushing Jaxon, just going as far down that other path as Jaxon wanted to go. But in the end, he'd been sweet and funny, sexy good company, and stepped back before Jaxon got in too deep.

That question had to remain unanswered. It would be too easy to fall into Kieran's arms and his bed and leave behind the doubts that had darkened the edges of Jaxon's world. He couldn't remember when the doubts started. Would they all go away once he and Danny said "I do"?

"Time to get going, Jax." Marc started humming again. Why did he seem happier than Jaxon did right now?

The room started tilting and Jaxon sat down on the bed. The dizziness passed after a few minutes and a glass of water.

"You steady, buddy?" Marc asked, hand on Jaxon's arm.

Jaxon looked at the hand. Did it do anything for him? Did he want to kiss Marc the way he wanted to do everything with Kieran? No. He wasn't sure whether he'd learned anything useful.

"Come on, Jax." Marc tugged him again.

As Jaxon followed him toward the door, he felt something under his foot. It was the room key and the note Kieran told him he had to read. He scooped them up and shoved them into his tux pocket, then slammed the door shut behind him as if that would keep the doubts from following him to the church.

ON SATURDAY, Kieran woke up later than he'd expected. He called Jaxon's room, but there was no answer. Had Danetta come by early to talk to Jaxon, or would she wait until after the wedding to tell him the truth? Kieran was sure if Jaxon had changed his mind after talking to her, he would have told Kieran.

Jealousy, excitement, trepidation all jostled for attention in his mind and gut as he showered and dressed. He was wearing one of his favorites: a blue silk-and-wool Zegna suit Alexa had picked out for him and insisted he wear for the wedding. He smiled at his reflection but then remembered he was here to write a story. He had to put aside his personal regard for Jaxon. No matter that he had begun to care entirely too much for Jaxon and that he might be making an irreparable mistake today.

While everyone else in town—and across the country, thanks to the teasers for Kieran's article *Gloss* had run on their web site— wondered whether Danetta would go through with the wedding, Kieran hoped like hell she wouldn't. Not because it would make a better column, but because… well, it might not be the best thing for Jaxon.

Yeah, Kieran couldn't even convince himself his concern was completely altruistic.

Jaxon deserved someone better than Danetta, someone who wouldn't lie to him, someone who loved him for all the right reasons. He felt sorry for Danny. She'd been through a lot and she hadn't put her own happiness above that of her father or mother or she would have moved away long ago. It didn't absolve her of the lies. Jaxon needed to know the truth.

Would he have wanted to marry her if she hadn't gotten pregnant? Only Jaxon would know. But Kieran had promised to let her tell Jaxon herself and he hoped he could trust her.

His cell phone beeped. Kieran raced to grab it, wishing he wasn't hoping Jaxon would call. Instead it was a text from Jeff, saying he'd gotten the message and was looking forward to Kieran's revisions, but he'd read and loved what was already sent.

A glance at the time meant Kieran would have to go directly to the church—without breakfast. Every bone in his body screamed for him not to go. But he needed to attend the wedding and not just for the column. He had to *see* Jaxon and Danetta get married in order to put this yearning for Jaxon behind him. He had to see Jaxon knowingly choose to stay with Danetta, even after having all the information.

Kieran had to *hear* Jaxon say "I do." Only then could he be certain there was nothing there for the two of them to pursue.

Then they could both get on with the rest of their lives.

JAXON AND Marc were already standing in their places by the time Kieran arrived. The church was packed. It seemed everyone in town wanted to be here firsthand to find out whether Danetta would go through with it this time. The overwhelming scent of flowers mixed with perfume and noise to make Kieran's head pound and his sinuses rebel.

Jaxon briefly caught Kieran's eye as Kieran was shown to a seat on the aisle about halfway back on the groom's side. Kieran's stomach churned, not from having drunk too much the night before, but from worry and fear. Had the woman sitting next to him heard it? She was chatting to the woman on the other side of her. Both wore wide-brimmed hats that battled for domination as they leaned together to gossip.

Jaxon turned again and nodded to Kieran. *Damn*, he looked fantastic in his tuxedo, even more handsome and desirable than Kieran had imagined. And he was smiling. He looked genuinely happy, Kieran thought morosely. A little too happy. Unless Jaxon was a saint, could he completely forgive Danetta for lying to him?

The others had forgiven her for running, but they hadn't asked her to marry them again. Still, they remained here to support her, despite what she'd put them through. He understood her reasons, but that wasn't enough to justify it. Was everyone in this town simply that tolerant? It made Kieran feel unworthy for ever holding a grudge.

The music started, and the first of the bridesmaids appeared at the door and moved up the aisle at a glacial pace. A cloud of perfume and roses arrived long before they did. Kieran didn't even glance at them because he couldn't take his eyes off Jaxon, and, Jaxon seemed to have fixed his gaze on Kieran, rather than on the bridesmaids.

Jaxon shifted his weight and fiddled in his pockets. He pulled something out and glanced at it—a piece of blue paper—and uncrumpled it as the bridesmaids continued their trek up the very long aisle.

Oh shit. Kieran recognized the note he'd written before talking to Danny. How had Jaxon gotten it?

Double shit. Kieran recalled stuffing it into his pocket with the room key. And he'd somehow lost the key during the party. A fleeting memory of Jaxon's arms around his waist up in the room flashed through Kieran's still-tipsy brain.

Had Jaxon taken the key and the note fell out too?

Triple shit.

Jaxon was whispering to Marc, showing him the paper as the bridesmaids moved noisily to their seats in a rustle of silk.

The discussion continued as the "Wedding March" announced that the bride had entered the church. Danetta walked slowly up the aisle, holding on to her father's arm, wearing an elegantly beaded V-necked dress with a softly ruffled skirt. She turned toward Kieran with a wide-eyed expression. As she passed by, even her makeup couldn't mask the red ringing her puffy eyes and nose. She gave Kieran a tentative smile before turning her gaze back to the front.

Jaxon's expression was markedly less cheerful the closer Danetta got to him. He glanced repeatedly at Kieran, who suddenly realized Danetta must not have told him the truth yet.

Danetta reached Jaxon. They turned to face the minister, who prepared to speak. Jaxon leaned down and whispered to Danetta.

"How could you lie to me about something *like that*?" Jaxon spoke angrily, loud enough for Kieran to hear, and certainly several rows behind him.

Then Jaxon turned and with a look of sadness and disgust, ran from the church.

A shocked roar erupted from the guests as he departed.

Danetta stood for a moment, mouth open as she processed the events. Marc put a hand on her arm and whispered into her ear. She pulled away, and Kieran could see her chest heaving with shock, embarrassment, and probably a dozen other emotions. She broke away from Marc and her father and walked over to Kieran.

Everyone was on their feet now.

"You promised me, Kieran."

He reached for her hands and she hit him with her bouquet, striking first his chest and then his face, the thorns from the roses digging into his cheek, ripping at his flesh. Kieran barely felt the pain.

"You, you bastard!" Danetta's voice broke and she sobbed rather than spoke the last word. "You lied. You told him without giving me a chance to explain any of it!" she cried out, repeating "You lied" over again, like some sort of desperate mantra, as she sobbed, while guests and bridesmaids rushed over, trying to calm her.

"I didn't tell him. I never gave him the note. I don't know how he got it. Honest."

"What am I going to do now?" Mascara ran down her face, like dreams that had just been washed away.

Kieran felt worse than ever. He wished he could do something for her, but her friends were milling around. He'd fucked this up so badly. He couldn't face Jaxon, and he couldn't face Jeff because there was no story here. Not one he wanted to tell anyway. There were just two people who had both been irreparably hurt because he'd come to town to try and make fools of them.

Instead, he'd been the biggest fool for thinking it was okay to fuck with other people's lives.

Chapter Twenty-Five

KIERAN WALKED slowly, taking the most roundabout route to the Trail Dust. He really wanted a drink, but if he started, he'd never stop. Maybe there was a way to fix this. He needed a clear head.

But his meddling might make it even worse.

When Kieran opened the door to his room, he found Jaxon waiting for him, sitting on the couch still in his tuxedo. His bow tie was untied and dangled around his neck. It would be incredibly sexy if he didn't look as miserable as anyone Kieran had ever seen.

On the table in front of Jaxon sat Kieran's room key—the gold one—and the crumpled-up note Kieran had written before he spoke to Danetta.

Now it dawned on him. Jaxon had put his hands around Kieran's waist and rubbed his ass the night before. He must have taken the key, and the note fell out of Kieran's pocket.

"Are you okay?" was all Kieran could think to say as he closed the door and walked to the couch where Jaxon sat cradling the half-empty bottle of tequila Kieran had been drinking the other night.

"I thought you were my friend," Jaxon said listlessly, and took a long swig from the bottle. A few drops of tequila trickled down his chin and he tried to lick them off.

"I am."

Jaxon picked up the note. "Then why didn't you tell me this!" He shook his fist then threw the crumpled paper at Kieran, and it bounced off his chest. Kieran wished it hurt as much as Danetta's thorns.

"Why didn't you *tell* me? Why?" Jaxon's voice shook.

"Let me have some of that," Kieran asked, and held out his hand for the tequila. Instead of taking a drink, he put it on the dresser on the other side of the room. The last thing Jaxon needed now was tequila.

"Tell me!"

"Because it wasn't my information to share. And because it's not the whole story."

"Then what is the whole story?" Jaxon's words were lost in an outraged sob.

"You should let Danetta tell you."

"I don't want to see her or speak to her or anything. God, I'm such a fucking fool. For listening to her. For thinking you're my friend. For throwing myself at you. You wouldn't take me when I offered. You must be laughing your big New York City ass off at the hicks in this town."

Kieran's heart shattered into more pieces with each cutting, hate-filled word Jaxon shouted. If he cut his arm off, it couldn't hurt more. He told himself he was making Jaxon's life easier by keeping Danetta's secret a little longer, but now he'd destroyed it even worse.

"I'm not laughing. I wish I were dead right now."

"So do I. Do you need any help with that?"

Kieran shook his head and turned toward the door. Staying here only upset Jaxon more.

"Don't go. Please?"

Kieran stopped with his hand on the doorknob, afraid to turn around.

"Kieran, tell me the whole thing. Help me figure this all out."

Slowly, Kieran turned and went back to the couch. He sat down and looked at the wreck of the man he had fallen for and wondered if he had let this happen. "What do you want to know?"

"Why didn't you tell me this sooner? About the lies? You knew.... Maybe we...."

"If I told you would you have believed me? Or would you assume I had selfish reasons for keeping you from marrying her?"

Jaxon nodded. "I can see that possibility. But you could have told me to talk to her."

"She needed to tell you herself. There's more to the story than what's in the note. A lot more. I didn't know everything when I wrote it. Then I went to see her last night, before the party. I told her what I'd found out and accused her of all sorts of things, and showed her the note."

"What could she have said to make you lie to me?"

"I didn't lie." Kieran saw anger flare in Jaxon's eyes again. "I didn't tell you anything because she promised me she would tell you—before the ceremony."

"She's a liar. Why did you believe her?"

"Because I know why she lied. I think you should listen."

"*You* won't tell me?"

"If you want to know, this is the only way."

"Fine." Jaxon crossed his arms over his chest and glared at Kieran.

"I'm texting her to come down here." Kieran pulled the phone out of his pocket.

"Now?"

"Yes. Don't get up or I'll tie you down."

"Why couldn't you have said that the other night?"

Kieran felt another stab when he saw Jaxon's expression was completely sincere.

"If we'd done something together, Kieran, I would have called the wedding off. I would have known it couldn't work."

"That's exactly why I didn't do anything. It had to be your conscious—sober and conscious—decision." There was no time for more of this discussion now. "She's coming down. I'll get out of here because you two need a chance to talk. Without me."

Jaxon nodded.

Kieran took one last look before he walked into the hallway. He had no idea whether Jaxon would be his friend or enemy next time they saw each other.

Coming down the hall was Danetta. She was still wearing the wedding dress, now stained with smeared makeup and flecks of blood. His blood.

"Good luck," he said. Sorry would have sounded so fucking inane. He turned away.

Danetta grabbed his hand. "Thank you." She gave him a quick hug.

She wasn't the monster he'd accused her of being in the note. Maybe they'd be able to work this out after all.

Chapter Twenty-Six

"COME IN," Jaxon said when he heard the tentative knock.

The door opened slowly, and he saw the satin shoe first. Then Danny came through, still in her dress. Her face looked awful. Jaxon probably looked as bad. He knew he felt worse.

"I owe you an explanation. First an apology." She started before she'd even closed the door behind her.

Jaxon didn't want to be anywhere near Danny right now, so he didn't invite her to sit on the couch.

She stood at the door, squeezing the fingers of her left hand with her right. She wasn't wearing the engagement ring anymore.

"Okay. I'm listening." It took every ounce—or gram or whatever they were supposed to say nowadays—of self-control to speak like an adult. He'd told his students a thousand times to speak calmly. Now he realized what a fucking hypocrite he really was because it was bloody impossible to be calm when he was so angry.

"I lied about being pregnant."

This time the information wasn't as shocking as discovering it while standing in front of the minister. Still, it threw into doubt everything he'd believed about their relationship. A thousand questions wrapped themselves around his brain but he couldn't manage more than to ask, "Why?"

"I really liked you. I didn't want to lose you."

"Why didn't you just wait and see how things turned out? Maybe we would have gotten here naturally. If we belong together."

"I knew you'd dump me if you ever came for a visit here."

He started to speak but she waved him silent.

"Once you met Mama, I figured you'd run. I'd run if the situation were reversed."

"You could have come to Austin. I'm sure there would have been a job you wanted there."

"It wasn't the job, Jaxon. I couldn't leave Daddy. I couldn't run off to a happy life and leave him here on his own to look after her."

"I wish you hadn't felt you needed to lie."

"I do too. I lied to you. And I lied to Marc and Jordan."

"What about Tom?"

"I really was pregnant with Tom. He was suddenly so sweet, and he stopped noticing how awful Mama could be. It was like some kind of magic spell."

"What happened?"

She shuffled her feet and twisted her fingers some more.

"Look, just come sit here. I'm not as mad as I was before."

She shook her head. Her veil fell off and she just kicked it away. He patted the couch and she came and sat at the other end.

"Tom and I were so excited. Then I fell when we were riding and lost the baby, a couple of weeks before the wedding."

Jaxon didn't believe her at first. But Danny wasn't crying now, wasn't trying to justify herself, which actually made him trust her more. "I'm sorry."

"It was early, and I was okay. Tom was more worried about me, but Mama… Mama…." She sobbed the word and had to pause to pull herself together. "Mama said Tom wasn't really interested in me and that he'd only wanted to marry me for the baby and soon I'd find out what marriage was all about. How she had once been a pretty, happy bride." She swallowed. "I didn't want to turn into Mama. I couldn't do that to Tom. He was so kind and wonderful. When I was walking down the aisle, I could hear all the things she warned me about, and I didn't want Tom to hate me and be sorry he married me. So I just turned around and ran. I thought I was doing him a favor.

"He ran after me, but I wouldn't come back to the church, and I wouldn't tell him why I ran. Everyone laughed at him for a while, but he didn't give up trying to talk to me. They laughed at that too. Finally I told him what Mama had said. We realized we weren't ready to get married if we couldn't talk through things. We probably would have split up, or not split up and been as unhappy as Mama predicted."

Jaxon just nodded. She was probably right. But he also knew Lorraine was in bad shape, he just hadn't realized what a terrible effect she'd had on Danny.

"I'm sorry about that. Really."

"Thanks." She leaned over to grab for tissues, and he handed her the box.

"Your dress is really beautiful. I didn't get to tell you before."

"Yeah, I know all the best wedding dress boutiques." She tried to laugh. Then she put a hand up to fix her hair but stopped and looked at Jaxon. "That doesn't explain what happened later. Or what I did to you."

"You can tell me another time."

"Sure. Another time." She gave another ironic laugh and smoothed the dress across her lap. She touched the spot where drops of blood stood out against the pale silk. "Oh dear. I hit Kieran with the bouquet." She put her hands over her mouth as if recalling some even worse horror.

"That explains the scratches on his face."

"I've really made a spectacle of myself today. Of you. I'm so, so sorry." She looked into Jaxon's eyes, but she seemed afraid to touch him and pulled her hands away as he reached out.

"Danny, did you want to run away today?"

She closed her eyes and shook her head.

It would have been so much easier for him if she had given a different answer. Did today change anything? Should they let it?

"Do you still want to get married?"

"To you?"

"Yes."

"I can't marry you, Jaxon. Even if you still wanted to. I wouldn't make a very good wife. I'm not ready to get married. Too many things I need to sort out before it would be fair to any man."

"It sounds like you've sorted some of them out already. I'm here if you need me."

"Jax, you're such a gentleman for saying so. Your Mama would be so proud of you."

"I wish your Mama was proud of you."

"Are you trying to get me to change my mind?" She smiled for the first time since she'd entered the room.

Jaxon didn't reply.

"Do you still want to marry me, Jaxon?" Before he could speak, she shook her head. "Don't answer. You're not ready either."

He felt like he'd failed her because he hadn't realized how damaged she was under the layers of confidence she'd put on every day just like makeup.

"I've seen things change between us. Inside of you. I know you had doubts you weren't willing to tell me about. Not that it's anywhere near as bad as what I've done."

He hoped she didn't know what she was talking about. Had it been so obvious?

"As much as today has been a disaster, I kind of think it's a good thing."

He moved toward her on the couch and pulled her close. She held on to his shoulder.

"I don't deserve a good man like you. But maybe *you* do."

He pulled back, then wished he hadn't. He couldn't look her in the eye.

"Jax, it's okay to wonder about things. And if it's a question you already know the answer to, then it's just one more reason we don't belong together."

"Why…? How…?"

"I never would have even guessed until I saw the way you and Kieran clicked, like two puzzle pieces that fit together. It wasn't quite so obvious, but once he arrived, I noticed all the ways you and I didn't fit together as well as I wanted us to."

"We were good together." Jaxon needed to make it true, so he wouldn't feel like he'd failed her.

"You and I were like a bowl of the best ice cream. That's really good. But you and Kieran are a hot fudge sundae."

He couldn't help smiling at her double entendres. Were they intentional?

"I didn't do anything with him."

"You should. I mean if you're interested. It's none of my business. I should just shut up right now." She started fanning her face and moved to get up.

"Now what?"

"I don't know. I've never been the one left at the church." She tried another weak smile. "There's a lot of commotion over this. I need to make my peace with some other people too. You don't deserve to be in the middle of any of this mess. I've done this, and I need to fix it."

He was too drained of emotion to process how he felt at the moment, but he knew he didn't want to have to discuss it a thousand more times. "I'll just stay at the Trail Dust for a few days. But, I don't want to look like I'm hiding."

"I'll take the blame. Don't you worry about that at all. But you should get out of Buckwheat Springs." She paused and a genuine smile curved her lips. "Just take the trip to Hawaii."

"Our honeymoon?"

"It's nonrefundable. Someone should enjoy it. We need some time and space. There are still things to sort out between us."

"I can't."

"You should. Really." She looked up into Jaxon's eyes, and he decided to believe her.

Chapter Twenty-Seven

KIERAN TOOK a deep breath before opening the door to his room. Jaxon had texted him when Danetta left and after he'd spoken with his parents, but Kieran gave him another twenty minutes alone. He had no idea whether Jax would still be angry with him. There had been no right thing for Kieran to have done. He had been hiding from Jaxon as much as giving him some space.

Treating himself to a hearty lunch in the Copper Caboose, he listened as a steady stream of Wheaties in varying degrees of indignation sat down at his booth and chatted or ranted about the events of the day.

Small-town attitudes and double standards mixed to create a toxic situation for Jaxon, Kieran quickly realized. He hoped his friend would be able to weather the spiteful opinions and comments from most of the people he'd spoken to.

A few people asked him what he'd done to get Danetta so upset, but he suggested they ask her directly. Hopefully the situation would change dramatically once people learned exactly what Danetta had been up to and for how long. It seemed likely Marc or Jordan might reveal Danetta's treachery, even if only to support and defend Jaxon. Tom, though, would probably never say anything; she hadn't lied to him.

"Hey," Jaxon said when Kieran finally entered his hotel room again.

"Hey." Kieran stayed by the door until Jaxon told him it was safe.

He sat in the chair by the desk and looked at Jaxon, who sat on the couch, still in the tux. Not looking as good as he had standing up in the church. At least he hadn't gotten into the tequila again. The bottle was capped and still on the desk.

"Thanks for making me talk to Danny." Jaxon took a long breath. "I'm sorry I put you in the middle. It wasn't fair to you. This wasn't your fault at all."

"It doesn't feel that way. It feels like it's all my fault."

"The problems Danny and I have aren't about you. They are about me and her. You were a little bit of a complication." Jaxon grinned. "But whether you were here or not, she still lied to me. And she didn't own up to those lies when she should have."

"Is that how you see it? You're awfully calm now."

"I'm stinking mad, but I'm too tired to show it."

"Do you want to talk at all?"

"Maybe later. I really want to get out of this damn tux. It's a waste."

Someone knocked at the door. Kieran got up and looked through the peephole.

"Who is it?" Jaxon asked.

"I don't know. Someone who wants to ask me more questions. I fended off enough of them at the Caboose while you and Danetta were talking. I figured it would take some of the pressure off."

"Why would they be looking for *you*?" Jaxon asked, looking confused. "I know they're out for my blood after I left Danetta at the altar, but—"

"Maybe because Danetta attacked me with her bouquet after you left. It's not rocket science to think I've got something to do with what happened."

"She did? Sorry. Yeah, you've got some blood on your face." Jaxon's voice came out toneless and distracted, as if he'd just noticed the red streaks.

Kieran touched his cheek and felt welts. He turned and looked in the mirror to see the damage. The thorns had left a few gashes on one cheek and there was some dried blood. Nothing major—he didn't need a plastic surgeon or anything, probably just some antiseptic.

"You should change your clothes, Jax. Do you have something to change into in your room upstairs?" Kieran forgot his face for the time being. "I don't mind going to get it for you."

"Yeah, thanks." Jaxon sounded exhausted. He fished in his pocket for the key and came up with the note as well. "This is your key. Somehow I ended up with it."

"I wish I'd put it in a different pocket. I guess that's how you got in here after you left the church?"

Jaxon nodded. "I don't have my key."

"I'll ask for one at the desk. Let me change first." He pulled his jacket off and hung it up, then slipped his pants off. He noticed Jaxon watching. He took off his shirt, curious whether Jaxon would keep watching or glance away. He didn't look away, and it cheered Kieran up more than it should have. Neither of them mentioned it, and Kieran slid into narrow jeans and an orange-and-pink-checked button-down.

"I like that shirt," Jaxon said. "Your wardrobe is much more interesting than mine."

"You're the principal in a dinky town in Texas. Stripes are probably too out there for you." Kieran laughed. "You can borrow a shirt. Don't think the pants'll fit."

"Thanks."

"I wouldn't go for anything pink just yet. Wait till you cross the state line."

Jaxon let out a real laugh. It sounded good and cheered Kieran up.

"All right. I'll grab something for you and be right back. Stick by the phone in case Mrs. Connors calls to make sure I'm allowed to get your key."

"Okay."

JAXON WAS wearing only a towel when Kieran returned with some clothes he'd stuffed into a brown-and-white plastic hotel laundry bag. "I hope these are okay with you. Jeans, underwear, socks, shoes." He thrust the bag at Jaxon and sat on the couch, mad at himself for looking at Jaxon's almost-naked body in the mirror.

"Thanks." Jaxon peered into the bag then tossed it onto the bed. "I hope it's okay to use the shower?"

"Sure." Kieran pulled out his laptop and made some notes about the wedding for his column. He didn't think he'd ever forget today, but the details would slip his mind soon enough. He had no idea what he was going to write or even what angle he could take. He'd deal with that later, once he got back to New York. By then, he doubted anyone in Buckwheat Springs would be talking to him about it. He'd spoken with a few people at the Caboose who had strong opinions about Jaxon, but if Danetta kept her word and came clean with the people who mattered most, soon the rest of town would know the truth, or at least enough of it.

The shower went off, and a few minutes later, Jaxon emerged from the bathroom in a cloud of steam, the towel wrapped precariously around his hips. This was Kieran's first chance to see much of his body, but Jaxon hadn't pretended he wasn't watching Kieran change clothes.

From the couch, Kieran could see Jaxon's upper body showed he still liked to keep in shape. He didn't have washboard abs or bulging biceps, but his chest showed firm, defined curves and planes and a sprinkling of light brown hair that ended beneath the towel.

In the mirror, Kieran watched Jaxon pull the towel off, but he'd turned so it was a rear view only. But a very nice rear, two smooth pale globes. *Turn around, please.* But Jax slid into the boxer briefs before he turned back toward Kieran. The pale yellow cotton was thin and revealed almost as much as it hid. It put a smile on Kieran's face, but if he stared too long, that wouldn't be the only part of him reacting.

He dragged his gaze back to the laptop as Jaxon finished dressing.

"Kieran?" Jaxon sat a foot away on the couch, enveloped in a cloud of motel shampoo aroma. Low-end motel shampoo aroma.

"Yeah?" He looked up and put the laptop on the coffee table.

"Can you tell me how you found out she'd lied about the baby?" Jaxon asked, voice wavering. He might have been able to forgive some of Danetta's lies, but it seemed that learning the truth about the baby had broken him.

Kieran explained how he'd figured everything out: with whom he'd spoken the day before and what he'd discovered. He didn't go over the discussion with Danetta in detail.

"How could she have lied to me about a baby? I was surprised when she said she was pregnant; we'd been careful, but birth control isn't 100 percent. But when she called me to tell me she'd lost it, I was really devastated. I felt so worried about her. I played right into her hands." Jaxon closed his eyes, and the tears finally broke through.

Kieran wanted to hold Jaxon in his arms to make him feel safe and loved, to let him know he wasn't a fool. Instead, he rubbed Jaxon's shoulder and waited to see what else Jaxon wanted or needed. After a while, Jaxon calmed down and wiped roughly at his face with tissues from a box Kieran brought over from the bedside table. He felt a little guilty at the memory of how he'd last used them.

"I'm sorry." Jaxon sounded suddenly self-conscious.

"Hey, this is a really huge thing for you to process. It's going to take time, and it's going to hurt. Just let me know what you need. Okay?"

"Thanks."

"Don't thank me."

"You told me how you found all this out, but why did you do it? Why did you start digging in the first place?"

The guilt settled heavier into Kieran's gut. "I just didn't understand why all the other men were so forgiving. One or two, maybe. But something seemed wrong here. Why did they all stay here? Why had you all become friends, and why didn't any of you feel any jealousy over the others? Something smelled bad. It's the kind of thing journalists pick up. This was like the Goodyear blimp it was so obvious there was much more to the situation."

"And you were digging so you could have a better story?"

"I came here to write a story. The blimp told me there was something worth finding out."

"Where did I—we—fit into your plan?"

"You want to know if I tried to find a way to ruin the wedding? So you wouldn't go through with it?" How the hell could he answer that one?

"Yes." Jaxon pressed his lips together and Kieran knew he had to tell the truth. Jaxon wouldn't put up with any more lies.

"No. I wanted to dig up some dirt; I won't deny that. But once we got to be—close, I needed to make sure there wasn't something you needed to know before you got married."

Jaxon sat back against the couch, looking a little more relaxed. "You did know something that would have stopped the wedding, but you didn't tell me. I'm sorry I accused you of sabotaging things. I should be thanking you for digging up what you did, no matter your motives."

Kieran watched Jaxon staring up at the ceiling. There was so much for him to deal with right now, but Kieran felt powerless to help. Offering too much would push Jaxon away. What was too much?

"She asked me to keep quiet about it all, not tell anyone about her being pregnant, even our parents. It's a small town, so I understood her situation. And then later, she said losing a baby was too painful to share with anyone else." Jaxon took a few shallow breaths. "All I wanted to do was comfort her and make her happy, so I went along with whatever she asked. I felt like it was my fault she was so unhappy. I would have done anything."

"It's not your fault any of it happened. You wouldn't have any reason to think she'd lied about any of it. She was very clever in how she got all of you to keep everything a secret so no one would figure out what she'd done."

"I feel like a complete idiot."

"You're just a guy who fell in love with a girl who wasn't quite what she appeared to be. It might not seem like it now, but it's for the best you found out in time."

"On the bright side, I don't have to eat any more of Lorraine's cooking."

They both broke into laughter. Kieran's stomach ached when they finally calmed down.

"Danetta lives with you, right?"

"Oh, fuck. Yeah. It's my house. I mean, I bought it for us. She wants to move back in with her parents, even though I said she could stay there until she found her own place. I'm mad at her, but I don't feel right sending her back there."

Kieran liked that Jaxon was still concerned for Danetta, even though she didn't really deserve it.

"What about your column?"

"I wasn't planning on writing about how she tricked you, or about the pregnancy, so don't worry."

"Maybe you should, sort of payback." Jaxon's tone was full of spite.

"Jax, you might want to focus on tying up loose ends here and not on revenge or retribution. It will all come out soon enough, and then you'll be off the hook as far as the town is concerned, trust me."

"You're probably right." Jaxon sighed and didn't look convinced.

THE EVENTS of the day soon came crashing down on Jaxon and he lay down on Kieran's bed for a nap. It was nearly eight o'clock when he finally woke again.

"I'm starving." Jaxon stretched like a lanky cat, the shirt tightening against his chest and outlining his body all too clearly.

"What do you want? I'll run out and get food. No one's knocked for the last half hour, but I'm not sure if you're ready to go out yet."

"I'm not ready. Do you mind? I don't care what you bring back. Surprise me." Then Jaxon paused. "On second thought, I've had enough surprises for one lifetime."

"I'll be back soon."

Chapter Twenty-Eight

KIERAN RETURNED with take-out cheeseburgers from Sam's. In times of stress, cheeseburgers beat out grilled chicken any day of the week.

"You've got some color back in your face." Kieran popped the last curly fry into his mouth.

Jaxon liked watching Kieran eat. The man enjoyed his food unabashedly.

"Damn, this burger is good," Jaxon said with his mouth full. "Better than whatever we were going to have at the reception."

"Didn't you get to choose anything for your own wedding?"

"I went along to the caterers to taste things, but Danetta made the final decisions. I can't believe what an idiot I was. When I look back, it's so obvious the way she manipulated me."

"Didn't she try to make you happy at all? I can't see her only expecting you to be concerned about *her* happiness. It's a problem when it's all uneven like that."

"Yeah, she did. She tried to do a lot. She worked hard, and then you know about Lorraine. Danny spent a lot of energy on her parents. They never gave back, so I was the only one trying to please her. I'm probably just remembering the worst of it right now." Jaxon finished his burger. Kieran had cleaned his plate long before.

"Hey, finish these fries for me." Jaxon pushed the Styrofoam box toward Kieran and tossed him some ketchup packets.

Kieran rarely turned down food, especially curly fries. He munched on Jaxon's leftover fries, now a routine with them.

"I never asked how things went with your parents."

"After I told my parents what you found out and how Danetta admitted everything, they understood why I ran out on her. I knew they would stand by me, but they deserved an explanation. Of course, it would have been better had I found out *before* she got down the aisle, but better late than never." Jaxon managed a laugh. "My dad even volunteered to help her move out before I get back."

"Get back from where?" Kieran asked. "Are you planning to stay at the Trail Dust until she moves out of your house?"

"I haven't told you everything about my discussion with Danny." Jaxon wasn't prepared to tell Kieran everything just yet. He'd start with the easy stuff and work up to the zinger. He shoved a large envelope across the table to Kieran. "I've got two tickets to what should be paradise."

Kieran peered into the envelope then dumped the contents onto the table. He narrowed his eyes at Jaxon. "You're going on the honeymoon?"

"Maybe." Jaxon slurped Coke, enjoying keeping Kieran in suspense. "The reservation is for two. You wouldn't let me go all by myself, would you?"

"Seriously? And you're inviting *me*?"

"Yes and yes," Jaxon confirmed. "The trip is already paid for, so why waste it? Plus, I need to get out of here for a while and let things blow over. I already have the vacation time booked at school."

"And me?"

"You can come along for moral support. Be Tonto, or Sancho Panza, or whoever."

"I don't do sidekick. I'm too tall." Kieran still hadn't jumped at the idea. Jaxon wondered whether he'd imagined Kieran's interest. He hadn't imagined the way Kieran had watched him get dressed. Had Jaxon only been a trophy straight guy? Easy to fuck because they'd never see each other again. Then again, Kieran hadn't fucked him, even though he'd offered himself. Heat prickled his ears at this possible new humiliation.

Better to get this over with. Jaxon pushed the food away. "I know we haven't talked about it since the other night, but it would be a good chance to get to know each other *better*." Was he too pushy? Too vague? He waited to see Kieran's reactions.

"You're not kidding?"

Jaxon shook his head. "Would you believe it was Danny's idea for me to take the trip?"

"I didn't see that coming."

There was more Kieran hadn't seen coming, but even Jaxon wasn't sure of the other part. He nodded. "I think she genuinely feels bad, and not just because we're not getting married. Her life is an even bigger mess than it was before, but she's not running and hiding." A tiny glimmer of respect formed in his heart.

"I don't know."

"We could... pick up where we left off the other night?" Jaxon raised his eyebrows.

Kieran's smile saddened. "I'm really tempted."

"Does it sway you if I tell you the trip's nonrefundable?"

Kieran let out a soft chuckle. "Oh, well, in that case, sure."

Should Jaxon be insulted that Kieran hadn't sounded eager to be with him? *Play it cool, Jax.* He kept the discussion neutral when he really wanted Kieran to pull him into his arms and make him forget about Danny and the wedding and show him a world he longed for. "I'm not sure if we can change the plane ticket, TSA being what they are."

"I can probably get the magazine to cover the airfare if you can't."

"So that's a yes?"

"Yes." Kieran's smile returned, brightening the room, and Jaxon's heart.

Jaxon was about to go on a honeymoon with Kieran Quinn. Absolutely the last thing he expected when he woke up that morning.

But he couldn't think of a better ending to the day.

KIERAN COULDN'T believe what he was hearing. Jaxon, with whom he was undoubtedly falling in love, had just asked him to go on a trip— a honeymoon—and had all but promised there would be sex.

His body already thrummed with the promise of Jaxon's touch, while his head reminded him that this was not the best thing for either of them right now. Jaxon was too vulnerable and needed time to process everything that had happened.

Kieran's heart was trapped painfully in between.

Jaxon appeared composed, even cheerful, right now; but Kieran was positive he'd break down soon. The last thing Jaxon needed was to start a new sexual relationship with another man. It would be hard enough for him to begin to understand his own sexuality, which he had clearly been questioning lately. This certainly wasn't the time for experimentation.

Kieran wanted to be with Jaxon, but he didn't want to end up as a rebound relationship.

"I'll go, under one condition." Kieran couldn't believe the words even as they left his mouth. "We go as friends. We don't go expecting anything more. You haven't even processed what's happened today, and starting something with me is probably more than you can handle right now. Okay with you?"

Jaxon looked a little relieved at Kieran's qualification. "Yes. We go as friends. You've stood behind me and helped me with everything today. You'd be good company for me right now. There's no one I'd rather go with."

"Not even Marc or Jordan?"

"No."

"Okay, then. Let me make some calls about the plane, and we leave—" Kieran glanced at the itinerary. "—at 8:00 a.m.? We'd need to leave—"

"By five." Jaxon was grinning.

Kieran was already reconsidering. Maybe if he didn't go to sleep at all tonight.... He glanced over at Jaxon and reminded himself spending the night together wasn't an option.

"My suitcase is all ready to go. It's upstairs in my room. I should get going." But Jaxon didn't get up.

This was going to be torture, but Kieran had to do it. "You should get some sleep. I'll call you once I've worked out things with New York."

"Okay." Jaxon got up and left.

Kieran placed a quick call to Jeff to make sure he had approval for an extended trip as long as he didn't miss any deadlines. Afterward, Kieran packed his bags and tried to get to sleep.

A week in Hawaii with Jaxon, he mused. Under any other circumstances, it would be a dream come true. But now, after what Jaxon had found out, it was likely Kieran would be a shoulder to cry on and nothing more. *It's a start*, he decided, and it would do for now.

Chapter Twenty-Nine

Tuesday
Kauai, Hawaii

IT WAS nearly 2:00 a.m., and Kieran was hunched over his laptop in their hotel room, trying to finish his column. He'd rewritten the entire first part, where he'd made Jaxon out to be a sucker for falling for Danetta. Kieran wanted to avoid violating Jaxon's privacy, revealing only what he considered necessary to the task of disclosing Danetta's lies. It took a lot of time and creativity to get a good column out of what Kieran was willing to discuss.

He leaned back and stretched, loosening the aching muscles in his back and neck, and glanced over at the bed where Jaxon slept soundly.

Jaxon. Kieran looked at him and sighed. The first two days of their stay had been spent swimming, snorkeling, and lazily sipping fruity cocktails at the hotel's beautiful private beach. They'd spent hours talking about how Jaxon was coping with everything and not a single minute talking about what had become exponentially more important: sex.

Kieran's inability to keep his eyes off Jaxon in Texas was nothing compared to having Jaxon's well-muscled, near-naked body right there all day, every day. Kieran wondered what he'd expected, coming to a tropical island for a week with Jaxon. Jax insisted Kieran got plenty of admiring glances from both men and women, but he barely noticed with his attention so focused on Jaxon.

Jaxon's fair skin meant he needed to apply sunscreen frequently, and only Kieran could reach all the places on his shoulders, back, and the backs of his legs. It was exquisite torture—but torture nonetheless—for Kieran to spread lotion on Jaxon every couple of hours, all the while remembering his promise not to venture beyond friendship this week.

Kieran's willpower was at an all-time low. He could swear Jaxon was taunting him by asking for sunscreen more frequently than strictly necessary. The sun brought out scattered clumps of caramel-colored freckles all over Jaxon. Kieran found himself gazing at them inappropriately, only to discover Jaxon watching him with a sly smile.

Being on the honeymoon package meant one bed in the room. Kieran struggled to resist Jaxon's flirtations. He wasn't tired enough to fall asleep yet, and he didn't want to lie in bed awake, listening to Jaxon's breathing against his ear, or feel the heat of Jaxon's body as he rolled up against Kieran during the night. Just thinking about the way Jaxon's skin felt made Kieran warm and tingly all over.

Kieran glanced at the bed. Jaxon had rolled onto his side, facing away from Kieran, but the sheet covering his body had slipped down. Kieran noticed the way his waist dipped in slightly above slim hips. The fallen sheet also revealed the smooth curve of Jaxon's naked ass. Wasn't Jax wearing boxers when he'd gone to bed?

Kieran enjoyed the view in spite of this discrepancy, his cock swelling.

Fuck. Kieran had spent plenty of time in the bathroom dealing with inconvenient and embarrassing hard-ons from looking at Jaxon or sharing a bed with him, and it seemed like he'd be making another trip soon. No harm in spending a few more minutes looking first. Jaxon shifted position again, now onto his back. The sheet tangled around his legs, and his cock sprang into view. From across the room Kieran could see Jaxon was hard—his cock dark and heavy, curving slightly along his abs, rising from a tangle of hair.

Kieran tried not to stare, but lost the battle even before it started. Jaxon had a cock every bit as gorgeous as the rest of him. Unbidden, Kieran's own cock ached and called for attention. Two full days of a swimsuit-clad Jaxon and now *this*? He felt like a six-foot-three-inch hard-on, and he didn't think he could last much longer. Why the fuck had they come to Hawaii? Why couldn't it have been Alaska? Jaxon would have had to keep all of his clothes on there, and Kieran wouldn't have needed quite so much self-control.

Unable to resist, Kieran palmed himself through his boxers as he got up and headed for the bathroom. On the way, he approached Jaxon, intending to pull the covers back up over Jaxon's increasingly irresistible body. As Kieran reached for the sheet, Jaxon grabbed his wrist.

"Kier, why don't you just come to bed?" Jaxon's voice was too soft, too inviting, and he made no move to hide his body while Kieran hovered at the bedside. "Instead of jerking off in the bathroom."

Fuck. Well, Kieran hadn't said he'd been subtle about it. "No, Jax. We had a deal." Kieran nearly choked on the words.

"I think your body wants to make a new deal." Jaxon's smirk was clear even in the low light as he gazed at Kieran's cock tenting his boxers. "I want you, Kier. I want you to touch me." Jaxon pushed the sheets away.

"I can't." Kieran wanted to. With every fiber of his being. But he wouldn't. No matter how much Jaxon wanted this. Even if Jaxon was ready to take the relationship in a new direction, Kieran wasn't.

He cared for Jaxon in a way that wouldn't make it easy for them to go their separate ways at the end of the week. If Kieran gave in now, it would hurt too much to give Jaxon up. And there was no way they could do otherwise: Kieran lived in New York, and Jaxon ran a school in a tiny Texas town where they'd eat him for breakfast if he showed up with a gay lover.

"Why not? I can see you want me, too."

"Because…." Kieran faltered. Honesty was the best policy. "Jax, you're making a game out of torturing me, and I'm out of willpower to resist. If we start something now, is it just going to end on Sunday? I'm beginning to care entirely too much about you to just say good-bye at the airport and go our separate ways. If we take things to the next level, it will kill me to let you go."

"Doesn't it matter that I feel the same way? That I'm falling in love with you, too?"

"How can you fall in love when you've only known me a week?" Kieran asked.

"You can fall in love in a week, and I can't? That doesn't make sense."

"But you've never been with a guy. It's a big step for you, especially after everything with Danetta. Wanting to do something and doing it are two entirely separate things."

"Someone I know explained it very well: it's not whether it's a guy or a woman, it's who I'm attracted to," Jaxon said, paraphrasing what Kieran had said to him a week earlier. "I happen to be attracted to *you*. I enjoy being with *you*. I want to be with you completely."

Kieran was silent.

"And who says we have to say good-bye on Sunday?" Jaxon continued. "If there's something real here, we'll figure out how to make it work. But we won't know for sure if we don't take this chance. Now." Jaxon pulled Kieran down to sit on the bed beside him, pressing his chest against Kieran's arm. Jaxon leaned in to brush his lips against Kieran's cheek and mouth.

"God, Jax, you are going to kill me, you know?" Kieran let Jaxon pull him into bed so they lay facing each other. Jaxon took possession of Kieran's mouth in a way that said he was absolutely serious about this.

Kieran let Jaxon kiss him, much the way he had in his motel room the week before. Jaxon kissed as greedily and passionately as before, practically consuming him until Kieran urgently needed air. The hunger in Jaxon's kiss extracted the very core of Kieran, making him feel as though Jaxon desperately needed him in order to stay alive. If this was how Jaxon kissed, Kieran wondered at the intensity with which Jaxon would make love. The prospect thrilled and frightened him.

Their hands explored each other's chests, backs, and arms. Touching Jaxon and being touched by him was as amazing as Kieran expected. He hadn't touched Jaxon's cock yet, though he wanted to, but he'd wait and take it slow for Jaxon's sake.

"Can I take your boxers off?" Jaxon asked. Kieran rolled onto his back and lifted his hips as Jaxon slid the shorts down. He got them as far as Kieran's knees and Kieran kicked them off the rest of the way. Kieran was about to find out if Jaxon was really ready for this or not.

Jaxon was on his left side, propped up on one elbow and staring at Kieran's cock with fascination. He started to reach out his hand and stopped.

"Can I touch you—your...?" Jaxon whispered.

"You can do whatever you want," Kieran told him. "Touch me however or wherever you want to."

Jaxon looked into Kieran's eyes before slowly reaching his hand out and touching Kieran's cock gently, using his fingertips to trace a line up the shaft. He nearly jumped when Kieran moaned softly at his caress. A few more tentative touches and Jaxon wrapped his hand loosely around Kieran.

"I don't want to do this wrong," Jaxon said.

"It works just like yours, Jax. You're not going to break it," Kieran reassured him.

"What do you like? How do you want me to do it?"

"Hey, it's cheating if I give you the answer before you even started the quiz, isn't it?" Kieran joked, lightening the mood enough so Jaxon smiled back. "Won't it be more fun to find out for yourself what I like?"

"Making education jokes?"

"It's true, isn't it? You remember better when you have to figure it out."

Jaxon stroked Kieran, gradually becoming more comfortable and applying more pressure, twisting his hand now and then. If Kieran moaned louder, Jaxon kept at whatever he was doing.

"I'd like it if you kissed me while you're at it." Kieran didn't think he'd seen anything more adorable than the look of concentration on Jaxon's face as he tried to please him.

Jaxon leaned over and kissed him softly while he continued stroking and pulling at Kieran's cock.

Kieran was close, but he wanted to last. He was defenseless. The feel of Jaxon's mouth on his sent Kieran over the edge. His body shuddered, and he groaned into Jaxon's mouth as a warning, but Jaxon hadn't understood. Kieran came, shooting hot, thick jets that ended up mostly on Jaxon's chest. The splatter surprised Jaxon, who let go of Kieran's cock and tensed up before he realized what had happened and relaxed, looking slightly embarrassed at his reaction.

Jaxon looked over at Kieran as if hoping for some comment on how he'd done. Kieran didn't say anything. He took Jaxon's hand and brought it to his mouth and lightly kissed the fingers, then gently licked a few drops of come off Jaxon's hand.

"But it's *your*—what does it taste like?" Jaxon asked with a slow smile as Kieran kept licking.

"Kind of salty, mainly," Kieran said.

Jaxon's smile widened as he brought his hand—and Kieran's—up to his mouth and took a tiny lick at the cloudy drops. He licked again, but Kieran couldn't read his expression.

Jaxon frowned. "It's, uh...."

"It's okay if you don't like it. You don't have to taste it if you don't want to."

"I do. It's just new." He took a few more licks. "It's you."

Kieran kissed Jaxon gently. "Now, I remember a little while ago you asked me to touch you." He leaned in and kissed Jaxon more forcefully, pulling his body close until he felt Jaxon's cock stiffen against his hip.

Jaxon lay on his back, drying streaks of come painted along his chest. Kieran was on his side, watching Jaxon's eyes.

"You still want this?" Kieran asked him.

"Yes."

KIERAN ROLLED toward Jaxon and caressed his chin and neck as they kissed, slowly working his hands down Jaxon's body. Jaxon's brain stopped working as he leaned in for the touch his body craved.

Finally, he was here with Kieran, both naked, about to do what Jaxon had imagined about for so long, but until he met Kieran he'd never experienced such an uncontrollable urge.

Kieran bent to lick at one of Jaxon's nipples. The tiny bud hardened in Kieran's hot mouth. Jaxon moaned and pressed up. Kieran treated the other nipple to the same attention. This time Jaxon didn't ask Kieran to stop.

"Oh God," Jaxon said as Kieran licked and sucked, hands moving farther down Jaxon's body.

He reached Jaxon's hard cock, paused, and whispered, "Beautiful" before reaching out to take hold.

Jaxon gasped as Kieran's hand wrapped around the shaft. The touch was gentle, but firm, and very skillful. He watched Kieran's large hand on him, giving him such incredible pleasure with a few simple touches.

This is what he'd craved. It wasn't simply the touch of another man. It was *Kieran.*

Kieran stroked firmly as his thumb spread precome around the crown, rubbing across the slit with perfect pressure and friction. Jaxon could barely contain his gasps and moans, so he gave up trying.

Almost as astonishing as the touch was watching Kieran's smile, his own visible enjoyment at the effect he had on Jaxon. He'd never seen anyone else so focused on making him feel wonderful, as if every groan and grunt brought pleasure to Kieran.

Kieran shifted position so he was sitting up and could use both hands. With one, he continued the stroking, while the other gently caressed and explored Jaxon's balls with a featherlight touch, gradually using more pressure as he discovered how Jaxon liked to be touched. He drew out the experience for Jaxon, still moaning and writhing under Kieran's hands.

Jaxon cried out when he came, startled with the intensity of his orgasm. Kieran's skillful hand captured most of Jaxon's come, and he reached toward the nightstand for some tissues and started to wipe his hand.

"Don't you want to taste me?" Jaxon asked, a little hurt Kieran hadn't.

"Of course I do, but I thought you didn't like getting messy, so I tried to catch it all." Kieran brought his hand to his mouth and licked at the remaining drops, eyes shining as he got a brand-new taste of Jaxon.

Jaxon pulled Kieran's hand up to his own mouth and tentatively lapped at drops of his own release. He hadn't realized how sexy this would be, licking his new lover clean. Danetta would have freaked if he'd done this with her. He pushed thoughts of her away and focused on Kieran and this beautiful new freedom.

"It tastes different." Jaxon glanced up at Kieran. "Is everyone different?"

"I haven't tasted *everyone*." Kieran raised an eyebrow. "I suppose so. But I don't care about anyone else."

Jaxon's heart trembled at the implication, at the intimacy in Kieran's low whisper. Then Kieran leaned over and kissed him before getting up and heading into the bathroom, returning with a warm washcloth. After cleaning up Jaxon, then himself, he climbed back into bed.

They lay in each other's arms for several minutes without speaking.

"How are you doing?" Kieran finally asked.

"Fine." Jaxon wanted to be fine right now. Wanted this to be perfect. And it was. Kieran knew just how to drive him crazy. But suddenly that skill made Jaxon uneasy.

"You don't sound completely fine." Kieran must have heard the change in Jaxon's tone. "Tell me what you're thinking. If this is too much, just let me know."

"It's not." Jaxon chose his words carefully. "It's just, is this any different from what you did with the guy in the bathroom at Sam's?" His voice came out smaller than he'd expected.

"Oh God, yes."

Jaxon wanted, needed, to believe it. "How? You made each other come and then walked away."

"And I'm not going anywhere right now. I'm still here with you. I wouldn't have come to Hawaii with you if all I wanted was a few fantastic orgasms."

"It was fantastic? I didn't really know what to do."

"It was fantastic because it was *you*." Kieran leaned over and planted a soft, sweet kiss at Jaxon's temple, and another at the corner of his mouth. The kisses weren't sexual, but the affection they contained washed away most of Jaxon's fears.

"Really?"

"Being with you isn't like being with anyone else. I said you could touch me any way you wanted, do anything you wanted. I don't do that with strangers. But I trust you with my body." Kieran stopped and looked away, as if gathering his thoughts. "I'm opening myself up to you, not just my body. I want you to know who I am inside, and I want to know you."

"I guess I understand."

"Are you sorry we did this?"

"No. What you said about trust. It just made me think of Danetta. I thought I could trust her, and—"

"Oh, Jax. I'm sorry!" Kieran pulled Jaxon into a tight embrace.

"I think it might be hard for me to trust you at first." Jaxon finally understood Kieran's initial reluctance to take their relationship physical. Once the magical high of physical pleasure abated, he was left with the cold reality of doubts his brain hadn't yet processed.

"I understand. Just take things at your own pace. If we do anything you're not sure about, just say the word and we'll stop. We need to both want this, or it won't work."

"I can't believe how understanding you are."

"I want you to be comfortable, and I want to make you happy, not just in a physical sense. That's easy. You deserve much more. I think Danetta expected you to make *her* happy, but I don't get the impression she was quite as concerned with *your* happiness as she should have been."

"When I step back and look at our relationship, I see you're right. I was so busy worrying about her, I didn't realize she was taking more than she was giving."

"You just tell me what makes you happy, and I'll try my best to do it." Kieran reached for Jaxon's hand and kissed the fingers.

The gesture ignited something deep inside Jaxon, physical hunger, but so much more. "Can I look at you some more? Your body, I mean?" They were in bed together but somehow it seemed an invasion of Kieran's body unless he got permission first.

Kieran laughed and lay back, welcoming Jaxon's explorations of his body with eyes and hands, from the top of his head all the way down to his toes. Watching Kieran's arousal grow just from Jaxon looking and touching was even more of a turn-on. Soon Jaxon hoped the exploration would venture far beyond mere caresses.

It was nearly sunrise when they fell asleep in each other's arms.

Chapter Thirty

Wednesday

AFTER A very leisurely and sexy room-service breakfast, Kieran and Jaxon hopped in their rental car and drove across the island for the first of the activities Jaxon and Danetta had booked. On horseback they toured the lush tropical rainforest, then rode down to a secluded beach for lunch, then snorkeling in a coral reef nestled in clean white sand. The water was crystal clear and bright with the rainbow colors of fish and other marine wildlife inhabiting the area.

The scheduled evening activity was a Honeymoon Sunset Dinner Sail.

"Jaxon, are you sure about this? I don't think it will be that much fun." Kieran didn't want him thinking too much about the wedding, and he wasn't sure whether they'd be welcome. "These cruises are always cheesy."

"Yeah. It'll be fun. You and a sunset, that's all I need." He kissed Kieran. "Come on."

They took the hotel shuttle with other couples to the Kukuiula Harbor. When they got to the ticket gate, a young woman was checking names off a passenger list.

"Lang," Jaxon said.

She flipped through the pages on her clipboard. "Yes, here you are. Mr. and Mrs.—" She put her hand over her mouth as she looked at Kieran and he smiled. "—Lang. Oh, we've made a dreadful mistake. I'll fix that right now to Mr. and Mr." Her flustered apology was well intended, and Kieran gave her a big smile. She returned a shaky laugh. "Have fun."

"We will." Jaxon grabbed Kieran's hand and dragged him up the gangplank to the little boat.

They might have been the only same-sex couple on the boat, but they acted like honeymooners—holding hands, kissing, and slow dancing. Kieran expected that Jaxon might be a bit shy to be seen with him, but Jaxon seemed to enjoy the surprised glances they got. He even made up an elaborate story about their wedding when someone asked about it during dinner. It bore absolutely no resemblance to Jaxon's disastrous wedding only days earlier.

Kieran found it hilarious how the women seemed hooked on every word Jaxon uttered. His good looks and charm attracted even women sitting next to their new husbands on their honeymoon.

It made Kieran wonder if maybe all of this was a dream. Had it really only been ten days earlier he'd met Jaxon, a straight guy about to be married, and now here they were, "honeymooning" in Hawaii and beginning a sexual and emotional relationship? Maybe the psychic had been right that finding his soul mate would be a surprise to both of them.

Could Jaxon be his soul mate? It was much too early to think like that. Two weeks ago he'd been in bed with an underwear model, but it was a Texas high-school principal who melted his heart and his doubts…. Kieran had never been happy—no, content—like this before. If only this week would never end.

Back in the room, Kieran reminded Jaxon he needed to finish his column and e-mail it to Jeff by midnight. With the time difference, Jeff would get it first thing in the morning New York time and then e-mail Kieran with any additional instructions.

Jaxon made quite a distraction. He lay in bed naked, watching Kieran work.

He was almost finished. "Fifteen more minutes. Just give me fifteen minutes and I'm all yours."

"You're going to teach me how to do a blow job tonight, right?" He blew a provocative kiss at Kieran.

How the hell could he work when Jaxon was offering a BJ?

Kieran wrapped it up in five and e-mailed the file to Jeff.

Then he hopped into bed with Jaxon.

Chapter Thirty-One

Thursday

KIERAN AND Jaxon took a day trip by air to the big island of Hawaii to visit the volcanoes and were exhausted by the time they got back to Kauai. They had a relaxing dinner at a well-known restaurant specializing in native fish and fresh, local ingredients. Kieran ordered a bottle of wine with their meal, which had the unfortunate effect of making Jaxon hornier than he already was. Throughout dinner Jaxon kept whispering, "Let's go back to the room" while trying to stroke Kieran's cock through his pants. Discretion was not Jaxon's strong suit.

"Jax, you probably don't want to get arrested for lewd behavior," Kieran said. "It might cause some problems with the school board."

"Can I get arrested for this?" Jaxon's hand moved in the direction of Kieran's crotch.

"Yes," Kieran lied. "Especially in Hawaii. They have all sorts of laws you wouldn't even expect."

"I don't believe you," Jaxon said defiantly, hand still on Kieran.

"Fine. But if I am right, you'll be in a whole heap o' trouble back home, won't you?" Kieran picked up Jaxon's hand and put it back in his own lap.

"Maybe." Jaxon behaved himself until they had nearly finished their meal. As he picked up his glass for the last few sips of wine, he very deliberately poured it onto Kieran's crotch and smiled triumphantly. "Oh, let me just help you clean that up!"

Kieran sat wide-eyed as Jaxon dabbed at him much more vigorously than was needed to clean up the spill.

"You're just lucky we were drinking white, or I'd be a little annoyed."

Jaxon gave an adorable wide-eyed shrug. "You'll need to change those, won't you?"

Back in the room, Jaxon was all over Kieran again as Kieran sat on the couch wearing dry sweats and flipping through channels on the television, pretending to ignore Jaxon. That proved to be impossible when Jaxon settled himself in Kieran's lap.

"Kier, I think we should do it tonight." He wrapped his arms around Kieran's shoulders.

"Do what?" Kieran cocked an eyebrow. He knew perfectly well what Jaxon was talking about.

"Real sex."

"Have we been having fake sex so far?" Kieran asked. "Were those fake orgasms, too? You have a spectacular career ahead of you in porn if you were faking all of that."

"You know what I mean."

"You're sure? You think you're really ready for that?" Kieran asked. "You need to be 100—no, 500 percent sure."

"Five hundred and one percent. A thousand percent."

Kieran pulled Jaxon close and leaned his forehead against Jaxon's. "Let's take things slow." He never imagined he'd be saying something like that to someone he wanted to make love to so badly. He couldn't remember the last time he'd even called it making love.

"I liked what we did last night. Are we still in Column A? I want to move to Column B." He kissed Kieran, slow and deep, until Kieran had to stop or he'd get both of them out of their clothing fast.

"Trust me, Jax. Fingers and cocks are entirely different. You may think the principle is the same, but when someone's cock is up someone else's ass, it's a whole new ball game."

"I *really* liked the fingers." Jaxon got up and tugged at Kieran's arm to pull him toward the bed.

As if Kieran could possibly have forgotten. The previous night, Kieran had used his finger inside of Jaxon, stretching him very gently and exploring his prostate so Jaxon could get an idea of how it felt. Then they reversed roles. Once Jaxon got over his initial squeamishness about putting a finger inside of Kieran's ass, he was like a kid with a new toy. The new toy being Kieran's prostate. Jaxon had been fascinated when he discovered that if he kept rubbing it, he could make Kieran come. Over and over.

Now Jaxon sat at the edge of the bed. He reached for the hem of his long-sleeved T-shirt and started to pull it up. Kieran took a deep breath as he gazed at Jaxon's defined chest and abs and his beautiful, tempting nipples came into view.

"What a tease you are," Kieran said when Jaxon slowed his movements, holding Kieran's gaze while the shirt was up near his shoulders.

"Maybe I need some help."

"I'm the one who needs some help." Kieran didn't think he could keep up with Jaxon. Even for a honeymoon suite, he wondered whether this bed had seen anything like Jaxon and whether it would ever be the same.

Kieran certainly wouldn't be.

He pulled Jaxon's shirt the rest of the way off and took off his own. Jaxon leaned forward to kiss Kieran's abs and peek down the waistband of his sweats. He pushed them down just enough to expose the head of Kieran's erection. Then he looked up into Kieran's face as he sucked the glans into his mouth.

Kieran couldn't breathe, and every nerve ending from his cock to his balls was on high alert. He tugged Jaxon off him with a finger under the chin.

"We can try 'real sex' if you're sure. Just remember, we can stop at any time."

"I won't want to stop."

"We haven't even started yet."

Jaxon leaned back and pulled Kieran by the waistband on top of him.

THEY WERE in bed, kissing and caressing, breath already ragged, both hard, their cocks brushing together and eliciting gasps and moans from them. A fresh bottle of lube and a few condoms were on the night table.

"Do you want to top or bottom?" Kieran asked.

"I want to do both," Jaxon said. "I want to try everything."

"Well, aren't you the eager one? You can only do one at a time, so choose wisely."

"What do you suggest?"

"If I top, then you'll learn how to do the prep. Then when you top, you'll know how to get me ready. But it's also a big step for you to take, and you can't go back and undo this."

"And if I top?"

"Then you just need to be really careful getting me ready. Once that's done, most of the mechanics should be the same as with a woman, except for the angles and the fact that I do have a cock down there. You already know where my prostate is, so you can figure out how to hit that spot." He paused. "Haven't you seen any gay porn?"

Jaxon's cheeks colored. "A little. But they don't give any instructions. They just bang away, and it's hard to tell exactly how to get what where."

Kieran laughed. Jaxon's inexperienced eagerness was sweet. It made Kieran even more concerned about hurting him, physically or emotionally.

"I want to top," Jaxon said decisively. "I want to make you come like I did last night with my cock and not my fingers. I liked all the noise you made."

Kieran was touched that Jaxon's desire was to please him and not simply please himself or to cross items off some sexual bucket list.

Kieran talked Jaxon through the prep, then Jaxon slipped a condom on and slicked more lube on himself. He looked down at Kieran, spread out in front of him, and smiled. He seemed a bit overwhelmed by the whole thing, but a look of determination crossed Jaxon's face. He touched the tip of his cock to Kieran's entrance.

"Go in slow, a little at a time. I'm not really used to this."

"Really? I thought you have a lot of sex."

"I guess it depends what you consider a lot." Kieran let the unintended insult roll off.

"Slow. Got it." Jaxon pushed in a tiny bit. He stopped. "Okay?"

"Not that slowly."

Jaxon pushed in a little more. It had been a long time since Kieran had bottomed, and he was tight, which made it feel even better as Jaxon slid in.

Jaxon's eyes opened wider and his breath caught in a soft gasp. "Oh God, Kier. It's so tight. Hot and tight," Jaxon blurted. "Like you're holding on to me." He kept sliding. "I'm not hurting you, am I?"

"No, just keep going like that." Kieran's body adjusted to accommodate Jaxon, and he let out a moan. "All the way in if you want." Jaxon pushed in deep. "God, Jax, it feels great."

"Oh, fuck, ahhh." Jaxon seemed unable to form words as his cock was buried to the hilt inside Kieran, his balls tickling Kieran's ass. "It's so good. I'm afraid to move, or I think I'll come."

"Just take a few breaths to calm down, then try moving." Kieran enjoyed the series of expressions flashing across Jaxon's features as he felt new sensations and tried new movements and angles. It didn't take Jaxon long to figure out how to brush Kieran's prostate, which reduced him to grunts and groans.

"Do I make you come first?" Jaxon asked. "I'm pretty close."

"I'll do that. You do whatever feels good for you." He wrapped his hand around his cock.

"I wanted to make you feel good."

"You are. You feel incredible inside me. Okay, you do it." Kieran let go.

Jaxon tried stroking and thrusting. "This takes coordination." He laughed. "I'm sorry I laughed."

"Laughing is good. This is supposed to be fun, not some kind of test you might fail. Lean forward." Kieran reached up to stroke Jaxon's cheek. "This time, let me."

"Okay." Jaxon's voice was shaky when he started moving, the pleasure overwhelming him again.

Kieran gasped, very close to the edge. He grabbed his cock and stroked in time with Jaxon's thrusts, and within moments Kieran came, shuddering and spasming, splashing their chests and abs.

"Oh God, Kier! I can feel you squeezing me. Oh wow." Jaxon let out a series of unintelligible words and sounds as he sped up his movements, losing the rhythm as orgasm began to overtake him. Kieran watched Jaxon's eyes flash green-black as he came, gasping and falling onto Kieran's come-streaked body.

"That was incredible," Jaxon said when he caught his breath again.

"Yeah, it was." Kieran's voice was low and raspy. Jaxon couldn't know how much Kieran meant that. He rarely bottomed, and he certainly had never been made love to as carefully, eagerly, and honestly as Jaxon just had. Watching Jaxon's discoveries was as incredible as the physical pleasure Jaxon had given him.

"I loved seeing your face and listening when I moved different ways," Jaxon said. "And the way you scrunched up your face just before you came. It was hot the way you grabbed your cock like that and…." Jaxon stopped. "I sound like a virgin, don't I?" He leaned over and licked at the come smeared on Kieran's abs. He certainly had gotten used to that quickly.

"Is there anything you didn't think was hot about it?" Kieran laughed as Jaxon's tongue tickled him and was relieved Jaxon had enjoyed his first experience so much.

"No. Except I think I'm gonna fall asleep." Jaxon slowly pulled out of Kieran and tossed the condom into a trash can next to the bed. He lay back down, wrapped his arms around Kieran, and—true to his word—fell sound asleep.

Kieran listened to Jaxon's even breathing against his ear for a while, enjoying the warmth and the now-familiar smell of him.

Jaxon had come into Kieran's life and turned everything upside down. Suddenly it was the most natural thing in the world to open up his heart and his body to Jaxon, in a way he never had with anyone else. And it was so easy to spend time with Jaxon, to fall in love with every little thing about him. But it frightened Kieran as much as it exhilarated him.

For now, everything between them was perfect. They could worry later about what would happen when the fantasy world of Kauai was behind them, when they were back in their real worlds, so far apart and very different.

Despite Jaxon's protestations, Kieran suspected he might have misgivings once the trip drew to a close. He wouldn't pressure Jaxon but feared he was rushing into this whole thing as a way of avoiding dealing with the Danetta wedding fiasco.

Kieran couldn't handle being a rebound relationship or a way for Jaxon to satisfy his curiosity. From the moment he climbed into bed at Jaxon's insistence Tuesday night, Kieran had let go, freed himself to fall in love with Jaxon, and he'd fallen hard. Now he was terrified by the possibility of Jaxon suddenly changing his mind or coming to his senses and realizing this had all been a mistake.

KIERAN WOKE during the night to discover Jaxon spooned tightly behind him, mouth hot and greedy, sucking at Kieran's ear and the back of his neck. Kieran was instantly hard as he felt Jaxon's cock against his lower back. He turned his head toward Jaxon and their mouths met for a long, deep kiss.

"Kier," Jaxon whispered, "I want you again. Can we...?"

"Yeah, me too." Kieran loved the way Jaxon asked so sweetly. He shifted position so he was on his stomach, facing the mirror on the wall opposite their bed, and pulled a pillow under his hips. Jaxon flipped the bedside lamp on and reached for the bottle of lube. When Kieran was ready, Jaxon slipped on a condom. He crouched between Kieran's legs and looked down at Kieran, spread open and waiting for him.

Kieran watched his face in the mirror. Jaxon hadn't seen things from this exact angle before and Kieran could tell from the expression on his face that he'd realized how vulnerable Kieran was like this. The sensation gave Jaxon an obvious rush. He slipped quickly and smoothly into Kieran, clearly enjoying the tight, hot grip once again. Jaxon watched himself in the mirror, catching Kieran's gaze.

Jaxon was more aggressive and rougher this time. Kieran loved it: the way Jaxon occasionally grabbed on to his hips as he slammed his cock deep into Kieran, the sounds Jaxon couldn't control as he groaned and grunted with each stroke. There was tenderness, too—a shared look that told Kieran this was about more than sex for Jaxon, too. Jaxon's hands caressed Kieran's body, and he whispered endearments into Kieran's ear as Jaxon's teeth grazed Kieran's neck and shoulders. After they both came, Jaxon didn't fall asleep. He held on to Kieran for dear life, and they kissed for a long time, until they both slept.

Chapter Thirty-Two

Friday

KIERAN AND Jaxon got up earlier than usual to have breakfast on the nearly deserted beach. They were both getting spoiled by the luxurious hotel and the amazing food. Kieran suspected it would take getting used to eating at even his favorite New York spots. Jaxon suggested a Hawaiian cooking class so Kieran could learn how to make some new favorite foods, but Kieran prided himself on never cooking. They chose to visit a historical sugar plantation over the cooking lesson.

Then in the afternoon, Kieran dared Jaxon to sign up for a surfing lesson. Two hours later, they'd learned the basics, and Jaxon had actually stood up and caught a wave. Being much taller, Kieran had more difficulty with balance and could barely manage to get onto his feet, much less stand up. He spent more time trying not to get nailed by his board when he fell off.

Exhausted, they headed back to the room for showers and a nap. But they didn't end up getting much rest and opted for a room-service dinner as they sat on the veranda watching the sunset smoldering through reds and oranges to pinks and purples.

Once the moon came up, they stayed on the balcony, and Jaxon reached for Kieran's hand. He wove his fingers through Kieran's and held on, watching the moon's reflections on the choppy waves. Kieran glanced out over the water, content even in the silence.

Jaxon wondered whether he and Danny would have had as much fun this week if they'd gone through with the wedding. What if Kieran had never come to Buckwheat Springs, never uncovered her string of lies? Would Jaxon now be this happy with her?

He doubted it.

She and everyone had been so focused on the wedding, without much consideration to being married. The wedding was one day; marriage was supposed to be forever. Could Jaxon have been satisfied to stay with her for the rest of his life? It was clear from the way he'd responded to Kieran that he'd been fooling himself into thinking he could.

"You okay?" Kieran's voice startled Jaxon out of unpleasant rumination.

"Yeah. Fine."

"I'm not so sure. Come over here." Kieran tugged Jaxon's hand, pulled him up, and settled him into Kieran's lap. He wrapped Jaxon in his arms and brought him in close for a kiss.

Jaxon's body caught fire immediately and his erection strained against his thin cotton trousers. Kieran brushed a hand across it and flicked his tongue across a nipple, making Jaxon gasp. He threaded his fingers through Kieran's soft hair and arched into the pleasure as Kieran sucked the other nipple.

Just a touch, a look from Kieran, aroused him. It felt wonderful, natural. Thank God he hadn't gone through with the wedding.

No. Thank Kieran.

Saturday

IT WAS their final full day in Hawaii, the last day of peace and tranquility and being alone together before they would need to face their real lives and problems again.

They went surfing first thing before spending the rest of the morning hiking in Waimea Canyon. By early afternoon it was too cloudy to enjoy the scenery, and they headed back to the hotel to get the couples massages Danetta had booked. It was perfect timing. After the surfing, hiking, and bedroom activities, they were both sore and in need of the relaxing pressure of the skilled masseuses.

Kieran and Jaxon spent their last sunset walking along the beach, holding hands in silence, just enjoying each other's company and storing up memories to get them through the inevitable separation that was quickly approaching.

Neither of them had much appetite during a late dinner. The unspoken anxiety around their inevitable good-byes was tangible. Back upstairs, they discovered a room-service cart with champagne—a farewell gift from the hotel. Kieran popped the cork and they sipped a glass each.

"Let's go down to the beach for one last swim," Jaxon suggested.

"Now?" Kieran asked. "It's late."

"No one else is down there now. It'll be romantic. I want to taste the salt on your skin after you've been in the ocean."

"I can't argue when you put it like that."

On the beach, they chased each other through the shallow surf, letting themselves be caught too easily, then kissing in waist-deep water as gentle waves splashed over them.

When they were too hungry for each other to continue on the beach, they made their way back to their room, shrugged off their hotel robes, and stood, arms around each other, kissing deeply. Jaxon wrapped his hand around Kieran's cock, which threatened to rip through the thin fabric of his swim trunks. Kieran had already gotten Jaxon's trunks off, and he ran his hands over the curve of his ass.

"Kier, tonight...." Jaxon had trouble getting the words out between kisses. "Tonight, I want you to make love to me. I want to bottom."

Kieran let go of Jaxon's lower lip.

"Are you sure?"

"Yes. I want to feel you inside me."

"Jax, *I'm* not sure—"

"Don't you want me?"

"God, yes, of course I do. Just, it's a big step for you."

"There is something here between us, isn't there?"

Kieran nodded, the knot in his chest expanding. He couldn't speak.

"Something that's big enough to last past this trip. To become serious, right?"

"Yes," Kieran whispered, not trusting his voice. "Absolutely. I was going to wait until later to bring it up, but I want you to come to New York for your summer break. Spend as long as you can with me while you decide what to do about your job in Buckwheat Springs. Maybe you can even look around for a new job in New York while you're up there."

"If there's something real between us, it can't possibly be the wrong thing for us... tonight."

"You'll come to New York?"

"Only if you make love to me tonight. Otherwise, no deal." Jaxon curled his mouth into a mischievous grin that made Kieran kiss him twice as passionately as before.

Jaxon lay on his back as Kieran kissed him, hands and mouth eventually traveling down Jaxon's throat. Kieran licked at the salt on his skin and sucked at his neck and collarbone. He moved slowly, drawing out the excitement and trying to put Jaxon at ease.

He traveled to Jaxon's chest and nipples next. Kieran had never met anyone with such sensitive nipples, and he enjoyed giving them proper attention while Jaxon squirmed and moaned beneath him. Moving farther down, Kieran finally reached Jaxon's cock, on which he lavished even more loving attention as he used one hand to get Jaxon ready. Kieran took his time, gently stretching and opening Jaxon so as to cause him the minimum amount of pain.

"You okay, Jax?"

"Um, I think so."

"Okay. Ready?" Kieran rolled on a condom and applied liberal amounts of lube. He knelt between Jaxon's knees.

"Are you sure it's going to fit?" Jaxon eyed Kieran's cock.

"I'm positive it will fit."

"I'm kinda scared now. But I don't want to stop."

"Don't be. It's me, okay? I'm going to take good care of you. I want to make it really good, and it will be. Just try to relax."

"I trust you." To Kieran those words meant everything.

"We can stop if you want, Jaxon."

"No! I want this. I really want *you*."

Kieran pressed the tip of his cock to Jaxon's hole. With one hand, he took Jaxon's cock and started stroking. Kieran waited until Jaxon relaxed and moaned a little at the touch before pressing inside just a tiny bit. Jaxon didn't react, so Kieran pushed in a bit more. This time Jaxon's eyebrows went up.

"Keep watching my face, Jax, and relax. Breathe," Kieran whispered.

Kieran slid in as slowly as possible, the incredible pressure building around him. He longed to drive himself into the heat but didn't give in to the instinct. He closed his eyes to concentrate on the sensations. He felt Jaxon relax around him. When he opened his eyes,

Jaxon was smiling. Kieran slid in easily. Then Jaxon's breath caught and Kieran stopped.

"You okay, Jax?"

"Yeah, I feel so full. It's good, and I can see how great it feels for you."

"You—*you* feel so good."

Jaxon smiled as Kieran pushed in again. Kieran leaned down to kiss him and slide in completely, then wrapped his arms around Jaxon and waited for him to relax and get used to the extraordinary sensation of Kieran's cock inside of him.

"It's like—I can't explain it, but like something was missing, and now, with you, everything's perfect," Jaxon whispered.

Kieran loved how Jaxon expressed his emotions so intensely. No other lover had ever said anything as beautiful to him.

"Yeah, *perfect*," Kieran repeated softly. "Let me know when you're ready for me to start moving."

"You're completely in? It didn't really hurt as much as I expected, only a little bit at first."

"I told you I was going to take care of you."

"You did. You have, since we met." Jaxon's eyes got shiny and he blinked then exhaled. "Okay, go ahead now."

In Jaxon's eyes Kieran saw a mirror of his own emotions, a mix of arousal, fascination, affection, and a hint of fear. Despite having had many lovers before, this time was something completely new for Kieran. He'd never been with someone who he cared so much for. He'd also never been anyone's first and took that very seriously. He was determined to make this the most amazing experience Jaxon had ever had.

"Now wrap your legs around me, Jax."

Kieran started with a slow rhythm until he could see—and hear—that Jaxon was enjoying the experience. Taking hold of Jaxon's hips, Kieran carefully shifted him to change angles and find what Jaxon liked best, occasionally brushing against Jaxon's prostate. Jaxon's eyes were half-closed. His hands skimmed over Kieran's shoulders and torso. When Jaxon's hand moved to take hold of his cock, Kieran gently deflected it.

"Jax, we're not nearly finished here, unless you want to come now. Or do you want more?"

"Oh God, yeah, more." Jaxon gasped and writhed on Kieran's cock.

Kieran was pleased to see Jaxon couldn't form a sentence—head thrown back, eyes half-closed, mouth open—and knowing he'd made Jaxon feel that good was a thrill in itself. He was also moved by the way Jaxon had given himself up willingly and lovingly to Kieran, trusting completely.

Almost from the instant he began moving inside of Jaxon, Kieran held back his own orgasm. Now he'd reached his limit. He gently took hold of Jaxon's cock, stroking him skillfully, thumb spreading the now-heavy stream of precome around the crown and squeezing along the shaft as he used his thumb on the sensitive spot under the head.

He heard Jaxon's breath hitch at the touch and watched Jaxon struggle to open his eyes, teeth digging into his full lower lip. Kieran focused on dragging his own cock against Jaxon's prostate as he stroked until Jaxon came.

The orgasm nearly surprised him, eyes open, glittering dark, as thick, hot jets of creamy come shot across his chest. "Oh, Kier. Oh God, oh fuck" was all Jaxon could manage to say.

Kieran leaned down onto Jaxon's chest, savoring the hot slickness of come and Jaxon's heaving chest as he fought for breath, body still shuddering from the intensity of his orgasm. Jaxon's hands came up and tangled in Kieran's hair, locking Kieran down, pulling him tightly against Jaxon's body.

"Oh, Kier."

Kieran covered Jaxon's mouth with his own and kissed him through the final aftershocks of orgasm, reveling in the tight spasms squeezing his cock and Jaxon's arms and legs holding him down. When Jaxon lay quiet with his hands still in Kieran's hair, a few quick, shallow thrusts were all Kieran needed, and he was coming, with Jaxon's name tumbling from his lips. He held Jaxon tightly, shuddering and groaning as he spurted his release inside of Jaxon, filling the condom.

Jaxon stroked Kieran's hair until Kieran's body stilled and he opened his eyes.

"That was the most amazing thing I've ever felt in my entire life." Jaxon was still slightly breathless, his voice low and gravelly.

"Me too." Kieran realized all of his weight was on Jaxon. "Oh, I'm crushing you."

"No, I like it. It's nice having you on me, and in me." He pulled Kieran's head down again for another kiss.

"It feels amazing."

"Is it always like that?"

"No."

"Oh." Jaxon pressed his lips together and looked away.

"It gets better," Kieran whispered and kissed his neck.

"I'd probably die if I felt anything better than that. I thought I was dying *this* time."

"Well, it's your loss if you don't want to try again."

"I didn't say that." Jaxon laughed.

Kieran slipped out and took care of the condom. "Let me go get something to clean up." He went into the bathroom, returning with a damp cloth to clean them up before sliding under the sheets again with Jaxon.

Jaxon rolled onto his side to face Kieran. "You're serious about what you said before? You want me to go to New York for the summer?"

"Unless you have something else you were planning. I imagine that trying to get together on weekends is going to get old real fast, and it won't be enough. We'll want more time together. It'll be a good opportunity to find out whether this is going to work long-term between us."

"I feel so comfortable with you, like we've known each other longer than only a couple of weeks."

"Me too. But this past week has been so unreal, especially after what happened with Danetta, and you leaving in the middle of your wedding. We need to spend time together in more normal circumstances."

"You have room for me in your place?"

"Yeah, of course. I don't live in a crappy little fifth-floor walk-up studio apartment. I have a nice place, in SoHo," Kieran said. "*Gloss* pays me a lot to be such an asshole in my columns."

"Sounds like you're a little disillusioned with your job?"

"It's not as easy to write bitchy, condescending columns as it used to be. I don't like it, and I don't want to keep doing it. I've been trying to branch out, but my editor rejects or rewrites anything I've written that isn't snarky and sardonic."

"You could move to Texas with me?"

"Right. You think we could live together in Buckwheat Springs?" Kieran let out an ironic laugh. "Being a gay couple in a little town in Texas sounds like a barrel of laughs to me."

"Good point." Jaxon yawned. He looked over at Kieran with an embarrassed smile.

"I think it's bedtime." Kieran turned off the lamp on the bedside table. He pulled Jaxon into his arms, with Jaxon's head resting on his chest. He didn't want this night to end, this week in paradise to end.

"Hey, Kier?" Jaxon asked after several moments of silence.

"Hmm?"

"So when are you going to show me 'better'?"

"My God, you're insatiable." Kieran wondered if Jaxon had been like this with Danetta. He fought off the urge to ask. "Think you can wait till the morning? I'd expect you might be a bit sore now anyway."

"Yeah, a little, but in a good way."

"Good night, Jax."

"Good night."

"I love you," Kieran whispered a few minutes later after working up the courage.

But Jaxon was already asleep. Kieran just listened to the sound of his breathing, regular and comforting, body pressed tightly against Kieran. A faint scent of salt water still clung to Jaxon's skin, blending with the musky smell of sex that permeated the room. The day had been perfect; but any day starting and ending with Jaxon would be.

Chapter Thirty-Three

Sunday

JAXON MADE sure they got up early enough to learn "better" from Kieran. He decided Kieran was absolutely right, but then he had been about everything they'd done together in bed. Afterward, they rushed to pack and have a quick breakfast before checkout.

While waiting for the airport shuttle, Kieran and Jaxon looked around in the hotel's gift shop, laughing at the typical Hawaiian souvenirs and wondering if maybe they should buy something but ultimately deciding not to, preferring to keep their week together more private and personal.

"Hang on." Jaxon stopped outside the shop. "There's actually something I do want to get. Wait here." He darted back into the store, leaving Kieran with the suitcases at the edge of the lobby. He was back in two minutes, carrying a small bag that he presented to Kieran.

Kieran opened it and pulled out a bright pink plastic orchid key ring. "Wow! How did you know I wanted one of those?" Kieran teased, holding out his hand as if Jaxon was going to put the ring on his finger.

"It's for your suitcase." Jaxon laughed and attached the key ring to Kieran's bag. "It's black and looks like 98 percent of the other bags out there. Now you can find it easily even at the airport in New York."

"O-kay, random," Kieran replied. "But, thanks." He gave Jaxon a kiss—just a brush of lips against a morning-stubbled cheek. "Now my suitcase looks gay, too. I'm guessing that's why you didn't get matching flowers for us?"

"Yeah, it's tough to be a gay suitcase in Texas, too."

"The airport shuttle is here already," Kieran said as a group of people with suitcases rushed toward the exit. Kieran and Jaxon followed slowly, wheeling their suitcases behind them, reluctant for their magical week to be over.

THE PLAN when Kieran and Jaxon left Texas was for Jaxon to return to Texas Sunday, while Kieran flew to New York. Those plans had been long since abandoned, and now Kieran would return to Buckwheat Springs for a few days, ostensibly to follow up on the fallout from the disastrous wedding for another column. No one in town would know the real reason he was there, and it would give them a few more days together to make plans for Jaxon's summer visit to New York.

They had a two-hour stopover in Los Angeles. After buying the largest coffees available at the first coffee cart they encountered, they wandered around the airport, killing time.

"Kier, there's a newsstand over there." Jaxon pulled on Kieran's arm. "I can't wait to read your column."

"Sure, Jax, if you want to." Kieran had long ago gotten over the excitement of seeing his words in print, and this had been such a difficult column to write—and one he'd had such a personal connection to—he preferred not to read it, but he could humor Jaxon.

Jaxon found *Gloss* on a rack and paid for it, then led Kieran over to a bench next to an enormous potted palm tree where he could start reading. Kieran put his laptop case on the floor between his feet and put his arm around Jaxon, leaning back against the bench.

There was something different, a little frightening, about having someone he cared for reading his work. It was more personal and revealing than when thousands of complete strangers read it. This column wasn't his best work. He'd struggled over the piece and then rushed the end to get into bed with Jaxon. Kieran felt self-conscious having Jaxon read it while he was sitting there.

Kieran felt Jaxon tense up. He looked over at Jaxon, who still had his gaze focused on the magazine, but Kieran couldn't tell what was wrong.

"That bad, is it?" Kieran joked.

"I wouldn't exactly say it's 'bad,'" Jaxon replied, his voice tight. "You have a really engaging style. And I guess it's very well written and amusing. Like this line: 'At first meeting Jaxon, I came to the conclusion that his IQ barely exceeded his waist size.'"

Kieran's heart pounded as a sickening sensation built in his gut. That wasn't in his final piece; it had been edited out of the first draft. He tried to grab the magazine away from Jaxon, but Jaxon wouldn't let go.

"'I wasn't quite sure whether Danetta was actually a witch or simply a highly skilled puppeteer. At dinner when Jaxon spoke, I couldn't even see Danetta's lips moving. A very impressive performance,'" Jaxon read. "Should I go on?"

"That's wrong! That's not the story I submitted!" Kieran raised his voice, attracting the attention of passers-by who eyed them suspiciously and moved to the other side of the terminal to avoid them.

"Oh, really? Then who wrote it? It has your name here at the top of the page and a little photo of you." Jaxon tapped his finger violently on the photograph as if he'd like to put out Kieran's eyes.

"It was, I…." Kieran gave up.

He had a good idea how this happened, and he was going to kill Jeff when he got back to the office, as slowly and painfully as possible. He'd research torture methods before he decided on one. Jeff had approved the final column Kieran e-mailed a few days earlier and never once hinted he'd make significant changes.

Kieran didn't have full control over what got published, and as features editor, Jeff could do this, but it would have been good to know in advance what he was planning to print. But, none of that would make Jaxon feel any better.

"I'm still waiting for your explanation, if you have one." Jaxon glared at Kieran, who avoided Jaxon's angry gaze. "Just tell me, did you write any of this?"

"It was in the very first draft, before I—we—anything happened between us." Kieran tried to explain. He took the magazine from Jaxon and skimmed the page. Everything he'd wanted to delete had been added back in, the part about the "X" in Jaxon's name, the Stepford comments, the matching shirt and skirt they'd been wearing when Kieran first met Danetta and Jaxon.

Kieran's heart was beating so loudly and heavily; he feared it would break right through his chest. He almost hoped it would so he could die instantly and be put out of the misery of seeing Jaxon's pained accusing stare.

The whole world was coming apart, and he didn't have a clue how to put it back together. "It was in the first draft I sent to my editor, but I told him to ignore it and to delete the files." The excuse sounded so pathetic, even Kieran hardly believed it.

"So you *did* write this? Even if you didn't submit it as part of your final story, these are your ideas and your words, right?"

"Yes," Kieran admitted in a tiny voice, utterly defeated.

"Is this really what you thought of me?" Jaxon grabbed the magazine back and stared at it again, as if maybe this time different words would appear on the page, less harsh and hurtful words.

"No, of course not!" Kieran shot back. "You know how I feel about you. Hasn't that been completely clear this past week? I love you."

Jaxon scoffed and looked away, ignoring the words. "You must have believed these things at some point, or you wouldn't have written them." Jaxon kept at Kieran, his voice even and insistent.

"Yes. No. That's not true. I don't really believe half the crap I write, I just take my impressions and exaggerate them. It's hyperbole, right? Just a form of—"

"I know what hyperbole is. I'm a fucking high school principal!" More people turned to stare, and an old lady nearby scuttled away like a frightened crab.

"I'm just explaining the style of humor I use. It's why my column is popular. People like—"

"People like to laugh at other people's problems or misfortune or confusion? Is that what you're going to say? People like to criticize others so they can forget how fucked up their own lives are? What *people* like is not the issue here. The issue is how you could have written these things, used my emotions and ideas about Danetta and about love and marriage in order to ridicule me—especially after what you found out, about how she'd lied...." Jaxon's voice trailed off.

"You know that's not what I wrote this past week and submitted. And I never would have ridiculed your idea of love or how happy you imagined you would be with her. Never. That's all too raw and personal right now. Besides, I never intended for *this* to be published."

"You mean you didn't think I'd ever see what you originally wrote?"

"That's not exactly what I meant, but I guess it's true enough." Kieran hung his head. He didn't have the strength to defend himself. It was hard enough to keep breathing without gasping. No matter what the reasons were that he had written these insults, Jaxon was right. Trying to make excuses wouldn't repair the pain Kieran had caused.

"This doesn't just make me look ridiculous to my family and friends, but to my students, their parents, the school board, and anyone I might come into professional contact with. Don't you see what you've done here? All in the name of entertainment and selling magazines!" Jaxon was out of breath as he went on. "But that isn't even the worst. Kier, I can't help but see this as a betrayal of everything I've shared with you this week. I shared my entire self, body and soul, with you. I can't believe I let myself be taken in by someone who thinks so little of me."

"Oh God, Jax. I'm so sorry. I never wanted to hurt you like this! I don't think those things, and I never wanted any of that to be published. When I wrote this, I couldn't admit I was falling in love with you. You were off limits, and I needed... I needed to find ways not to fall for you. If I really had these opinions about you, how *could* I fall in love with you?"

"Maybe you don't actually think you love me," Jaxon said coldly. "Maybe you just saw me as a challenge to get me into your bed. This past week might have been fodder for another heartless column."

"Do you really think that?" Kieran's voice sounded shocked and subdued.

"What I think is that I don't want to see or talk to you right now. Maybe not ever. Go get on a plane back to New York and leave me alone. I can't take any more lies and deceit. After everything that happened with Danetta, now I find out that you're no better than she is. Just go." Jaxon's voice was cold and cruel.

Jaxon got up, then glanced at the magazine he still held in his hand. Glowering, he turned and threw it at Kieran, hitting his cheek, then strode away without a backward glance. Compared to the hole Jaxon had just ripped through his heart, he barely noticed the magazine being flung in his face.

Kieran sat on the bench in the middle of the airport, crumpled magazine by his side, and watched Jaxon Lang walk out of his life. He had never felt so miserable. The worst part of it was that nearly everything that Jaxon said had been true. Kieran had written those hurtful things, and he had ridiculed Jaxon's ideas about love and marriage, and he hadn't considered the consequences at the time. Even if Kieran didn't feel that way now, he'd displayed a severe lack of respect for Jaxon, and Jaxon had every right to react the way he did.

Kieran felt even worse that he'd hurt Jaxon again. Kieran had found out about Danetta's deceit and manipulations and saved Jaxon from a marriage built on lies, only to break him again with more lies. It killed Kieran that he had been the one to shatter Jaxon's happiness once more.

Kieran looked in the direction Jaxon had gone. It would be easy to find him and catch up to apologize. But Jaxon wouldn't listen right now. Kieran's wit and humor had gotten him ahead in journalism, but it had just destroyed his chance at earning Jaxon's love.

Chapter Thirty-Four

JAXON HAD wanted to do so much more than just throw the magazine at Kieran and walk away. Ironic that he understood why Danetta had attacked Kieran with her wedding bouquet.

Kieran Quinn had burst into their lives two weeks ago, and in that short span of time had managed to do more damage than a hurricane. Jaxon couldn't believe what a fool he'd been to fall for the man. He'd listened to Kieran talk about love and sex and attraction, but he'd been spinning a web of lies way worse than what Danetta had done. Jaxon couldn't forgive her lies, but Kieran's duplicity and *hypocrisy* hurt even more.

Kieran was so fucking sanctimonious about it all, about how he was saving Jaxon from Danetta. Sure, he'd saved Jaxon from her, and then he'd gone and done the exact same thing to him. Was Kieran any better than Danetta?

The flight home took forever. The empty seat next to Jaxon was a constant reminder Kieran was gone. He dreaded his return to Buckwheat Springs, where everyone would have surely read the column. The only saving grace was that no one knew that for the past week Jaxon had shared his bed and body with Kieran. Jaxon had opened himself wide and left himself completely vulnerable to Kieran's charm. All he had to show for it was a week full of beautiful memories he couldn't bear to think about.

In Amarillo, Jaxon headed straight for the baggage claim, retrieved his suitcase, and sat down to wait for Sam to pick him up. He'd mulled over the decision long and hard before calling her from Los Angeles, but he needed a ride back to town and knew she wouldn't ask too many questions. He wasn't up to spending any time with Marc or Jordan and couldn't ask Tom—not with Laura about to have their baby any time now.

Sam had been the logical choice, but she was late, so he sat on his own in the nearly empty airport. The rest of the passengers from Jaxon's flight collected their bags and departed. One bag remained on the belt, going around and around: Kieran's suitcase. It had the pink plastic orchid Jaxon had attached to it in the hotel lobby just before they left for the airport. Jaxon felt sick to his stomach at the sight of yet another reminder of what a fool he'd been to trust Kieran so quickly.

Sam entered the baggage claim area, and Jaxon's spirits rose. He walked over to meet her, and she gave him a warm embrace.

"I'm sorry for being late. Hope you weren't waiting too long."

"It's fine. I don't have anywhere I need to be right now."

She glanced at him, but didn't say whatever she might be thinking. As they walked out of the airport, Jaxon looked back and saw an airport employee pull Kieran's suitcase off the conveyor belt.

"Jaxon, honey, I can't wait to hear all about your trip!" Sam said as they walked to her pickup.

"I'm really tired, Sam. I'm not feeling much like talking now if that's okay with you." Jaxon knew she'd respect his request.

"Sure, honey. Long day of traveling can really take it out of you. I know it probably wasn't really a vacation for you, dealing with everything that's happened."

They drove in silence for a few minutes until they'd gotten out of town and onto the nearly deserted state road heading for Buckwheat Springs. Sam concentrated on the road while Jaxon stared out the window listlessly. It was pitch black outside except for the headlights on Sam's truck, the stars, and a tiny sliver of moon.

"You want to talk about anything, sweetie?" Sam's voice was comforting, not inquisitive.

"No." What was he going to say? Heaviness pressed against his chest. He put his forehead against the window, cool against his heated skin.

"Well, just in case you change your mind, I'm right over here." Sam gave his leg a reassuring squeeze. "And I'm real good at keeping secrets."

"I know."

"Well, you know, you look good. All tanned and healthy and—"

Jaxon's head whipped around and he glared at Sam until she stopped talking.

"Oh." She sounded like she'd been slapped and Jaxon felt like an ass. "I didn't realize I wasn't allowed to talk either." She turned the radio on, flipping around the dial and settling on a lively Mexican station.

They drove for less than five minutes before Jaxon couldn't take it anymore and reached out to the radio, twisting the dial violently until he found another station to listen to.

"Well, at least now I know there's really someone home inside that gorgeous bod over there."

"What the fuck do you want from me?" Jaxon snapped again, wishing he'd taken a bus. Hell, walking might have been better than this. Since when did Sam get so chatty?

"I think you need to get yourself together before you go to school tomorrow," she said. "People are going to be talking, maybe even asking you direct questions, and you can't react like that. And *they* might not be asking with your best interests at heart. I'm here to listen if there's anything you want to get off your chest with a friend."

"Thanks." He realized she hadn't responded with heat or malice, just warmth and worry. "I'm sorry I snapped at you."

"No, problem. I know it's all been horrible, and it's going to be rough for a while, after what Danetta—"

"It has nothing to do with Danetta." The words had slipped out before Jaxon could stop himself. He concentrated on the darkness outside again. Maybe Sam would pretend she hadn't heard him.

"Oh" was all Sam said, but she pulled the truck over to the shoulder. "Do you want to talk about it anyway?"

Jaxon stared out of his window for a few minutes, avoiding Sam's gaze. It all hurt so much, and he needed to tell somebody.

"I know it's going to sound crazy"—he continued staring into the distance—"but I kind of met someone else. Just listen before you start tsk-tsking me, okay? The timing is so fucked up, but in a way, it doesn't have anything to do with Danetta. I mean, things were sort of there between us before…."

He didn't know how to explain any of this. He didn't know how he felt about Kieran or the realizations he'd come to in order to convey it to someone else. But he was hurting and knew Sam wanted to help.

"Go on. Take your time. I'm not tsk-tsking or judging."

"We went to Hawaii together, and it didn't turn out quite the way I had expected."

"Ah," Sam said. "That someone wouldn't happen to be a tall, dark, and handsome journalist, now would it?"

How had she known? Had everyone in town seen something between them?

"Was it so obvious?" Jaxon asked, looking out the window. He couldn't face her.

"No, I don't think so. But I'm pretty good at picking up on little things."

"Because you're a bartender, and you're good at reading people?"

"No. Because *I'm* gay."

Jaxon's head shot around again. "You are?"

"Have you ever seen me with a guy?"

Jaxon shook his head.

She continued, "I have a girlfriend who lives near Amarillo. But my point is I can see when two people are attracted to each other, and I definitely saw that between the two of you. I admit I was surprised at first when I saw your reaction to him, but I have to tell you, Kieran looked at you in a way I've never seen Danetta look at you. That boy was in love with you the day he met you; I'd bet a month's salary on that."

"What do you mean?"

"He looked kinda fascinated with you, and not just a physical attraction—though I could tell there was plenty of that, too. Danetta sometimes looks—looked—sorta like she owned you and took you for granted. I don't think she appreciated you very much, but it's not really my place to say."

"No, it's okay. I don't mind." He paused, glancing away from Sam's intense stare. He had to get the weight off, but he didn't want to spill his guts to Sam no matter how supportive she was. She put a hand on Jaxon's arm, and he turned toward her. "About Kieran. We had such a great time together in Hawaii. It was perfect. Then—did you read his column? The things he wrote about me?" Jaxon couldn't keep the hurt, the betrayal, from his voice.

"I read it. I can see why you're upset."

"He said that his editor published the first draft and not the one he submitted while we were in Hawaii. I know he didn't intend for that to be published and he was sorry it happened, but it doesn't change the fact he wrote it." The words tumbled out on their own now. "I told him I couldn't trust him any more than I could trust Danetta and left him in the middle of the airport in L.A." Jaxon gasped for breath when he finished.

"I can't say whether or not you should believe him or accept his apology, Jaxon. That's for you to decide. But I'm here if you want to talk about how you're feeling. It might not mean much, but I don't think people really believe all that stuff he writes. They might laugh at his humor, but I doubt anyone has changed their opinion of you after reading the article. Most people just see it as entertainment, like television. It's amusing, but it's not real."

He took a breath before asking the thing he'd tried not to think about. "What are people saying? About me, Danny, the wedding?"

Sam rubbed a hand across her lips. "Lots of things. Mostly 'bout Danny. She admitted she'd made some mistakes and hadn't been honest with you. Your dad and Marc Rossiter helped her move her things out. Marc's got that big house...." She paused.

Marc, too, had bought a nice house before his abandoned wedding.

"Marc's letting her stay till she gets back on her feet."

"It's better for her not to stay with her parents. Sam, am I a bastard because I don't want to see her?" Jaxon asked, gazing out into the distance, watching tumbleweeds roll past in the moonlight.

"No. I think it's understandable. At least at first. You probably should find a neutral place for a chat before too long and smooth things over."

"So it wouldn't be cool if I egged her car?"

They laughed for a few minutes, breaking the tension. He'd fantasized with Kieran about things he could do but wouldn't. People judge character by how you act under adversity. Jaxon was not going to let Danny or Kieran push him to do something he'd regret.

"Sun's gonna come up if we stay here any longer! You ready?"

He leaned over and hugged Sam and she got back on the road. "Thanks for listening."

"Anytime, sugar. Anytime."

Chapter Thirty-Five

Buckwheat Springs

JAXON EXPECTED Buckwheat Springs to be different upon his return. Despite Sam's reassurances, he was convinced people would see him as a villain for walking out of his wedding. So he was pleasantly surprised to discover that wasn't the case.

While no one went out of their way to tell him, many people were so horrified upon finding out what Danetta had done that they forgave Jaxon. At least for the time being, Danetta had used up the goodwill Buckwheat Springs had for her treatment of her former grooms. People had lost respect for her, and her behavior was no longer charming or quirky. Everyone knew about Lorraine's problems and sympathized with Danetta and Bert to some extent, but that didn't excuse what she'd done to her ex-grooms.

Most folks treated Jaxon as kindly as they had before the wedding fiasco. Even Kieran's column painting him as a fool hadn't caused much of a stir; as Sam predicted, people saw it for what it was, entertainment. A few laughs and it was forgotten.

But none of this erased the sting of Kieran's words.

Thankfully, no one noticed or cared that Jaxon had gone to Hawaii with Kieran. A few asked how he liked Hawaii and he gave honest answers. Most people were glad he at least got the honeymoon.

At home he erased any lingering traces of Danetta around his house and memories of what had been a wonderful week with Kieran. He'd moved into the guest bedroom, vowing to remove every bit of frill and lace as soon as possible. But he'd gotten used to sleeping next to Kieran and the bed felt empty and cold without him.

Jaxon's first week back at work was agony with Kieran withdrawal symptoms. If not for the hectic pace of the school year's final week and the senior class's graduation ceremony, his misery over what had happened between him and Kieran would have been multiplied.

How could he have fallen for Kieran like that? He'd never done more than think about being with a man, much less falling in love with one, but Kieran had blown into town, and everything in Jaxon's life had turned upside down. Kieran had been charming and confident and funny, and seemed so attracted to and interested in Jaxon.

Somehow it was worse that Kieran had been the one to insist they go to Hawaii as friends. It made Jaxon want Kieran all the more, trying to break him down. Maybe that reluctance for a physical relationship simply had been an act, Jaxon merely a challenge to get the straight guy into bed just before his wedding? Had he enjoyed watching Jaxon throw himself into such an intense physical relationship?

Kieran had insisted he was falling in love with Jaxon, had *acted* as if he was. What Jaxon couldn't reconcile was that loving, sweet, tender Kieran with the two-faced asshole who had written so many hurtful things in the column.

But in the middle of the night when he lay awake and looked over at the empty side of the bed, it wasn't Danetta he missed; it was Kieran. Kieran had gotten into his very soul in a way that Danetta never had. He hadn't loved her as much as he'd thought; he'd been in love with the *idea* of her and the perfect life he imagined he was supposed to have.

It hadn't been Jaxon's idea of a perfect life. But then, neither was the week he'd spent with Kieran. It hurt like hell to still have these emotions for Kieran and know there was nothing left of what they'd shared.

But Jaxon couldn't forget the feel of Kieran's hands on him, the way Kieran kissed him—gentle at times, demanding and hungry at others. He couldn't shake the physical memory of making love with Kieran. As amazing as it had been to make love to Kieran, it couldn't compare to how incredible it felt having Kieran inside him.

Jaxon had wanted it so badly at the time and was still amazed by how tender—and *loving*—Kieran had been. It had honestly been the most unbelievable physical experience of Jaxon's life. He would prefer that it had been painful and ugly, so he could hate Kieran for touching him, but that was impossible. Physically, it had been beyond amazing, but emotionally it had been even more powerful. Kieran was everything Danny never was or could be.

Kieran made him feel whole.

Jaxon lost count of how many nights he woke up that first week back, his body craving Kieran, his cock painfully hard and demanding attention. He tried to think of someone else as he stroked himself, seeking release that never satisfied him.

THE SECOND Monday home, Jaxon walked to school dreading the week ahead. It promised nothing but unending paperwork, reports, and schedules for the following school year. All the staff had summer fever, and even with the a/c on full blast, the heat remained a distraction.

Staff chitchat would be of summer travel and relaxation. Trips with the kids, chores they'd promised the husband or wife. Jaxon couldn't take listening to the rising excitement in everyone's tone. Not when his world was falling apart. He'd have no summer with Kieran or the trip to Savannah he and Danetta had planned. He closed his office door with more force than necessary and hoped no one understood why.

At lunchtime Jaxon wandered into the staff break room to refill his mug with fresh coffee and noticed a group of staff members engaged in a lively discussion. Jaxon heard someone mention Kieran's name. Someone from the group looked up.

"Jaxon, what did you think of Kieran Quinn's column?" Mavis Beach, a history teacher asked.

Jaxon walked over, feigning nonchalance, resigned to the fate of having to discuss the column yet again.

"I'm tired of talking about the whole wedding thing. Isn't there something better to discuss?"

"No, not the one about the wedding," Jack Murphy, an English teacher, said. "It's yesterday's column. He apologized for what he wrote. He's even resigned from the magazine. He wrote a really personal column this time. The first and last one that was about him, he said."

"What?" Jaxon couldn't believe what he'd heard. Kieran certainly owed more than a few people an apology. In Hawaii, Kieran had told Jaxon he was getting tired of the snark and humor at people's expense, how he wanted to write something different. Had he been telling the truth after all?

"I have a copy at my desk if you want to read it," Mavis offered before running off. She returned a moment later with *Gloss* in hand. Jaxon took the proffered magazine, though he wasn't sure he wanted to read it.

He thanked her and returned to his office. Part of him wanted to see what all the fuss was about. The other part wasn't sure it was ready to read anything Kieran had written, or see the face he couldn't forget in the little photograph at the top of the page. Jaxon sipped coffee, staring at the magazine without opening it—without even touching it. *I'll read the column when I finish this mug.*

Jaxon drank so slowly the coffee turned cold before he was half-finished. He frowned and swallowed an unsatisfying mouthful. Best to just get it over with and move on, he decided, and turned to the table of contents to find the column.

Kieran had indeed apologized—not specifically for the wedding column or anything he'd written about Jaxon, but in general to all the people he ever embarrassed, hurt, or betrayed. Over the years he'd written a good many unkind things about people in the name of humor and entertainment, and he was ashamed of it. Kieran hadn't realized exactly how much power his words had to harm other people until something he wrote hurt a person who was very important to him.

By the time he understood exactly the pain he'd caused, he wrote, it had been too late. He'd found himself sitting alone in the middle of an airport, unable to find any words to express how sorry he was. So even though it might be too little, too late, Kieran wanted to apologize not only to that one special person, but to everyone he'd hurt over the years. He hoped that by revealing something embarrassing and humiliating about himself, rather than his usual targets, that he might prove his sincerity. This would be his last column for *Gloss*; he was resigning, rather than continue what he'd been doing.

Jaxon appreciated the apology, surprised it had been made in such a public way, but it did impress Jaxon with its honesty. Rather than calling to apologize, Kieran had used his column and his words hoping to right the wrongs he'd done, not only to Jaxon, but to many other people before him. It was a fitting choice.

That evening Jaxon settled himself at Sam's bar. At seven o'clock on a Monday, the place was empty except for the two of them. The jukebox played random selections no one was listening to. Sam opened a bottle of beer for Jaxon. He'd been in at some point on most days since he'd come back, just for a quick chat or a bit of friendly support.

He'd gotten a few interested glances from other patrons but hadn't responded. Unlike Kieran, mindless sex in the men's room wasn't going to cure the ache in his heart.

"Did you see what he wrote?" Jaxon asked.

"Yep, I did." It was impossible to interpret her tone.

"What do you think?"

"I think you couldn't have asked for a more public and sincere apology than that. It's still up to you whether to forgive him or try to rebuild your relationship. But I reckon he'd have written 'Jaxon Lang, I'm sorry, and I love you' if he could do it without outing you."

"You think so?" Jaxon was still skeptical. Sam was far more sentimental than he'd expected from a worldly bar owner.

"Honey, I know so." She shut her mouth quickly and Jaxon was immediately suspicious.

"You talked to him!" He pointed the beer bottle in accusation. "You called him to talk about me?"

"No, he called me here, asking about you." She held her hands up in surrender. "Now before you go getting all hot under the collar and shouting traitor, just listen. He knew you wouldn't talk to him. But he was real worried about you."

"You told him what we've been talking about? What I told you?" Jaxon couldn't believe that another person close to him had betrayed him. He wasn't sure he'd trust his own mother at this point.

She shook her head. "Of course not! I'm on your side, sugar. I told him you were pretty upset about what he'd written and how he'd sorta lied and betrayed you like Danetta had. That's no more than you told him yourself, right?"

Jaxon nodded, his anger waning.

Sam went on. "But he wanted to find a way to apologize to you even if he couldn't win you back. All that mattered was you believe he was genuinely sorry for hurting you so much."

"Does he think I'm just going to accept his apology and take him back? 'Cause I'm not!"

"He knows you're not ready to trust him now, but you shouldn't let that keep you from trusting someone else in the future. I think he's learned his lesson in the worst possible way, and he doesn't expect anything from you."

"Well that's good. I don't have anything left for him anymore." Jaxon took a long swig of beer to keep Sam from seeing the tear sliding down his cheek. *Maybe if I keep saying it, I'll start believing it myself.*

LYING IN bed that night, Jaxon recalled how Kieran had acted when they were in Hawaii. Kieran had made it clear to Jaxon before they'd ever left Buckwheat Springs, before Jaxon had even left Danetta, that he wanted more than a physical relationship.

And during their trip together, *Kieran* had been the one to try and slow things down physically, when Jaxon had been ready and eager—impatient—to take the next step. Kieran had forced Jaxon to wait and make sure he was completely ready emotionally as well as physically before they went beyond kissing. That wasn't how you acted with a fling.

Could Kieran really have fallen in love with him, and meant everything he'd written in his last column? He had also been betrayed by his editor after seeing his own name on work he hadn't intended to be published.

Kieran's feelings had been genuine, and like Jaxon, they'd hit him so suddenly he hadn't been able to process them properly. Kieran had exaggerated his first negative impressions, but looking back on the relationship with Danetta, some of Kieran's observations weren't that far from the truth. Jaxon had been under her thumb to a certain extent and hadn't cared because he thought he was happy with Danetta.

Jaxon's yearning—emotional and physical—for Kieran hadn't diminished, which had made this all the more painful to endure. But he couldn't cover up the emotions with work and indignation. It had been so much easier to move on from Danetta because he no longer cared for her. Pushing her out of his life had been welcome relief.

Jaxon wasn't as upset with Kieran as he was with himself. He'd rushed into a serious relationship with Danetta; then he'd rushed into things with Kieran. He hadn't wanted to make the same mistakes with Kieran, and he'd used the misunderstanding about the column as an excuse to push Kieran away.

Now he'd had the time and distance to know who and what he wanted: Kieran.

It was Jaxon's turn to apologize.

Unable to sleep, Jaxon called directory assistance in New York in order to get Kieran's phone number, but it was unlisted. He had to wait until morning to try the *Gloss* office and see if they had home contact information. But when office hours arrived and he called the magazine, he had no luck. They confirmed that Kieran did not work there anymore but refused to release personal information about him.

Neither of them had expected there would be any need to exchange contact information in Hawaii, not when they were both coming back to Texas together. Why didn't he get Kieran's phone number or address?

He called Sam from his office as soon as he knew she'd be at the saloon.

"Heya, sugar, what's up this mornin'? You don't need a drink this early, do ya?"

"No." Jaxon laughed and paused a beat. He didn't want to sound like he'd been waiting to call for hours. "You wouldn't happen to have Kieran's number? You said he called, but maybe...."

"Sorry, sweetie. He didn't leave it, and we don't have caller ID on this ancient piece of horse pucky."

Jaxon pressed his lips together so he wouldn't betray his disappointment. "It was worth a try. Got any other ideas? The magazine won't release personal info."

"No I sure don't. But if Kieran calls again, I promise to get a number."

Jaxon disconnected, overwhelmed by hopelessness. All he knew was that Kieran's apartment was in SoHo; he didn't even have a clue what street it was on.

He remembered Kieran mentioning his two closest friends also wrote for *Gloss*. Alexa Something, the food writer and Brad Something-Else, the film critic. He grabbed his copy of *Gloss*—he'd given in and bought the one with Kieran's final column in it.

Yup, there they were: Alexa Harrington and Brad Raines, with their e-mail addresses. They could give him Kieran's contact information. He opened his e-mail program and... stopped.

This wasn't the way to handle something this important. He got up and locked his door, then phoned the *Gloss* office.

"Can I speak with Alexa Harrington, please?"

"Just one moment."

"Alexa." She had a cultured, New England voice, like a young Katharine Hepburn. Jaxon already had a good feeling about this.

"Hi, we haven't met, but I'm a friend"—was that the way to describe it?—"of Kieran Quinn. Jaxon Lang."

"Jaxon!"

"Yes."

"With an *X*?" She toned her voice down to a whisper.

"Yes." He also lowered his voice, though he wasn't sure why.

"Oh my God!" He heard muffled voices in the background. "Let me give you a call right back. What's your number?"

Two minutes later his phone rang.

"Sorry, Jaxon, I had to get somewhere private. Too many big ears around a magazine office."

"That's okay."

"So, you're Jaxon. I've heard a lot about you from Kieran."

What had he been saying? "I hope nothing too terrible."

"I can't repeat any of it. But I'm glad as hell you're calling."

"I'm not sure if this is appropriate, but I wanted to know how Kieran is. I don't have his contact information."

"I can give you his number. I'm sure he'd be thrilled to hear from you."

For the first time in weeks, Jaxon felt a little warmth deep inside where it had been icy-cold since that morning in LAX. "I don't want to talk to him on the phone. I need to do this in person. Do you think that's a good idea?" Even if she thought it was a terrible idea, he would go anyway.

"That's a fantastic idea. How soon can you get here?"

"Next Tuesday."

"Can you get here sooner?" She sounded as panicky as he felt about the idea of the trip.

"I can't get out of work before that."

"Okay, take the first flight on Tuesday. Let me know if you can make it sooner. I'll pay whatever it costs to change your ticket."

"Why? What's going on?" He stopped himself from asking if Kieran had been with someone else. It would serve Jaxon right if that happened. He could have avoided this.

"Nothing." Her forced cheerfulness was patently obvious. "Let me know what flight you're coming in on. I can send a car for you."

"That's not necessary. I'll take a cab."

"You've never been to New York, have you?"

"No."

"Use the magazine's car. It's the least they can do, considering what happened."

"Thanks." He was about to hang up. "Hey, Alexa? Please don't tell Kieran I'm coming."

"Why not?"

"In case he doesn't want to see me. It would be... embarrassing."

"Trust me, sweetie, he wants to see you." She sounded just like Sam. "Call me!"

She hung up, but Jaxon was relived he had a plan and an ally.

He went online and booked a flight to New York. He'd go and win Kieran back. Some things just had to be done in person.

Chapter Thirty-Six

THE POUNDING in Kieran's head wouldn't go away. He grabbed for the glass on the nightstand, but it was empty. There was a bottle of some headache meds, and he reached for it. Who needed water?

The bottle was empty.

The pounding had gotten louder.

His phone rang. Alexa. He didn't want to talk to her so he ignored it. Ten seconds later a text arrived.

Open the fucking door!

It hadn't been his head after all. He dragged himself out of bed and made it to the front door, knocking a bottle off a table in the living room.

He looked to make sure it was empty as he walked to the door.

Alexa was standing on the doorstep. He opened the door to let her in.

"Kieran, you should put some pants on. Underwear first, though." She pushed her purse in front of his crotch and averted her gaze. Then she stopped, pulled the purse away and stared. "Oh, very nice. You have no idea how many disappointed ladies there must be. Mmm-mmm-mmm."

"Is it time to go out already?" He looked for the clock.

"Pants?"

"Fine." He found some slung over a chair and pulled them on. "Happy?"

"Not particularly, but it's better if I don't see what I'm missing."

He dropped onto the couch while she picked up empty bottles from the floor and counter. "Did you eat recently?"

"Yeah. I got delivery from that place over on Thompson with the meatloaf. Are you running for busybody of the year or something? You've got my vote."

"I'm just worried about you." She walked up behind him, draped her arms over his shoulders, and kissed his cheek. "The Robinson Crusoe look is out this year, didn't you know?"

"Lex, stop it."

"Have a shower, and I'll take you to lunch. Anywhere you want."

"I'll think about it in the shower."

"Good man." She patted his head, and he swatted at her hand.

But he got up and took a shower. He did feel better. And he was starving. A constant diet of tequila and meatloaf sandwiches wasn't as satisfying as it sounded. He noticed his middle was softer and thicker than he remembered. He stood in front of the mirror in profile and realized he was letting himself get into bad shape.

But who was there to notice? Alexa was the only one who'd seen him naked since that last morning with Jaxon in Hawaii.

Waves of nausea washed over him, hot and stifling, and he splashed cold water over his face until he felt a little more human. Would he ever feel normal again? Whatever normal felt like. That was hazy. Finally, he pulled on the last clean pair of jeans he had and a shirt from last season.

When he got back to the living room, it was cleaner than he'd seen it before. He heard the sound of the washing machine from the room behind the kitchen.

"Lex, are you doing my laundry?"

"Only because I love you."

"I love you too." He planted a kiss on the top of her head and held her close for a few minutes. "Thank you."

They walked a couple of blocks to Balthazar. The host knew Alexa—everyone who worked at a restaurant in Manhattan did—and brought them to a table in the front where they could watch people strolling by. He let her order and stuck with Perrier because she refused to order any alcohol until after dinner.

"Will you help me pack when we get back?"

"Pack?" Alexa tensed up. "Pack what?"

"My suitcase. I'm going away."

She choked and spit out some bread crumbs. "Away?"

"I need a break. I'm thinking about Peru. Is this a good time of year to go to Peru? Who's the travel guy? I should ask him."

"No. It's not a good time for Peru."

"What about Fiji?"

"Nope. September."

"Istanbul? Rome? Outer Mongolia?"

She rejected all of them.

"You don't fucking know what you're talking about." Why didn't she want him to go away?

"Don't go yet. You're not yourself."

Aha. "Who am I?" He got a sneer in return. "Are you worried I'll do something dangerous while I'm gone? Or someone dangerous?" He tried to smile. He didn't feel like doing anyone. At least not anyone but Jaxon. He'd already talked Lex's ear off about that, and he wasn't about to start again.

"Yes. I'm worried."

"Hey, don't be. Really. I won't jump off a cliff or drink my own volume in gin or anything. Seriously." He reached for her hand over the table, and she held it, then brought it to her face. She was crying. "Oh, shit, Lex. Don't cry."

"Let's go somewhere together? I've got some time off in a few weeks."

"I really need a change of scenery sooner. I'm afraid I am going to do something desperate if I don't."

"Where's the one place in the city you've been dying to eat at?"

"Per Se?"

"Well I've got a reservation there for next week."

"Really?" He had wanted to go there for a long time. It was one of the toughest reservations for a normal person. "When?"

"Next Wednesday evening."

"I won't be around next week. I told you."

"Per Se? Come on! I want to cheer you up, and you've been hinting around about it—not very subtly—for months."

"Why don't you want me to leave before Wednesday?"

"Besides dinner at Per Se?" Her voice and her eyebrows rose.

"Yeah."

"No reason."

She was up to something. That dinner reservation was too convenient. He sat back in his chair and watched her face for telltale signs. He didn't see any, but he still wasn't satisfied. "Fine. I won't leave till Thursday. Happy?"

"Blissful." She stole a bite of duck confit off Kieran's plate, popped it into her mouth, and moaned.

WHEN KIERAN got back to his apartment, he went online looking for a vacation spot that caught his eye. Half a dozen looked promising.

Trekking in Nepal? A casino in Monte Carlo? Hiking in Switzerland? He psyched himself up for a trip he'd never forget.

Who was he kidding? He wouldn't enjoy any of these places. He glanced toward the kitchen to see if he still had any tequila in the place. If not, he'd call a different shop for a delivery. They knew his voice at the closest one and the one two blocks farther in the opposite direction.

But first he phoned Per Se.

"Hello, this is Brad from *Gloss*. I'm Alexa Harrington's assistant. Can I verify the reservation for next Wednesday? We may need another spot at the table."

"Hold please, Brad."

But Alexa didn't have a reservation for any day next week. Not under her own name or any of the aliases she used when she wanted to dine incognito.

She'd lied to Kieran.

Screw her and her BS. He logged into the travel site and booked the trip that most appealed to him. He was flying out on Tuesday.

Chapter Thirty-Seven

Buckwheat Springs

JAXON'S WEEK and weekend went by at a snail's pace. He had three school board meetings on Monday or he would have left for New York days ago.

As the last meeting wrapped up, he breathed a sigh of relief at the official end to the school year and sent his staff home early. That evening, Sam took Jaxon with her to her girlfriend's house near the airport, where he would spend the night before Sam dropped him at the terminal first thing on Tuesday morning. Jaxon was on his way to New York at last.

Tuesday
New York City

WHEN JAXON walked through the arrival doors at JFK, he saw a liveried driver holding a sign:

Jackson Long

Close enough. The *Gloss* car was a roomy town car, and the driver was cheerful and entirely too chatty. He'd assumed Jaxon was a VIP being flown in for some special event, and Jaxon went along in case Alexa might get in trouble otherwise.

As they crossed the Williamsburg Bridge into Manhattan, Jaxon's stomach knotted with excitement and fear. The well-known skyline gave him a sense of familiarity he didn't have here, especially when he had no idea how his visit to Kieran would play out.

On the phone the night before, Alexa had sounded excited. She wouldn't give him any information on Kieran but assured him she hadn't spoiled the surprise.

He looked up at the tall buildings surrounding him, blocking out the afternoon sun. Despite the heat of the day, Jaxon felt a slight chill go through him. What if she was wrong, and when Jaxon arrived, Kieran didn't want him anymore? Sam said Kieran knew he'd lost Jaxon. What if he'd already moved on, found a new lover?

He couldn't, wouldn't give up without a fight. He'd make sure Kieran knew how Jaxon really felt, how much he'd missed him, and what a fool he'd been not to believe him. He had to know how things could be between them. He just had to try.

Jaxon couldn't believe how much traffic there was. It took half an hour to go what was probably only half a mile. *I could walk faster.* But of course he didn't know his way around. Finally, the car stopped in front of a distinguished-looking old building.

A cacophony of car horns, idling engines, squealing bus brakes, and beeping at the pedestrian walkways greeted him. The streets even smelled different. On the ground, New York was busy, bustling, with an exhilaration he felt in every pore. No wonder Kieran loved it here. It was so different from Texas.

Bike messengers whizzed by at daredevil speed as he retrieved his suitcase, tipped the driver, and walked to the front door. Before he made it across the sidewalk, a woman leading four dogs on leashes went past. The smallest, a white terrier, got his leash tangled with Jaxon's suitcase for a moment before Jaxon freed the animal.

A doorman in red and black livery stood outside and opened the door for Jaxon once he'd extricated himself from the terrier. He entered, wheeling his suitcase behind him.

Wow, Kieran sure lives in some fancy place. Definitely *not* the fifth-floor walk-up he'd originally imagined.

The lobby area was spacious and impressive. A black-and-white checkerboard marble floor was accentuated by a round mosaic in the center depicting flames overlaying a compass. The walls were pale paneled wood—the interior designers probably called it "biscuit" or "eggshell" so they could charge more—with inscrutable modern art on the walls.

A reception desk seemed a football field length away. Another liveried man stood behind it and nodded when Jaxon entered. Then he walked toward the elevator.

"Where you goin', mister?" the man at the distant desk asked. "You need to get announced first around here. No one goes up there without a key or gettin' announced." Apparently the lobby was his territory, and he made the rules—or at least enforced them.

Only then did Jaxon realize there was no button on the elevator, only a keyhole. Kieran wasn't kidding when he said he lived in a nice place, but he hadn't mentioned the high security.

"I'm here to see Kieran Quinn." Jaxon walked over to the desk, rolling his suitcase across the marble expanse. The middle-aged man sitting behind the desk wore an engraved gold nametag that said "Kurt." He had a grizzled gray beard and gravelly voice that might have had a touch of the South in it, buried under several decades of Brooklyn.

"Mr. Quinn is not at home at present." Kurt's voice was eerily reminiscent of the *Gloss* receptionist—he wondered whether there was some sort of training school for that—and Jaxon felt his heart sinking. He glanced at his watch. It was nearly 5:00 p.m. Could Kieran have gone to that bar this early, looking for someone else? Maybe he was just at the gym. Jaxon could wait, assuming Kurt allowed that sort of thing.

"I don't suppose you know where he went or when he'll be back?" Jaxon ventured, knowing it was probably useless.

"I'm sorry, sir, I wouldn't know," Kurt replied.

Of course not. Jaxon bristled. The staff was probably not supposed to reveal any information about the tenants in a place like this anyway.

"But he did have a couple of suitcases with him, so I have a feeling he's going to be gone for a while. Usually he leaves instructions for us when he travels, but he rushed right out just before you got here, actually; didn't say nothing." Kurt shook his head and tsked, as if leaving town without instructions to the building staff should be considered a felony. His speech had gotten more casual and friendly, for which Jaxon was grateful. Maybe Kurt would come around after all and offer some help.

"He had suitcases?" Jaxon repeated, let down. Where had Kieran gone? On a nice vacation to forget about Jaxon? To find someone new? *With* someone new? Jaxon wondered why Alexa hadn't mentioned Kieran was going away.

"Yeah," Kurt confirmed. "Left like five minutes before you walked in. How's that for bad timin'? You got a suitcase, too. Looks like you came in from out-of-town, huh?" Kurt asked. Suddenly he was very friendly, when he didn't have any information.

"Thanks, anyway." Jaxon turned away from the desk. He had Kieran's cell phone number from Alexa; maybe he could still catch him before he left town. Maybe Jaxon could convince Kieran to stay. "Do you have a phone I can use? Mine's not getting any bars in here. I'm going to try calling Kieran's cell."

"Sure, Mister. For a friend of Mr. Quinn, sure." Kurt motioned to a phone in the corner of the lobby. "Use that one. Not very private, but it works. No more payphones around anymore, you know."

"Thanks." Jaxon walked over to a large, black, old-fashioned rotary dial phone on an antique table crafted of dark, polished wood. He pulled Kieran's number from his pocket and dialed. The phone went directly to voice mail, and Jaxon hung up. He didn't know what to say even if he did leave a message.

He tried another number.

"Alexa?"

"Jaxon! Where are you?"

"I'm in Kieran's lobby, but—"

"Won't he let you in?"

"He's not here. The doorman said he left earlier with suitcases."

"That lying fucker. He wasn't supposed to leave till after Wednesday."

"What? Where did he go?"

"I don't know. I tried everything I could to keep him here till you arrived, short of telling him you were coming. He and I have dinner plans for tomorrow. Or he thinks we do, but I made the reservation for the two of you. I didn't think he'd slink out of town like this. Oh damn. I should have just told him."

"It's okay. I took a chance trying to surprise him. It's my own fault. This is all my fault." Jaxon dropped into the chair next to the phone. He felt hot and the room spun. He pulled at his collar for more air.

"Jaxon, don't worry. You'll come stay with me until I can get Kieran's ass back to the city."

"Oh no. I'll find a hotel and rebook my return flight."

"You'll do no such thing. I insist. It's my fault he left." She gave Jaxon her address. "I'm at the office, but I can get there in about thirty minutes. I'll call the front desk to let you in."

"Thanks."

What a disaster. After a few minutes of cursing himself again, Jaxon made his way over to the desk. "Can you help me find this address? Is it walking distance or should I get a cab?"

Kurt looked at the address. He nodded and scratched the back of his head. "Oh, this is about three blocks from here. You got one of those rolling suitcases so it should be ten minutes walking or so." He gave directions. As he was finishing up the desk phone rang.

Jaxon nodded thanks and collected his bag, then headed across the spacious lobby for the front door.

"Yes, oh sure. I wondered what you wanted us to do.... Of course," Kurt's voice echoed across the polished floors. "And, Mr. Quinn?"

That got Jaxon's attention, and he turned toward Kurt. *Kieran* was calling the lobby of his apartment building?

"What should I tell your friend who came by to see you?" Kurt asked into the phone. Jaxon's heart did a series of flips as he rushed back to the desk. He held out his hand, hoping he could speak directly with Kieran. "You don't know when you'll be back? ... I'll tell him. He's still here in the lobby, on his way over to Broome Street. ... He's got a suitcase with him, too, isn't that funny?" Kurt chuckled into the phone like he was chatting with his best friend. He looked up at Jaxon and covered the mouthpiece. "Where you visitin' from, Mister?"

"Texas. Buckwheat Springs!" He hoped for a chance to talk with Kieran, but Kurt repeated the information into the phone, nodded a few times as he said good-bye, and hung up.

Kieran hadn't asked to speak to him. Jaxon's heart plummeted along the downward part of the rollercoaster, again.

"Did he say anything when you told him I was here?" Jaxon asked. Kieran had to know it was Jaxon. Had he come to New York for nothing, then? Had Kieran already moved on?

"He hopes you have a nice visit here in New York," Kurt relayed with a cordial smile, as if that should make Jaxon happy.

"Oh."

"You wanna leave a message?" Kurt offered. "He calls every few days to check for messages, you know."

"No, thanks." Jaxon turned and headed for the door. Another wave of loneliness and desolation crashed down on him as he wheeled his suitcase toward the entrance.

The doorman opened the door as Jaxon approached, but before he could walk through it, he was nearly knocked over, then grabbed and pulled into an embrace by someone entering. Someone tall.

Kieran.

"Jax! I can't believe you're here!" Kieran pulled Jaxon back into the lobby, and Jaxon was forced to let go of his suitcase and let himself be swept along by Kieran's excitement.

Kieran swung him around on top of the mosaic flames, and it felt like something from a silly sentimental movie Jaxon would never be caught dead watching. But right now there was nothing he wanted more than to be in Kieran's almost painfully exuberant embrace.

Until Kieran kissed him.

This time there was nothing held back in the kiss. Jaxon poured out all of his love and desire and relief, and Kieran responded hungrily, taking hold of Jaxon in a way that sent pleasurable electric shocks throughout Jaxon's entire body, reminding him of just how badly he'd missed Kieran—body and soul—during the difficult weeks they'd been parted.

Kieran's lips crushed Jaxon's, and he tasted blood, but he simply let himself be carried away with the relief and passion, absorbing the familiar smell and relishing the scratch of the dark stubble he'd come to love. He opened himself up to welcome Kieran in, wanting him so badly he'd probably explode from longing and pent-up desire.

And Kieran drank in Jaxon's essence, tongue darting into Jaxon's mouth and exploring every curve and corner, making it clear that Kieran was home, belonged here. Jaxon wanted to lose himself, give himself up completely to the desire coursing through his body.

Jaxon wrapped his arms around Kieran's neck, fingers instinctively tangling in the familiar soft locks. He pulled Kieran's head down, wanting him as close as possible. For long, delicious minutes, they reacquainted themselves with taste and feel.

When Jaxon took a breath, he remembered they were still in the middle of the lobby, with Kurt and the doorman looking on.

But Jaxon kissed Kieran back even more fiercely, not caring who was watching. *Let them look. Let everyone see how lucky I am to be here with Kieran.*

Jaxon was most definitely going to have a very nice visit to New York after all.

Chapter Thirty-Eight

KIERAN'S PHONE buzzed in his back pocket. It was just enough to break the spell. Probably just as well because Kieran wanted more than kisses from Jaxon, and that wouldn't go over well in the lobby. He knew that from experience.

Jaxon let go and stepped back, chest rising and falling, sucking in air the way Kieran was.

The phone buzzed again. "What?"

Jaxon frowned.

"Sorry, hello? Lex, I'm kind of busy right now." Kieran noticed Kurt trying to get his attention and pointing to the bags. "Hang on. Thanks, please take them all upstairs" He turned his attention back to Alexa as he put an arm around Jaxon and planted a kiss on his temple.

"I don't know where you are, but get your ass home right now, Kieran Quinn, or you'll be very sorry."

"I am home. Well, almost. I'm in the lobby with Jaxon."

"You are? Never mind."

The elevator door opened, and they went inside. Kieran pulled Jaxon in for another kiss while Alexa babbled in his ear.

Jaxon pulled away and grabbed the phone. "Hi, Alexa. He came back just as I was about to head to your place."

Kieran grabbed the phone back as the elevator landed on his floor. "Bye now, Lex. I'll talk to you in a few days." He glanced at Jaxon, who looked adorably delectable. "Maybe next week. I've got company."

"But wait, I have to tell y—"

Kieran jammed the phone in his back pocket, opened the door, then stopped before stepping inside. "Should I carry you over the threshold or something?"

"Why?"

"Isn't that post-honeymoon tradition?"

"I'm not very traditional, at least not anymore."

"I am." Kieran smiled and pulled Jaxon over his shoulder in a fireman's carry and deposited him on the couch. Then he went down on his knees and brought Jaxon in for a more private NC-17 kiss.

"Would it be rude to get some water or something? I came here directly from the airport."

"Sorry. Sure." Kieran let go and opened the fridge. There was nothing in there but a few bottles of Perrier. He grabbed one and two glasses and brought them in to Jaxon.

Jaxon drained his glass. "Thanks."

"Would you like a tour of the place?" Kieran glanced around, grateful Alexa had helped him clean up, both the apartment and himself.

Jaxon nodded and smiled, a kind of sweet, shy look Kieran had missed so much it hurt to see it. "Definitely. As long as the tour starts in the bedroom."

Kieran just stared at him.

Jaxon stood up, erection straining against the fabric of his jeans. "What are you waiting for, Kier? I intend to get to Column B before I walk out that door again." He grinned and raced across the living room with Kieran on his tail.

He glanced in each door as he passed until he got to the biggest bedroom and flopped down on the bed as Kieran stood in the doorway. Kieran saw Jaxon's arousal, but for a moment memories of the other men who had been in this room, in this bed, flooded over him, leaving a heavy layer of shame in their wake.

It was too late to take Jaxon into another bedroom.

Jaxon kicked his shoes off, then realized Kieran hadn't come toward the bed.

"What's wrong? Did I get this wrong and you can't forgive me for pushing you away?" He stood up, not meeting Kieran's gaze.

A knife sliced through Kieran's heart. "No, no. There's nothing for me to forgive. I was wrong." He sat on the edge of the bed. "It hurt so much to come home knowing I'd probably never see you again. And it hurts in a different way that you came here for me."

"Kieran, I love you. It was a matter of time before my brain figured out what my heart already knew." He stroked Kieran's cheek, and Kieran laid his palm over Jaxon's hand, pressing it closer.

"I love you. With my heart and my brain."

"What about your body?"

Kieran nodded.

"Do you have stuff?"

"Yes."

Jaxon rolled over and opened the drawer, then he looked back at Kieran, but Kieran closed his eyes.

"What's *that*?" Jaxon's tone was playful.

"That's Column C, or maybe D."

"How long before we get there?"

"Seriously?" Kieran's heart was beating like a metronome on the highest setting and not because Jaxon was so close.

"Yes." He took Kieran's hand again. "I know I'm not the first guy you've slept with."

Understatement.

"Or the first one you've had here. That's okay. It doesn't bother me." He straddled Kieran's lap and started kissing his way down Kieran's throat, undoing buttons one at a time and planting kisses along the way until Kieran was hard and out of breath. Then Jaxon moved away and started pulling his own clothes off. Kieran's mouth watered at the sight of his heavy, swollen cock. He'd missed touching it, sucking it, feeling it inside him.

"I just want to know one thing before we go further."

"Anything." Kieran really meant it.

"As long as we're together, it's just me. Are you ready for monogamy?"

"You're the first man who's shown me how much I want that. Yes."

Jaxon stepped forward, and Kieran took the head of his cock into his mouth, then a few more inches.

"Slow down."

"I missed you."

"I can tell." Jaxon grabbed handfuls of Kieran's hair and laughed. "Can you finish that in the shower?"

"You sure?"

"Yeah. I want to bottom."

Under warm water, Kieran reacquainted himself with every beautiful inch of Jaxon's cock, as slowly and gently as possible until Jaxon begged him for an orgasm. By that time, Kieran's cock was throbbing and his balls ached. His hair was still dripping down his chest and back when he got Jaxon back in bed.

"You ready for Column B?"

"Oh yes." Jaxon was on his back, playing with Kieran's balls, as Kieran leaned across him to get lube and condoms from the drawer. He cupped them and let them tumble out of his hand.

"Having fun?"

Jaxon just licked his lips, and Kieran worried he'd shoot all over him just from desire.

"How about you get on your hands and knees?" Kieran put a hand under Jaxon's shoulder to get him moving. Jaxon bent forward and Kieran knelt behind him. He squeezed Jaxon's ass and reciprocated the ball play.

"This is Column B? Doggie style?"

"Just wait. You're so impatient."

Kieran kissed and scraped his teeth along the round, fleshy parts of Jaxon's shapely ass.

Jaxon let out a giggle. "Your stubble is tickling me!"

More squeezing and kissing, then Kieran spread Jaxon's cheeks wide to expose his asshole. He circled it with a fingertip until he felt Jaxon relax a little. Then he planted a very soft kiss right on the pink pucker. Another kiss and then he dragged his tongue across it like it was a lollipop.

Jaxon squirmed. "Oh! Mmm." He relaxed even more and let out a pleasurable sigh.

Kieran kept licking, then he pushed just the tip of his tongue inside, but the ring of muscle was too tight. He worked away until he got an inch or so of his tongue in there.

"That's not your finger, is it?"

"Nwwow," Kieran replied against Jaxon's ass. He pushed in deeper and alternated that with licking around the outside. Jaxon tasted of soap after their thorough shower.

"Aaaah. Ummm. Ohhhh God, that feels good."

Kieran pulled his tongue out.

"More? Please?"

He pushed back and played a little more.

"Is this Column B?"

Kieran pulled out again. "This is Column B. If you do this to me, it's Column C."

"Let's finish Column B first."

Kieran smiled and pulled a condom onto himself. He loved Jaxon's eagerness and curiosity. It was going to be fun introducing him to new things. After applying more lube, he slid inside Jaxon smoothly and easily, and it felt like home.

Jaxon instinctively pushed up against his strokes, and they got a good rhythm going. When he paused to catch his breath and kiss Jaxon's back, Jaxon looked up.

"Kier, can we rotate? I want to watch in the mirror. I can't see your face this way."

A scene flashed through Kieran's brain of the last guy he'd fucked here, watching in the mirror—Todd the underwear model. But with Jaxon, it wouldn't be the same. They shifted position so they were in profile in the mirror. Jaxon smiled as he watched Kieran thrusting into him.

It was so much sexier than with Todd. Jaxon caught Kieran's eye and looked like he was loving every minute of it too, hard again and moaning. Kieran fucked up against his prostate until he had Jaxon shuddering and coming again. Then he took his own orgasm. It lasted forever, floating him on a warm golden cloud as Jaxon held his gaze in the mirror. Every muscle in his body tensed up, and a bubble of white-hot pleasure seemed to singe every nerve ending.

He fell back exhausted, and Jaxon curled up beside him until he caught his breath. Then carefully, Jaxon pulled the condom off, wrapped it up, then bent over to lick Kieran clean. He used just the amount of pressure Kieran could tolerate in his sensitized state. Then they kissed and held each other.

The buzzing phone pulled them out of their post-coital cocoon of bliss.

"I'll get it." Jaxon leaned down, pulled Kieran's discarded jeans onto the bed, and grabbed the phone. "Alexa." He handed it to Kieran.

"Busy."

"Wait, no. I—"

"I don't talk to liars."

"What did I lie about?"

"Dinner reservation at Per Se?"

She chuckled merrily.

"It's not funny. I called, and they didn't have anything this week under any of your pseudonyms."

"Because I made the reservation under *your* name. For tonight. For you and Jaxon."

He tried to sit up, but his body was Jell-O. "What?"

"That's what I wanted to tell you. Jaxon called me and we arranged his visit, but you were being a douche nozzle with your stupid vacation plans. I had to make sure you didn't leave town before he got here."

"Oh." Kieran looked up, and Jaxon wore a charming guilty expression Kieran wanted to kiss right off. "Tonight?"

"Yes. At seven. You have forty-five minutes to get there."

"I don't suppose you could push it back an hour?"

Jaxon shook his head. "Two hours."

"Two hours, Lex?"

"I'll see what I can do. I hope you're having a nice reun—" Kieran disconnected. He looked at Jaxon. "Two hours, huh?"

"That gives us time to reunite some more."

"I think you'll put me in the hospital if we reunite like that in the foreseeable future."

"Oh." Jaxon licked his kiss-bruised bottom lip. "What if I do something from Column C to you?"

"That's very tempting."

"Does that place deliver?"

"Per Se? It's one of the most exclusive restaurants in town. There's a three-month wait for tables."

"But do they deliver?" Jaxon lay down and curled up against Kieran's side.

"Should I cancel?"

"No. We should do something special to celebrate today."

Kieran kissed the top of Jaxon's head and lay back. How did he get so lucky? He was with Jaxon again, both able to put the mistakes and misunderstandings behind them, ready to move forward together.

A piece of paper had fallen out of his pocket when Jaxon got the phone from his jeans. He leaned over to pick it up and handed it to Jaxon.

Jaxon looked at the folded paper. "What's this? Not one of your famous notes?"

"Open it."

"Tell me first."

"It's the boarding pass for the plane I missed when I came back here after talking to Kurt."

Jaxon glanced at Kieran, then unfolded the paper. His eyebrows rose, and he caught Kieran's eye again. "You were flying to Texas? To see me?"

"Some things need to be done in person. Like apologies." He brushed his lips against Jaxon's honey brown hair.

"I love you, Kieran."

They kissed again in a tangle of arms and legs. Jaxon pressed close, his hips moving against Kieran, who felt the heaviness of another erection stirring. Jaxon looked up with his wicked smile and peeled back the sheets, kissing his way down Kieran's torso.

"So, is there anything after C?"

EM LYNLEY has worked finance, the wine industry and high-tech, though she'd rather be writing hot man-on-man romance. She spent 10 years as an economist and financial analyst, including a year as a White House Staff Economist, but only because all the intern positions were filled. Tired of boring herself and others with dry business reports and articles, her creative muse is back and naughtier than ever. She has lived and worked in London, Tokyo and Washington, D.C., but the San Francisco Bay Area is home for now.

Contact EM:
Website: http://www.emlynley.com
Blog: http://emlynley.livejournal.com
Twitter: @emlynley
Facebook: http://www.facebook.com/emlynley

Bound for Trouble

By EM Lynley

Daniel "Deke" Kane is a broken man, facing the end of his career in the FBI. He's on desk duty after a botched drug raid left the suspects and two children dead. He's got one chance to prove himself, or the only thing he'll be investigating is the Help Wanted ads.

Ryan Griffiths has been on the run for ten years. Forced onto the streets when his father kicked him out, Ryan earns his living in other men's beds. Finding his john dead in a hotel room drives him under the radar until a favorite client gives him a chance at a safe, clean life. But Ryan's relatively stable new world shatters when Deke Kane catches up with him.

When Deke's tasked to take down a drug dealer with terrorist ties and a taste for the dark side of BDSM, his only chance to get close is the suspect's interest in Ryan, and he convinces Ryan to become a confidential informant. In return, Deke offers Ryan immunity from his past. As Ryan falls under the drug lord's domination, Deke finds himself falling for Ryan.

http://www.dreamspinnerpress.com

Dirty Dining

By EM Lynley

Jeremy Linden's a PhD student researching an HIV vaccine. He's always short of money, and when biotech startup PharmaTek reduces funding for his fellowship, he's tempted to take a job at a men's dining club as a serving boy. The uniforms are skimpy, and he's expected to remove an item of clothing after each course. He can handle that, but he soon discovers there's more on the menu here than fine cuisine. How far will he go to pay his tuition, and will money get in the way when he realizes he's interested in more from one of his gentlemen?

Brice Martin is an attorney for a Silicon Valley venture capital firm. When he's asked to take a client to the infamous Dinner Club, he finds himself unexpectedly turned on by the atmosphere and especially by his server, Remy. He senses there's more to the sexy young man than meets the eye. The paradox fascinates him, and he can't get enough of Remy.

Their relationship quickly extends beyond the club and sex. But the trust and affection they've worked to achieve may crumble when Jeremy discovers Brice's VC firm is the one that pulled the plug on PharmaTek—and Jeremy's research grant.

http://www.dreamspinnerpress.com

Hostile Takeover

EM Lynley

Years ago, Chase Richards and Mathias Tobler fell in love while training for the US Olympic fencing team. Afterward, they even attended the same business school so they could be together. Then Chase left Mathias alone and heartbroken in Italy. But all of that is ancient history by the time Chase thunders back into Mathias's safe, settled life with a business deal.

There's no way Mathias is going to do business with Chase. He spent nine years picking up the pieces and has moved on in life—and love. But Chase won't give up without a fight: he concocts a scheme to manipulate the market and take over the Tobler family business. If Mathias wants to save it, he'll have to face off against Chase over crossed sabers.

Chase has a reputation as an unscrupulous corporate raider, but the Tobler business holds little interest for him. In reality, he wants Mathias. Chase must win him back—by any means necessary—before Mathias gives his heart to someone else. But how does a cold-blooded corporate raider convince the man he loves that his heart really isn't made of stone?

Out of the Gate

By EM Lynley

British actor Wesley Tremayne thinks he's close to hitting the big time—a film career—with his role as a hunky explorer on a popular American TV show. Success should be just around the corner, as long as he keeps his sexual orientation a secret. Wes's best friend and beard, Julia Compton, forms the other half of a glamorous Hollywood couple that's merely a façade.

Evan Taylor left his acting career behind five years ago without looking back. He's always been more comfortable around horses than people—especially Hollywood types. His new life training racehorses is a dream come true, but increasing financial problems and an abusive boyfriend have him doubting himself and his choices.

Then Wes and his friends buy a third-rate racehorse—partially for publicity—and send him to Evan's stable. Wes's friendship with Evan soon develops into an overpowering attraction he can't act on. He's never met a man like Evan, but if there's any chance for a future together, Wes must choose between a career he loves and the man he adores.

http://www.dreamspinnerpress.com

Delectable

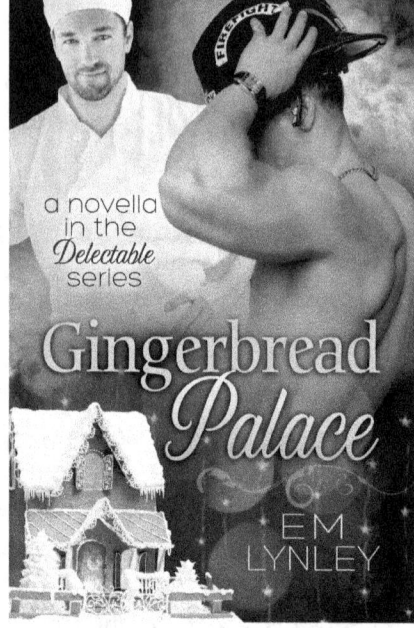

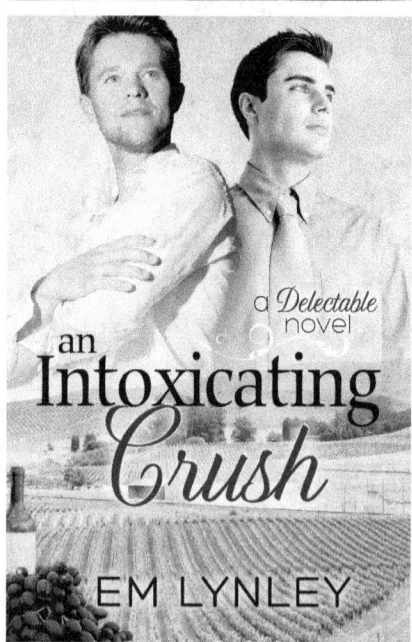

http://www.dreamspinnerpress.com

Lighting the Way Home

Delectable Series

By EM Lynley & Shira Anthony

World-class chef Joshua Golden is homesick for Paris before he even arrives in New York, but he'll endure it—his parents need him to help run the family restaurant while his mother recovers from surgery. Running a place so far beneath his talents is bad enough, but bad turns to worse when Josh discovers his former best friend and lover, Micah Solomon, is living at his parents' house with his ten-year-old son, Ethan.

For ten years, Josh has done his best to forget how Micah shattered his heart into tiny pieces. Now Micah's back, fresh out of prison, and helping out at the restaurant. Micah may not be the kind of sous chef Josh is used to, but he is more helpful and supportive than any of the other employees. But Josh finds it hard to keep his distance when, time after time, Micah proves himself a better man than Josh thought. Reluctantly, Josh realizes there is more to Micah than his lousy life choices… but that doesn't mean Josh is ready to forgive him.

http://www.dreamspinnerpress.com

Precious Gems

PUMPKIN
Rolls AND Porn
SOUNDS

KRIS T. BETHKE

http://www.dreamspinnerpress.com

www.ingramcontent.com/pod-product-compliance
Lightning Source LLC
Chambersburg PA
CBHW070108260626
47160CB00004B/1370